THE
STORIES
OF
EVA
LUNA

THE
STORIES
OF
EVA LUNA

Isabel Allende

TRANSLATED FROM THE SPANISH BY
Margaret Sayers Peden

BANTAM BOOKS
NEW YORK · TORONTO · LONDON
SYDNEY · AUCKLAND

*This edition contains the complete text
of the original hardcover edition.*
NOT ONE WORD HAS BEEN OMITTED.

THE STORIES OF EVA LUNA

*A Bantam Book / published by arrangement with
Macmillan Publishing Company*

PRINTING HISTORY
Originally published in Spain as Cuentos de Eva Luna *by
Plaza & Janés Editores, S. A., Barcelona*

*Some of these stories have previously appeared in
Granta, The Irish Times,
Latin American Literary Review, and ZYZZYVA.
Atheneum edition published 1991
Bantam export edition / September 1991
Bantam trade paperback edition / February 1992*

Library of Congress Cataloging-in-Publication Data

Allende, Isabel.
  [Cuentos de Eva Luna. English]
  The stories of Eva Luna / Isabel Allende : translated from the
Spanish by Margaret Sayers Peden.
    p. cm.
  Translation of: Cuentos de Eva Luna.
  ISBN 0-553-55003-9
  I. Title.
PQ8098.1.L54C8413 1992   91-30581
863—dc20   CIP

Published simultaneously in the United States and Canada

*Bantam Books are published by Bantam Books, a division of Bantam
Doubleday Dell Publishing Group, Inc. Its trademark, consisting of the
words "Bantam Books" and the portrayal of a rooster, is Registered in U.S.
Patent and Trademark Office and in other countries. Marca Registrada.
Bantam Books, 666 Fifth Avenue, New York, New York 10103.*

PRINTED IN THE UNITED STATES OF AMERICA

OPM   0 9 8 7 6 5 4 3

For William Gordon, for times shared

CONTENTS

vii

CONTENTS

The King ordered the Grand Vizier to bring him a virgin every night, and when the night was over, he ordered her to be killed. And thus it had happened for three years, and in all the city there was no damsel left to withstand the assaults of this rider. But the vizier had a daughter of great beauty, named Scheherazade . . . and she was very eloquent, and pleased all who heard her.

A THOUSAND AND ONE NIGHTS

PROLOGUE

YOU untied your sash, kicked off your sandals, tossed your full skirt into the corner—it was cotton, if I remember—and loosened the clasp that held your hair in a ponytail. You were shivering, and laughing. We were too close to see one another, each absorbed in our urgent rite, enveloped in our shared warmth and scent. You opened to me, my hands on your twisting waist, your hands impatient. You pressed against me, you explored me, you scaled me, you fastened me with your invincible legs, you said a thousand times, come, your lips on mine. In the final instant we glimpsed absolute solitude, each lost in a blazing chasm, but soon we returned from the far side of that fire to find ourselves embraced amid a riot of pillows beneath white mosquito netting. I brushed your hair back to look into your eyes. Sometimes you sat beside me, your legs pulled up to your chin and your silk shawl over one shoulder in the silence of the night that had barely begun. That is how I remember you, in stillness.

You think in words; for you, language is an inexhaustible thread you weave as if life were created as you tell it. I think in the frozen images of a photograph. Not an image on a plate, but one traced by a fine pen, a small and perfect memory with the soft volumes and warm colors of a Renaissance painting, like an intention captured on grainy paper or cloth. It is a prophetic moment; it is our entire existence, all we have lived and have yet to live, all times in one time, without beginning or end. From an indefinite distance I am looking at that picture, which includes me. I am spectator and protagonist. I am in shadow, veiled by the fog of a translucent curtain. I know I am myself, but I am also this person observing from outside. I know what the man on the rumpled bed is feeling, in a room with dark beams arching toward a cathedral ceiling, a scene that resembles a fragment from some ancient ceremony. I am there with you but also here, alone, in a different frame of consciousness. In the painting, the couple is resting after making love; their skin gleams moistly. The man's eyes are closed; one hand is on his chest and the other on her thigh, in intimate complicity. That vision is recurrent and immutable; nothing changes: always the same peaceful smile on the man's face, always the woman's languor, the same folds in the sheets, the same dark corners of the room, always the lamplight strikes her breasts and cheekbones at the same angle, and always the silk shawl and the dark hair fall with the same delicacy.

Every time I think of you, that is how I see you, how

I see us, frozen for all time on that canvas, immune to the fading of memory. I spend immeasurable moments imagining myself in that scene, until I feel I am entering the space of the photograph and am no longer the man who observes but the man lying beside the woman. Then the quiet symmetry of the picture is broken and I hear voices very close to my ear.

"Tell me a story," I say to you.

"What about?"

"Tell me a story you have never told anyone before. Make it up for me."

Rolf Carlé

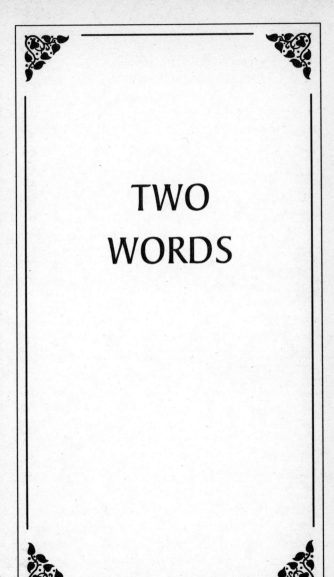

TWO
WORDS

SHE went by the name of Belisa Crepusculario, not because she had been baptized with that name or given it by her mother, but because she herself had searched until she found the poetry of "beauty" and "twilight" and cloaked herself in it. She made her living selling words. She journeyed through the country from the high cold mountains to the burning coasts, stopping at fairs and in markets where she set up four poles covered by a canvas awning under which she took refuge from the sun and rain to minister to her customers. She did not have to peddle her merchandise because from having wandered far and near, everyone knew who she was. Some people waited for her from one year to the next, and when she appeared in the village with her bundle beneath her arm, they would form a line in front of her stall. Her prices were fair. For five centavos she delivered verses from memory; for seven she improved the quality of

9

dreams; for nine she wrote love letters; for twelve she invented insults for irreconcilable enemies. She also sold stories, not fantasies but long, true stories she recited at one telling, never skipping a word. This is how she carried news from one town to another. People paid her to add a line or two: our son was born; so-and-so died; our children got married; the crops burned in the field. Wherever she went a small crowd gathered around to listen as she began to speak, and that was how they learned about each others' doings, about distant relatives, about what was going on in the civil war. To anyone who paid her fifty centavos in trade, she gave the gift of a secret word to drive away melancholy. It was not the same word for everyone, naturally, because that would have been collective deceit. Each person received his or her own word, with the assurance that no one else would use it that way in this universe or the Beyond.

Belisa Crepusculario had been born into a family so poor they did not even have names to give their children. She came into the world and grew up in an inhospitable land where some years the rains became avalanches of water that bore everything away before them and others when not a drop fell from the sky and the sun swelled to fill the horizon and the world became a desert. Until she was twelve, Belisa had no occupation or virtue other than having withstood hunger and the exhaustion of centuries. During one interminable drought, it fell to her to bury four younger brothers and sisters; when she realized that her turn was next, she decided to set out across the plains in the direction of the sea, in hopes that she might trick death along the way. The land was eroded, split with deep cracks, strewn with rocks, fossils of trees and thorny bushes, and skeletons of animals bleached by the sun. From time to time she ran into families who, like her, were heading south, following the mirage of water. Some had begun the march carrying their belongings on their back or in small carts, but they could barely move their own bones, and after a while they had to abandon their possessions. They dragged themselves along painfully, their skin turned to lizard hide and their eyes burned by the reverberating glare. Belisa greeted them with a wave as she passed, but she did not stop, because she had no strength to waste in acts of compassion. Many people fell by the wayside, but she was so stubborn that she survived to cross through that hell and at long last reach the first trickles of water, fine, almost invisible threads that fed spindly vegetation and farther down widened into small streams and marshes.

Belisa Crepusculario saved her life and in the process accidentally discovered writing. In a village near the coast, the wind blew a page of newspaper at her feet. She picked up the brittle yellow paper and stood a long while looking at it, unable to determine its purpose, until curiosity overcame her shyness. She walked over to a man who was washing his horse in the muddy pool where she had quenched her thirst.

"What is this?" she asked.

"The sports page of the newspaper," the man replied, concealing his surprise at her ignorance.

The answer astounded the girl, but she did not want to seem rude, so she merely inquired about the significance of the fly tracks scattered across the page.

"Those are words, child. Here it says that Fulgencio Barba knocked out El Negro Tiznao in the third round."

That was the day Belisa Crepusculario found out that words make their way in the world without a master, and that anyone with a little cleverness can appropriate them and do business with them. She made a quick assessment of her situation and concluded that aside from becoming a prostitute or working as a servant in the kitchens of the rich there were few occupations she was qualified for. It seemed to her that selling words would be an honorable alternative. From that moment on, she worked at that profession, and was never tempted by any other. At the beginning, she offered her merchandise unaware that words could be written outside of newspapers. When she learned otherwise, she calculated the infinite possibilities of her trade and with her savings paid a priest twenty pesos to teach her to read and write; with her three remaining coins she bought a dictionary. She poured over it from *A* to *Z* and then threw it into the sea, because it was not her intention to defraud her customers with packaged words.

One August morning several years later, Belisa Crepusculario was sitting in her tent in the middle of a plaza, surrounded by the uproar of market day, selling legal arguments to an old man who had been trying for sixteen years to get his pension. Suddenly she heard yelling and thudding hoofbeats. She looked up from her writing and saw, first, a cloud of dust, and then a band of horsemen come galloping into the plaza. They were the Colonel's men, sent under orders of El Mulato, a giant known throughout the land for the speed of his knife and his loyalty to his chief. Both the Colonel and El Mulato had spent their lives fighting in the civil war, and their names were ineradicably linked to devastation and calamity. The rebels swept into town like a stampeding herd, wrapped in noise, bathed in sweat, and leaving a hurricane of fear in their trail. Chickens took wing, dogs ran for their lives, women and children scurried out of sight, until the only living soul left in the market was Belisa Crepusculario. She had never seen El Mulato and was surprised to see him walking toward her.

"I'm looking for you," he shouted, pointing his coiled whip at her; even before the words were out, two men rushed her—knocking over her canopy and shattering her inkwell—bound her hand and foot, and threw her like a sea bag across the rump of El Mulato's mount. Then they thundered off toward the hills.

Hours later, just as Belisa Crepusculario was near death, her heart ground to sand by the pounding of the horse, they stopped, and four strong hands set her down. She tried to stand on her feet and hold her head high, but her strength failed her and she slumped to the ground, sinking into a confused dream. She awakened several hours later to the murmur of night in the camp, but before she had time to sort out the sounds, she opened her eyes and found herself staring into the impatient glare of El Mulato, kneeling beside her.

"Well, woman, at last you've come to," he said. To

speed her to her senses, he tipped his canteen and offered her a sip of liquor laced with gunpowder.

She demanded to know the reason for such rough treatment, and El Mulato explained that the Colonel needed her services. He allowed her to splash water on her face, and then led her to the far end of the camp where the most feared man in all the land was lazing in a hammock strung between two trees. She could not see his face, because he lay in the deceptive shadow of the leaves and the indelible shadow of all his years as a bandit, but she imagined from the way his gigantic aide addressed him with such humility that he must have a very menacing expression. She was surprised by the Colonel's voice, as soft and well-modulated as a professor's.

"Are you the woman who sells words?" he asked.

"At your service," she stammered, peering into the dark and trying to see him better.

The Colonel stood up, and turned straight toward her. She saw dark skin and the eyes of a ferocious puma, and she knew immediately that she was standing before the loneliest man in the world.

"I want to be President," he announced.

The Colonel was weary of riding across that godforsaken land, waging useless wars and suffering defeats that no subterfuge could transform into victories. For years he had been sleeping in the open air, bitten by mosquitoes, eating iguanas and snake soup, but those minor inconveniences were not why he wanted to change his destiny. What truly troubled him was the terror he saw in people's eyes. He longed to ride into a town beneath a triumphal arch with bright flags and flowers everywhere; he wanted to be cheered, and be given newly laid eggs and freshly baked bread. Men fled at the sight of him, children trembled, and women miscarried from fright; he had had enough, and so he had decided to become President. El Mulato had suggested that they ride to the capital, gallop up to the Palace, and take over the government, the way they had taken so many other things without anyone's permission. The Colonel, however, did not want to be just another tyrant; there had been enough of those before him and, besides, if he did that, he would never win people's hearts. It was his aspiration to win the popular vote in the December elections.

"To do that, I have to talk like a candidate. Can you sell me the words for a speech?" the Colonel asked Belisa Crepusculario.

She had accepted many assignments, but none like this. She did not dare refuse, fearing that El Mulato would shoot her between the eyes, or worse still, that the Colonel would burst into tears. There was more to it than that, however; she felt the urge to help him because she felt a throbbing warmth beneath her skin, a powerful desire to touch that man, to fondle him, to clasp him in her arms.

All night and a good part of the following day, Belisa Crepusculario searched her repertory for words adequate for a presidential speech, closely watched by El Mulato, who could not take his eyes from her firm wanderer's legs and virginal breasts. She discarded harsh, cold words, words that were too flowery, words worn from abuse, words that offered improbable promises, untruthful and confusing words, until all she had left were words sure to touch the minds of men and women's intuition. Calling upon the knowledge she had purchased from the priest for twenty pesos, she wrote the speech on a sheet of paper and then signaled El Mulato to untie the rope that bound her ankles to a tree. He led her once more to the Colonel, and again she felt the throbbing anxiety that had seized her when she first saw him. She handed him the paper and waited while he looked at it, holding it gingerly between thumbs and fingertips.

"What the shit does this say," he asked finally.

"Don't you know how to read?"

"War's what I know," he replied.

She read the speech aloud. She read it three times, so her client could engrave it on his memory. When she finished, she saw the emotion in the faces of the soldiers who had gathered round to listen, and saw that the Colonel's eyes glittered with enthusiasm, convinced that with those words the presidential chair would be his.

"If after they've heard it three times, the boys are still standing there with their mouths hanging open, it must mean the thing's damn good, Colonel" was El Mulato's approval.

"All right, woman. How much do I owe you?" the leader asked.

"One peso, Colonel."

"That's not much," he said, opening the pouch he wore at his belt, heavy with proceeds from the last foray.

"The peso entitles you to a bonus. I'm going to give you two secret words," said Belisa Crepusculario.

"What for?"

She explained that for every fifty centavos a client paid, she gave him the gift of a word for his exclusive use. The Colonel shrugged. He had no interest at all in her offer, but he did not want to be impolite to someone who had served him so well. She walked slowly to the leather stool where he was sitting, and bent down to give him her gift. The man smelled the scent of a mountain cat issuing from the woman, a fiery heat radiating from her hips, he heard the terrible whisper of her hair, and a breath of sweetmint murmured into his ear the two secret words that were his alone.

"They are yours, Colonel," she said as she stepped back. "You may use them as much as you please."

El Mulato accompanied Belisa to the roadside, his eyes as entreating as a stray dog's, but when he reached out to touch her, he was stopped by an avalanche of words he had never heard before; believing them to be an irrevocable curse, the flame of his desire was extinguished.

During the months of September, October, and November the Colonel delivered his speech so many times that had it not been crafted from glowing and durable words it would have turned to ash as he spoke. He traveled up and down and across the country, riding into cities with a triumphal air, stopping in even the most forgotten villages where only the dump heap betrayed a human presence, to convince his fellow citizens to vote for him. While he spoke from a platform erected in the middle of the plaza, El Mulato and his men handed out sweets and painted his name on all the walls in gold frost. No one paid the least attention to those advertising ploys; they were dazzled by the clarity of the Colonel's proposals and the poetic lucidity of his arguments, infected by his powerful wish to right the wrongs of history, happy for the first time in their lives. When the Candidate had finished his speech, his soldiers would fire their pistols into the air and set off firecrackers, and when finally they rode off, they left behind a wake of hope that lingered for days on the air, like the splendid memory of a comet's tail. Soon the Colonel was the favorite. No one had ever witnessed such a phenomenon: a man who surfaced from the civil war, covered with scars and speaking like a professor, a man whose fame spread to every corner of the land and captured the nation's heart. The press focused their attention on him. Newspapermen came from far away to interview him and repeat his phrases, and the number of his followers and enemies continued to grow.

"We're doing great, Colonel," said El Mulato, after twelve successful weeks of campaigning.

But the Candidate did not hear. He was repeating his secret words, as he did more and more obsessively. He said them when he was mellow with nostalgia; he murmured them in his sleep; he carried them with him on horseback; he thought them before delivering his famous speech; and he caught himself savoring them in his leisure time. And every time he thought of those two words, he thought of Belisa Crepuscario, and his senses were inflamed with the memory of her feral scent, her fiery heat, the whisper of her hair, and her sweetmint breath in his ear, until he began to go around like a sleepwalker, and his men realized that he might die before he ever sat in the presidential chair.

"What's got hold of you, Colonel," El Mulato asked so often that finally one day his chief broke down and told him the source of his befuddlement: those two words that were buried like two daggers in his gut.

"Tell me what they are and maybe they'll lose their magic," his faithful aide suggested.

"I can't tell them, they're for me alone," the Colonel replied.

Saddened by watching his chief decline like a man with a death sentence on his head, El Mulato slung his rifle over his shoulder and set out to find Belisa Crepus- culario. He followed her trail through all that vast coun- try, until he found her in a village in the far south, sitting under her tent reciting her rosary of news. He planted himself, spraddle-legged, before her, weapon in hand.

"You! You're coming with me," he ordered.

She had been waiting. She picked up her inkwell, folded the canvas of her small stall, arranged her shawl around her shoulders, and without a word took her place behind El Mulato's saddle. They did not exchange so much as a word in all the trip; El Mulato's desire for her had turned into rage, and only his fear of her tongue prevented his cutting her to shreds with his whip. Nor was he inclined to tell her that the Colonel was in a fog, and that a spell whispered into his ear had done what years of battle had not been able to do. Three days later they arrived at the encampment, and immediately, in view of all the troops, El Mulato led his prisoner before the Candidate.

"I brought this witch here so you can give her back her words, Colonel," El Mulato said, pointing the barrel of his rifle at the woman's head. "And then she can give you back your manhood."

The Colonel and Belisa Crepusculario stared at each other, measuring one another from a distance. The men knew then that their leader would never undo the witchcraft of those accursed words, because the whole world could see the voracious-puma eyes soften as the woman walked to him and took his hand in hers.

WICKED
GIRL

AT the age of eleven, Elena Mejías was still a scrawny whelp of a girl with the dull skin of solitary children, a mouth revealing gaps still unfilled by second teeth, mouse-colored hair, and a prominent skeleton, much too large for the rest of her, that threatened to poke through at the elbows and knees. Nothing about her betrayed her torrid dreams, nor presaged the sensuous creature she would become. Among the nondescript furnishings and faded draperies of her mother's boardinghouse, she went completely unnoticed. She was like a melancholy little waif playing among the dusty geraniums and enormous ferns in the patio, or trooping back and forth between the kitchen range and dining room tables to serve the evening meal. On the rare occasion some boarder took notice of her, it was only to ask her to spray for cockroaches or to fill the watertank in the bathroom when the creaking pump failed to draw water to the second floor. Her mother, exhausted by heat and the grind of running her board-inghouse, had no energy for tenderness or time to devote to her daughter, so she failed to notice when Elena began to change into a different creature. She had always been a quiet, shy child absorbed in mysterious games, talking to herself in corners and sucking her thumb. She emerged from the house only to go to school or the market; she seemed uninterested in the noisy children of her own age playing in the street.

The transformation of Elena Mejías coincided with the arrival of Juan José Bernal, the Nightingale, as he liked to call himself and as a poster he tacked to the wall of his room loudly proclaimed. Most of the boarders were students or employees in some obscure division of city government. Real ladies and gentlemen, Elena's mother always said, for she prided herself on not taking just anyone under her roof, only respectable persons with a visible means of support, good manners, and enough money to pay a month's room and board in advance, who were also disposed to live by the regulations of her boardinghouse—more fitting for a seminary than a hotel. A widow has to think of her reputation and be able to command respect; I don't want my home turned into a haven for bums and perverts, her mother frequently repeated, so no one, especially Elena, would ever forget. One of the girl's responsibilities was to spy on the guests and keep her mother informed of any suspicious behavior. Eternal stealth exaggerated the ethereal air of the child who moved in an aura of silence, vanishing in the shadows of a room only to appear suddenly as if returning from another dimension. Mother and daughter shared the many chores of the boardinghouse, each immersed in her silent routine, feeling no need to communicate with the other. In truth, they spoke very little, and when they did, during the brief freedom of the hour of the siesta, it was about the clients. Sometimes Elena tried to embellish the gray lives of those transitory men and women who passed through the house leaving no trace of a memory by attributing to them some extraordinary event, coloring their lives through the gift of some clandestine love affair or tragedy, but her mother had an infallible instinct for detecting her fantasies. She also knew when her daughter was hiding something from her. She had an unassailable practical sense and a clear notion of everything that went on under her roof. She knew exactly what each lodger was doing at any hour of the night or day, how much sugar was left in the pantry, who was being called when the telephone rang, and where the last person had left the scissors. She had once been a cheerful, even pretty, young woman; her frumpy dresses barely restrained the impatience of a still-young body, but all the years spent scratching out a living had slowly drained away her spirit and zest for life. When Juan José Bernal came to inquire about a room, however, all that changed for her, and for Elena as well. The mother, seduced by the Nightingale's pretentious manner of speaking and the hint of fame represented by the poster, ignored her own rules and accepted him as a guest, despite the fact he did not in any way fit her image of the ideal boarder. Bernal told her that he sang at night and therefore needed to rest during the day; that he was between engagements and thus could not pay the month in advance; and that he was extremely fussy about his food and hygiene—he was a vegetarian, and he needed to shower twice a day. Amazed, Elena watched, without comment or question, as her mother wrote the name of the new guest in her book and then showed him to his room, struggling with his heavy suitcase while he bore the guitar case and the cardboard tube containing his treasured poster. Camouflaged against the wall, Elena followed them up the stairs, noting the new guest's intense appraisal of the cotton skirt clinging to her mother's sweaty buttocks. As she went into the room Elena flipped the switch, and the great blades of the ceiling fan began to turn with the screech of rusted metal.

Bernal's arrival signaled an immediate change in the household routine. There was more work now, because Bernal slept until the other guests had left for their various employments; he tied up the bath for hours on end; he consumed an astounding quantity of rabbit food, which had to be prepared especially for him; he was constantly on the telephone; and he made liberal use of the iron for touching up his dress shirts—without any charge for this unusual privilege. Elena came home at siesta, when the sun was blazing and the day languishing beneath a terrible white glare, but even at that hour Juan José Bernal would still be fast asleep. As her mother had ordered, Elena would remove her shoes to keep from disturbing the artificial quiet of the house. She was aware that her mother was changing day by day. She could see the signs from the very beginning, long before the residents began to whisper behind her mother's back. First it was the fragrance that clung to her mother and lingered in the rooms as she passed through. Elena knew every corner of the house, and her long training in spying led her to the perfume bottle behind the packets of rice and tins of conserves on the pantry shelf. Next she noticed the dark pencil outlining her mother's eyelids, the touch of red on her lips, the new underclothes, the immediate smile when finally Bernal came down in the evening, his hair still wet from the bath, and sat in the kitchen to wolf down strange dishes fit for a fakir. Her mother would sit across from him and listen while he recounted episodes from his life as an artist, punctuating every adventure with a deep laugh.

For several weeks, Elena hated that man who was claiming all the space in the house and all her mother's attention. She was repelled by the brilliantine-slick hair, the polished nails, the excessive zeal with a toothpick, the pedantry, the brazen assumption they all would serve him. She wondered what her mother could see in the man: he was nothing but a small-time adventurer, a bar entertainer whom no one had ever heard of, why, he might be an out-and-out scoundrel, as *señorita* Sofía, one of their oldest boarders, had suggested in whispers. But then one warm Sunday evening when there was nothing to do and time seemed to have stopped within the walls of the house, Juan José Bernal appeared in the patio with his guitar; he installed himself on a bench beneath the fig tree and began to strum a few chords. The sound drew all the guests, who peered out one by one, at first with a certain timidity—unsure of the reason for this unusual occurrence—and then with increasing enthusiasm; they hauled out the dining room chairs and set them in a circle around the Nightingale.

The man had an ordinary voice, but he had a good ear, and sang with a certain charm. He knew all the stock boleros and rural ballads of the popular repertoire, and a few songs from the Revolution sprinkled with blasphemies and four-letter words that made the ladies blush. For the first time that Elena could remember, there was a festive air in the house. When it grew dark, they lighted two kerosene lamps and hung them in the trees, and brought beer and the bottle of rum reserved for treating colds. Elena was trembling as she filled the glasses; she felt the heartrending words of the songs and the lament of the guitar in every fiber of her body, like a fever. Her mother was tapping her toe to the rhythm. Suddenly she stood up, took Elena's hands, and the two began to dance, immediately followed by all the others, including *señorita* Sofía, all fluttering and nervous giggles. For an endless moment Elena danced, moving to the cadence of Bernal's voice, held tight against her mother's body, breathing in the new flowery scent, blissfully happy. Then she felt her mother gently pushing her away, pulling back to dance alone. With her eyes closed and her head tipped back, her mother swayed like a sheet drying in the breeze. Elena stepped from the floor, and all the dancers returned to their seats, leaving the mistress of the boardinghouse alone in the center of the patio, lost in her dance.

After that night, Elena saw Bernal through new eyes. She forgot that she had detested his brilliantine, his toothpicks, and his arrogance, and whenever she saw him or heard his voice she remembered the songs he had sung the night of that impromptu fiesta and again felt the flush on her skin and the confusion in her heart, a fever she did not know how to put into words. She watched him when he was not looking, and little by little noticed things she had not at first appreciated, his shoulders, his strong, muscular neck, the sensual curve of his heavy lips, his perfect teeth, the elegance of his long, fine hands. She was filled with an insupportable longing to be close enough to him to bury her face against his dark-skinned chest, to hear the resonance of the air in his lungs and the beating of his heart, to smell his scent, a scent she knew would be sharp and penetrating, like good leather or tobacco. She imagined herself playing with his hair, examining the muscles of his back and legs, discovering the shape of his foot, dissolving into smoke and filtering down his throat to inhabit his entire body. But if he happened to look up and meet her eyes, Elena, trembling, would run and hide in the farthest and densest corner of the patio. Bernal had taken possession of her thoughts; she could not bear how time stopped when she was away from him. In school, she moved as if in a nightmare, blind and deaf to anything except her inner thoughts, where there was room only for him. What was he doing at that moment? Perhaps he was sleeping face down on the bed with the shutters closed, the room in darkness, the warm air stirred by the blades of the fan, a trail of sweat marking his spine, his face sunk in the pillow. At the first sound of the bell marking the end of the day, she ran home, praying he was not yet awake and she would be able to wash and put on a clean dress and sit down to wait for him in the kitchen, pretending to do homework so her mother would not burden her with household chores. Later, when she heard him leaving his bath, whistling, she was tormented by impatience and fear, sure that she would die of pleasure if he touched her, even spoke to her, dying for him to do just that but at the same time ready to fade into the furniture, because although she could not live without him, neither could she endure his burning presence. Stealthily, she followed him everywhere, waited on him hand and foot, tried to divine his wishes and offer whatever he needed before he asked, but always moving like a wraith, not wanting to reveal her existence.

Elena could not sleep at night because he was not in the house. She would get up from her hammock and roam the first floor like a ghost, working up courage finally to tiptoe into Bernal's room. She would close the door behind her and open the shutter a crack to let in the reflection from the street to light the ceremonies she invented to enable her to claim the bits of the man's soul left behind in his belongings. She stood staring at herself in the oval of a mirror as black and shiny as a pool of dark mud, because he had looked at himself there and the vestiges of their two images could blend together in an embrace. She walked toward the glass, eyes staring, seeing herself through his eyes, kissing her own lips with a cold hard kiss that she imagined warm as Bernal's lips. She felt the surface of the mirror against her breast and the tiny grapes of her nipples hardened, generating a dull pain that flowed downward to an exact point between her legs. She sought that pain, again and again. She took a shirt and boots from Bernal's clothespress and put them on. She walked a few steps around the room, very careful not to make any noise. Still in his clothes, she burrowed through his

drawers, combed her hair with his comb, sucked his
toothbrush, licked his shaving cream, caressed his dirty
clothes. Then, without knowing why, she took off her
nightdress, his boots and shirt, and lay naked on Bernal's bed, greedily inhaling his scent, invoking his
warmth to wrap herself in. She touched every inch of
her body, beginning with the strange shape of her skull,
the translucent cartilage of her ears, the sockets of her
eyes, the opening of her mouth, and continued down
her body, sketching all the bones, folds, angles, and
curves of the insignificant whole of herself, wishing she
were as immense and heavy as a whale. She imagined
her body filling with a sweet, sticky liquid like honey,
swelling, expanding to the size of a mammoth doll, until
she overflowed the bed and the room, until her tumes-
cence filled the entire house. Exhausted, she would
doze for a few minutes, weeping.

Then one Saturday morning, watching from her window, Elena saw Bernal walk up to where her mother
was bent over the trough scrubbing clothes. He laid his
hand on her waist and she did not move, as if the weight
of that hand were part of her body. Even from a
distance, Elena could see his gesture of possession,
her mother's attitude of surrender, their intimacy, the
current that joined them in a formidable secret. Elena
broke out in a sweat, she could not breathe, her heart
was a frightened bird in her rib cage, her hands and
feet tingled, her blood rushed until she thought it would
burst her fingers. That was when she began to spy on
her mother.

One after another, she discovered the clues she
sought; at first it was only a glance, an overly long

greeting, a complicitous smile, the suspicion that beneath the table their legs were touching and that they were inventing pretexts to be alone. Finally, one night as she was returning from Bernal's room after performing her lover's ritual, she heard a sound like the whisper of an underground stream coming from her mother's room, and she realized that all that time, every night while she believed Bernal was out singing for a living, the man had been just across the hall, and while she was kissing his memory in the mirror and breathing in the trace of his presence in the sheets, he had been with her mother. With the skill learned from many years of making herself invisible, she glided into the room and saw them locked in their pleasure. The fringed lampshade glowed with a warm light that exposed the lovers on the bed. Her mother was transformed into a round, rosy, moaning, opulent siren, an undulating sea anemone, all tentacles and suckers, all mouth and hands and legs and orifices, rolling and turning and cleaving to the large body of Bernal, who by contrast seemed rigid and clumsy, moving spasmodically like a piece of wood tossed by inexplicable high winds. Until that moment the girl had never seen a man naked, and she was taken back by the essential differences. His masculinity seemed brutal to her, and it was a long time before she could overcome her terror and force herself to look. Soon, however, she was conquered by fascination and watched with absolute attention to learn from her mother the formula she had used to snatch Bernal from her, a formula more powerful than all Elena's love, all her prayers, her dreams, her silent summons, all her magic ceremonies contrived to draw him to her. She was sure that her mother's caresses and sighs held the key to the secret, and if she could learn them, Juan José Bernal would sleep with her in the hammock hung every night from two large hooks in the room of the cupboards.

Elena spent the following days in a haze. She lost interest in everything around her, even Bernal himself, whom she stored in a spare compartment of her mind, and she submersed herself in a fanciful reality that completely replaced the world of the living. She continued to follow her routines by force of habit, but her heart was not in anything she did. When her mother noticed her lack of appetite, she attributed it to oncoming puberty—though Elena still looked too young—and she found time to sit alone with her and explain to her the joke of having been born a woman. Elena listened in sullen silence to the peroration about Biblical curses and menstrual flow, convinced that none of that would ever happen to her.

On Wednesday Elena felt hungry for the first time in almost a week. She went into the pantry with a can opener and a spoon and devoured the contents of three cans of green peas, then peeled the red wax from a Dutch cheese and ate it as she would an apple. Immediately after, she ran to the patio, doubled over, and vomited a vile green soup over the geraniums. The pain in her belly and the bitter taste in her mouth restored her sense of reality. That night she slept tranquilly, rolled up in her hammock, sucking her thumb as she had in her cradle. Thursday morning she woke happy; she helped her mother prepare coffee for the boarders and ate breakfast with her in the kitchen. Once at school, however, she complained of terrible pains in her stomach, and she writhed so and asked so often to go to the bathroom that by midmorning her teacher gave her permission to go home.

Elena made a long detour, consciously avoiding familiar streets, and approached the house from the back wall, which overlooked a ravine. She managed to scale the wall and jump into the patio with less difficulty than she had expected. She had calculated that at that hour her mother would be in the market and, as it was the day for fresh fish, it would be a while before she returned. The house was empty except for Juan José Bernal and *señorita* Sofía, who had been home from work a week because of an attack of arthritis.

Elena hid her books and shoes under some bushes and slipped into the house. She climbed the stairway, hugging the wall and holding her breath, until she heard the radio thundering from the room of *señorita* Sofía and felt more calm. The door to Bernal's room opened with a push. It was dark inside, and for a moment, having just come from the brilliant daylight outside, she could see nothing. She knew the room from memory, however; she had measured that space many times and knew where each object was, the precise place the floor squeaked, how many steps it was from the door to the bed. She waited, nevertheless, until her eyes adjusted to the darkness and she could see the outlines of the furniture. A few moments more and she could see the man on the bed. He was not sleeping face down, as she had imagined so often, but lying on his back on top of the sheets, wearing only his undershorts, one arm was outflung and the other across his chest, and a lock of hair had fallen over his eyes. Instantly, all the fear and impatience that had accumulated for days disappeared, leaving Elena cleansed, with the calm of one who knows what she has to do. It seemed to her she had lived that moment many times; she told herself she had nothing to fear, this was a ceremony only slightly different from those that had gone before. Slowly, she stripped off her school uniform down to the cotton panties she dared not remove. She walked to the bed. She could see Bernal better now. Gingerly, she sat on the edge of the bed near his hand, concentrating on not adding even one wrinkle to the sheets. She leaned forward slowly, until her face was only a few centimeters from his and she could sense the warmth of his breath and the sweet scent of his body; then with infinite care she lay down beside him, extending each leg so cautiously he did not even stir. She waited, listening to the silence, until she resolved to rest her hand on his belly in an almost imperceptible caress. With that touch a suffocating wave flooded her body; she feared the sound of her heart was echoing through the house and would surely wake Bernal. It was several minutes before she recovered, and when she realized he had not moved, she relaxed, and let her arm fall limp—its weight, in any case, so slight it did not alter his sleep. Recalling her mother's movements, as her fingers crept beneath the elastic waist of his undershorts, Elena sought Bernal's lips and kissed him as she had so often kissed the mirror. Still asleep, Bernal moaned; he wrapped one arm around the girl's waist while his free hand took hers to guide her and his mouth opened to return her kiss, as he whispered his lover's name. Elena heard him name her mother, but rather than drawing back, she pressed even more closely to him. Bernal took her by the waist and pulled her atop him, settling her on his body as he began the first movements of love. Then, sensing the extreme fragility of that birdlike skeleton on his chest, a spark of awareness flashed through the cottony fog of sleep, and he opened his eyes. Elena felt his body tense, felt herself seized by the ribs and thrown aside so violently she fell to the floor, but she sprang to her feet and ran back to the bed to embrace him again. Bernal slapped her full in the face and leapt from the bed, terrorized by who knows what ancient prohibitions and nightmares.

"Wicked, *wicked* girl!" he screamed.

The door opened, and *señorita* Sofía was standing in the threshold.

Elena spent the next seven years with the nuns, three more attending college in the capital, and then began working in a bank. In the meantime, her mother married her lover and the two of them continued to run the boardinghouse until they had saved enough money to retire to a small house in the country, where they grew carnations and chrysanthemums to sell in the city. The Nightingale hung the poster proclaiming his artistry in a gilt frame, but he never sang in a nightclub again, and no one missed him. He never accompanied his wife when she visited her stepdaughter, and he never asked about her—not wanting to stir up doubts in his own mind—but he thought of her constantly. The child's image had stayed with him, intact, untouched by the years; she was still the passionate girl he had rejected. If truth were known, as the years went by, the memory of those light bones, that childish hand on his belly, that baby tongue in his mouth, grew to be an obsession. When he embraced the heavy body of his wife, he had to concentrate on those visions, meticulously invoking Elena's image to awaken the always more diffuse impulse of pleasure. Now in his middle years, he went to stores that sold children's clothing and bought cotton underpants and pleasured himself, stroking them and stroking himself. Then he would be ashamed of such salacious moments and he would burn the panties or bury them in a deep hole in the patio in a vain attempt to put them out of his mind. He began to loiter around schools and parks where he could stand at a distance and watch the prepubescent girls who for an all-too-brief moment bore him to the abyss of that unforgettable Thursday.

Elena was twenty-six when she visited her mother for the first time, bringing her boyfriend, an army captain who for years had been begging her to marry him. The two young people—he, not wanting to seem arrogant, in civilian clothes, she laden with presents—arrived on one of those cool November afternoons. Bernal had awaited that visit like a jittery teenager. He stared at himself in the mirror at every opportunity, scrutinizing his image, wondering whether Elena would see any change, or whether in her mind the Nightingale had remained immune to the ravages of time. He had prepared for the meeting, practicing every word and imagining every possible answer. The only possibility

37

he failed to consider was that in the place of the smoldering child who had consigned him to a life of torment he would find an insipid and quite shy young woman. Bernal felt betrayed.

As it grew dark, after the euphoria of the arrival had worn off and mother and daughter had exchanged all their latest news, they carried chairs to the patio to enjoy the cool of evening. The air was heavy with the perfume of carnations. Bernal suggested a glass of wine, and Elena followed him into the house to bring glasses. For a few moments, they were alone, face to face in the narrow kitchen. Bernal, who had waited so long for this opportunity, held Elena by the arm while he told her how it had all been a terrible mistake, how he had been half asleep that morning and had no idea what he was doing, how he had never meant to throw her to the floor or call her what he did, and would she please take pity on him and forgive him, and maybe then he could come to his senses, because for what seemed a lifetime he had been consumed by a constant burning desire for her that fired his blood and poisoned his mind. She stared at him, speechless, not knowing what to answer. What wicked girl was he talking about? She had left her childhood far behind, and the pain of that first rejected love was locked in some sealed compartment of memory. She did not remember any particular Thursday in her past.

CLARISA

CLARISA was born before the city had electricity, she lived to see the television coverage of the first astronaut levitating on the moon, and she died of amazement when the Pope came for a visit and was met in the street by homosexuals dressed up as nuns. She had spent her childhood among pots of ferns and corridors lighted by oil lamps. Days went by slowly in those times. Clarisa never adjusted to the fits and starts of today's time; she always seemed to have been captured in the sepia tints of a nineteenth-century portrait. I suppose that once she had had a virginal waist, a graceful bearing, and a profile worthy of a medallion, but by the time I met her she was already a rather bizarre old woman with shoulders rounded into two gentle humps and with white hair coiled around a sebaceous cyst the size of a pigeon egg crowning her noble head. She had a profound, shrewd gaze that could penetrate the most hidden evil and return unscathed.

Over the course of a long lifetime she had come to be considered a saint, and after she died many people placed her photograph on the family altar along with other venerable images to ask her aid in minor difficulties, even though her reputation for being a miracle worker is not recognized by the Vatican and undoubtedly never will be. Her miraculous works are unpredictable: she does not heal the blind, like Santa Lucia, or find husbands for spinsters, like St. Anthony, but they say she helps a person through a hangover, or problems with the draft, or a siege of loneliness. Her wonders are humble and improbable, but as necessary as the spectacular marvels worked by cathedral saints.

I met Clarisa when I was an adolescent working as a servant in the house of Le Señora, a lady of the night, as Clarisa called women of her occupation. Even then she was distilled almost to pure spirit; I thought at any minute she might rise from the floor and fly out the window. She had the hands of a healer, and people who could not pay a doctor, or were disillusioned with traditional science, waited in line for her to relieve their pain or console them in their bad fortune. My *patrona* used to call her to come lay her hands on her back. In the process, Clarisa would rummage about in La Señora's soul with the hope of turning her life around and leading her along the paths of righteousness—paths my employer was in no hurry to travel, since that direction would have unalterably affected her commercial enterprise. Clarisa would apply the curative warmth of the palms of her hands for ten or fifteen minutes, depending on the intensity of the pain, and then accept a glass of fruit juice as payment for her services. Sitting face to face in the kitchen, the two women would have their chat about human and divine topics, my *patrona* more on the human side and Clarisa more on the divine, never straining tolerance nor abusing good manners. Later, when I found a different job, I lost sight of Clarisa until we met once again some twenty years later and reestablished a friendship that has lasted to this day, overcoming the many obstacles that lay in our way, including death, which has put a slight crimp in the ease of our communications.

Even in the times when age had slowed her former missionary zeal, Clarisa persevered steadfastly in her good works, sometimes even against the will of the beneficiaries—as in the case of the pimps on Calle República, who had to bear the mortification of the public harangues that good lady delivered in her unwavering determination to redeem them. Clarisa gave everything she owned to the needy. As a rule she had only the clothes on her back, and toward the end of her life it was difficult to find a person any poorer than she. Charity had become a two-way street, and you seldom could tell who was giving and who receiving.

She lived in an old rundown three-story house; some rooms were empty but some she rented as a storehouse for a saloon, so that the rancid stench of cheap liquor always hung in the air. She had never moved from the dwelling she had inherited from her parents because it reminded her of an aristocratic past, and also because for more than forty years her husband had buried himself alive in a room at the back of the patio. He had been a judge in a remote province, an office he had carried out with dignity until the birth of his second child, when disillusion robbed him of the will to accept his fate, and like a mole he had taken refuge in the malodorous cave of his room. He emerged only rarely, a scurrying shadow, and opened the door only to hand out his chamber pot and to collect the food his wife left for him every day. He communicated with her by means of notes written in his perfect calligraphy and by knocks on the door—two for yes and three for no. Through the walls of his room you could hear asthmatic hacking and an occasional longshoreman's curse intended for whom, no one never knew.

"Poor man, I pray that God will soon call him to His side, and he will take his place in the heavenly choir," Clarisa would sigh without a suspicion of irony. The opportune passing of her husband, however, was one grace Divine Providence never granted, for he has survived to the present day. He must be a hundred by now, unless he has already died and the coughs and curses we hear are only echoes from the past.

Clarisa married him because he was the first person to ask her, and also because her parents thought that a judge would be the best possible match. She left the sober comfort of her paternal hearth and reconciled herself to the avarice and vulgarity of her husband with no thought of a better fate. The only time she was ever heard to utter a nostalgic comment about the refinements of her past was in regard to a grand piano that had enchanted her as a girl. That is how we learned of her love for music and much later, when she was an old woman, a group of us who were her friends gave her a modest piano. It had been over sixty years since she had been anywhere near a keyboard, but she sat down

44

on the piano stool and played, by memory and without hesitation, a Chopin nocturne.

A year or so after her marriage to the judge, she gave birth to an albino daughter, who as soon as she began to walk accompanied her mother to church. The tiny creature was so dazzled by the pageantry of the liturgy that she began pulling down drapes to "play bishop," and soon the only game that interested her was imitating the ecclesiastical ritual, chanting in a Latin of her own invention. She was hopelessly retarded; her only words were spoken in an unknown tongue, she drooled incessantly, and she suffered uncontrollable attacks during which she had to be tied like a circus animal to prevent her from chewing the furniture and attacking guests. With puberty, however, she grew more tractable, and helped her mother around the house. The second child was born into the world totally devoid of curiosity and bearing gentle Asian features; the only skill he ever mastered was riding a bicycle, but it was of little benefit to him since his mother never dared let him out of the house. He spent his life pedaling in the patio on a stationary bicycle mounted on a music stand.

Her children's abnormality never affected Clarisa's unalterable optimism. She considered them pure souls immune to evil, and all her relations with them were marked by affection. Her greatest concern was to save them from earthly suffering, and she often asked herself who would look after them when she was gone. The father, in contrast, never spoke of them, and used the pretext of his retarded children to wallow in shame, abandon his career, his friends, even fresh air, and

45

entomb himself in his room, copying newspapers with monklike patience in a series of stenographic notebooks. Meanwhile, his wife spent the last cent of her dowry, and her inheritance, and took on all kinds of jobs to support the family. In her own poverty, she never turned her back to the poverty of others, and even in the most difficult periods of her life she continued her works of mercy.

Clarisa had a boundless understanding of human weaknesses. One night when she was sitting in her room sewing, her white head bent over her work, she heard unusual noises in the house. She got up to see what they might be, but got no farther than the doorway, where she ran into a man who held a knife to her throat and threatened, "Quiet, you whore, or I'll slash your throat."

"This isn't the place you want, son. The ladies of the night are across the street, there where you hear the music."

"Don't try to be funny, this is a robbery."

"What did you say?" Clarisa smiled, incredulous. "And what are you going to steal from me?"

"Sit down in that chair. I'm going to tie you up."

"I won't do it, son. I'm old enough to be your mother. Where's your respect?"

"Sit *down*, I said!"

"And don't shout, you'll frighten my husband, and he's not at all well. By the way, put that knife down, you might hurt someone," said Clarisa.

"Listen, lady, I came her to rob you," the flustered robber muttered.

"Well, there's not going to be any robbery. I will not

let you commit a sin. I'll *give* you some money of my
own will. You won't be taking it from me, is that clear?
I'm giving it to you." She went to her purse and took
out all the money for the rest of the week. "That's all I
have. We're quite poor, as you see. Come into the
kitchen, now, and I'll set the kettle to boil."

The man put away his knife and followed her, money
in hand. Clarisa brewed tea for both of them, served
the last cookies in the house, and invited him to sit with
her in the living room.

"Wherever did you get the notion to rob a poor old
woman like me?"

The thief told her he had been watching her for days;
he knew that she lived alone and thought there must be
something of value in that big old house. It was his first
crime, he said; he had four children, he was out of a
job, and he could not go home another night with empty
hands. Clarisa pointed out that he was taking too great
a risk, that he might not only be arrested but was
putting his immortal soul in danger—although in truth
she doubted that God would punish him with hell, the
worst might be a while in purgatory, as long, of course,
as he repented and did not do it again. She offered to
add him to her list of wards and promised she would not
bring charges against him. As they said goodbye, they
kissed each other on the cheek. For the next ten years,
until Clarisa died, she received a small gift at Christmastime through the mail.

Not all Clarisa's dealings were with the indigent; she
also knew people of note, women of breeding, wealthy
businessmen, bankers, and public figures, whom she
visited seeking aid for the needy, with never a thought

for how she might be received. One day she presented herself in the office of Congressman Diego Cienfuegos, known for his incendiary speeches and for being one of the few incorruptible politicians in the nation, which did not prevent his rising to the rank of Minister and earning a place in history books as the intellectual father of an important peace treaty. In those days Clarisa was still young, and rather timid, but she already had the unflagging determination that characterized her old age. She went to the Congressman to ask him to use his influence to procure a new modern refrigerator for the Teresian Sisters. The man stared at her in amazement, questioning why he should aid his ideological enemies.

"Because in their dining room the Little Sisters feed a hundred children a day a free meal, and almost all of them are children of the Communists and evangelicals who vote for you," Clarisa replied mildly.

That was the beginning of a discreet friendship that was to cost the politician many sleepless nights and many donations. With the same irrefutable logic, Clarisa obtained scholarships for young atheists from the Jesuits, used clothing for neighborhood prostitutes from the League of Catholic Dames, musical instruments for a Hebrew choir from the German Institute, and funds for alcohol rehabilitation programs from viniculturists.

Neither the husband interred in the mausoleum of his room nor the debilitating hours of her daily labors prevented Clarisa's becoming pregnant again. The midwife advised her that in all probability she would give birth to another abnormal child, but Clarisa mollified her with the argument that God maintains a certain equilibrium in the universe, and just as He creates some things twisted, He creates others straight; for every virtue there is a sin, for every joy an affliction, for every evil a good, and on and on, for as the wheel of life turns through the centuries, everything evens out. The pendulum swings back and forth with inexorable precision, she said.

Clarisa passed her pregnancy in leisure, and in the proper time gave birth to her third child. The baby was born at home with the help of the midwife and in the agreeable company of the two inoffensive and smiling retarded children who passed the hours at their games, one spouting gibberish in her bishop's robe and the other pedaling nowhere on his stationary bicycle. With this birth the scales tipped in the direction needed to preserve the harmony of Creation, and a grateful mother offered her breast to a strong boy with wise eyes and firm hands. Fourteen months later Clarisa gave birth to a second son with the same characteristics.

"These two boys will grow up healthy and help me take care of their brother and sister," she said with conviction, faithful to her theory of compensation; and that is how it was, the younger children grew straight as reeds and were gifted with kindness and goodness.

Somehow Clarisa managed to support the four children without any help from her husband and without injuring her family pride by accepting charity for herself. Few were aware of her financial straits. With the same tenacity with which she spent late nights sewing rag dolls and baking wedding cakes to sell, she battled the deterioration of her house when the walls began to sweat a greenish mist. She instilled in the two younger children her principles of good humor and generosity with such splendid results that in the following years they were always beside her caring for their older siblings, until the day the retarded brother and sister accidentally locked themselves in the bathroom and a leaking gas pipe transported them gently to a better world.

When the Pope made his visit, Clarisa was not quite eighty, although it was difficult to calculate her exact age; she had added years out of vanity, simply to hear people say how well preserved she was for the ninety-five years she claimed. She had more than enough spirit, but her body was failing; she could barely totter through the streets, where in any case she lost her way, she had no appetite, and finally was eating only flowers and honey. Her spirit was detaching itself from her body at the same pace her wings germinated, but the preparations for the papal visit rekindled her enthusiasm for the adventures of this earth. She was not content to watch the spectacle on television because she had a deep distrust of that apparatus. She was convinced that even the astronaut on the moon was a sham filmed in some Hollywood studio, the same kind of lies they practiced in those stories where the protagonists love or die and then a week later reappear with the same faces but a new destiny. Clarisa wanted to see the pontiff with her own eyes, not on a screen where some actor was costumed in the Pope's robes. That was how I found myself accompanying her to cheer the Pope as he rode through the streets. After a couple of hours fighting the throngs of faithful and vendors of candles and T-shirts and religious prints and plastic saints, we caught sight of the Holy Father, magnificent in his portable glass cage, a white porpoise in an aquarium. Clarisa fell to her knees, in danger of being crushed by fanatics and the Pope's police escort. Just at the instant when the Pope was but a stone's throw away, a rare spectacle surged from a side street: a group of men in nun's habits, their faces garishly painted, waving posters in favor of abortion, divorce, sodomy, and the right of women to the priesthood. Clarisa dug through her purse with a trembling hand, found her eyeglasses, and set them on her nose to assure herself she was not suffering a hallucination.

She paled. "It's time to go, daughter. I've already seen too much."

She was so undone that to distract her I offered to buy her a hair from the Pope's head, but she did not want it without a guarantee of authenticity. According to a socialist newspaperman, there were enough capillary relics offered for sale to stuff a couple of pillows.

"I'm an old woman, and I no longer understand the world, daughter. We'd best go home."

She was exhausted when she reached the house, with the din of the bells and cheering still ringing in her temples. I went to the kitchen to prepare some soup for the judge and heat water to brew her a cup of camomile tea, in hopes it would have a calming effect. As I waited for the tea, Clarisa, with a melancholy face, put everything in order and served her last plate of food to her husband. She set the tray on the floor and for the first time in more than forty years knocked on his door.

"How many times have I told you not to bother me," the judge protested in a reedy voice.

"I'm sorry, dear, I just wanted to tell you that I'm going to die."

"When?"

"On Friday."

"Very well." The door did not open.

Clarisa called her sons to tell them about her imminent death, and then took to her bed. Her bedroom was a large dark room with pieces of heavy carved mahogany furniture that would never become antiques because somewhere along the way they had broken down. On her dresser sat a crystal urn containing an astoundingly realistic wax Baby Jesus, rosy as an infant fresh from its bath.

"I'd like for you to have the Baby, Eva. I know you'll take care of Him."

"You're not going to die. Don't frighten me this way."

"You need to keep Him in the shade, if the sun strikes Him, He'll melt. He's lasted almost a century, and will last another if you protect Him from the heat."

I combed her meringue hair high on her head, tied it with a ribbon, and then sat down to accompany her through this crisis, not knowing exactly what it was. The moment was totally free of sentimentality, as if in fact she was not dying but suffering from a slight cold.

"We should call a priest now, don't you think, child?"

"But Clarisa, what sins can you have?"

"Life is long, and there's more than enough time for evil, God willing."

"But you'll go straight to heaven—that is, if heaven exists."

"Of course it exists, but it's not certain they'll let me in. They're very strict there," she murmured. And after a long pause, she added, "When I think over my trespasses, there was one that was very grave . . ."

I shivered, terrified that this old woman with the aureole of a saint was going to tell me that she had intentionally dispatched her retarded children to facilitate divine justice, or that she did not believe in God and had devoted herself to doing good in this world only because the scales had assigned her the role of compensating for the evil of others, an evil that was unimportant anyway since everything is part of the same infinite process. But Clarisa confessed nothing so dramatic to me. She turned toward the window and told me, blushing, that she had not fulfilled her conjugal duties.

"What does that mean?" I asked.

"Well, I mean I did not satisfy my husband's carnal desires, you understand?"

"No."

"If you refuse your husband your body, and he falls into the temptation of seeking solace with another woman, you bear that moral responsibility."

"I see. The judge fornicates, and the sin is yours."

"No, no. I think it would be both our sins. . . . I would have to look it up."

"And the husband has the same obligation to his wife?"

"What?"

"I mean, if you had had another man, would your husband share the blame?"

"Wherever did you get an idea like that, child!" She stared at me in disbelief.

"Don't worry, because if your worst sin was that you slighted the judge, I'm sure God will see the joke."

"I don't think God is very amused by such things."

"But Clarisa, to doubt divine perfection *would* be a great sin."

She seemed in such good health that I could not imagine her dying, but I supposed that, unlike us simple mortals, saints have the power to die unafraid and in full control of their faculties. Her reputation was so solid that many claimed to have seen a circle of light around her head and to have heard celestial music in her presence, and so I was not surprised when I undressed her to put on her nightgown to find two inflamed bumps on her shoulders, as if her pair of great angel wings were about to erupt.

The rumor of Clarisa's coming death spread rapidly. Her children and I had to marshal an unending line of people who came to seek her intervention in heaven for various favors, or simply to say goodbye. Many expected that at the last moment a significant miracle would occur, such as, the odor of rancid bottles that pervaded the house would be transformed into the perfume of camelias, or beams of consolation would shine forth from her body. Among the visitors was her friend the robber, who had not mended his ways but instead become a true professional. He sat beside the dying woman's bed and recounted his escapades without a hint of repentance.

"Things are going really well. I rob only upper-class homes now. I steal from the rich, and that's no sin. I've never had to use violence, and I work clean, like a true gentleman," he boasted.

"I will have to pray a long time for you, my son."

"Pray on, Grandmother. It won't do me any harm."

La Señora came, too, distressed to be saying good-bye to her beloved friend, and bringing a flower crown and almond-paste sweets as her contribution to the death vigil. My former *patrona* did not know me, but I had no trouble recognizing her despite her girth, her wig, and the outrageous plastic shoes printed with gold stars. To offset the thief, she came to tell Clarisa that her advice had fallen upon fertile ground, and that she was now a respectable Christian.

"Tell Saint Peter that, so he'll take my name from his black book" was her plea.

"What a terrible disappointment for all these good people if instead of going to heaven I end up in the cauldrons of hell," Clarisa said after I was finally able to close the door and let her rest for a while.

"If that happens, no one down here is going to know, Clarisa."

"Thank heavens for that!"

From early dawn on Friday a crowd gathered outside in the street, and only her two sons' vigilance prevented the faithful from carrying off relics, from strips of paper off the walls to articles of the saint's meager wardrobe. Clarisa was failing before our eyes and, for the first time, she showed signs of taking her own death seriously. About ten that morning, a blue automobile with Congressional plates stopped before the house. The chauffeur helped an old man climb from the back seat; the crowds recognized him immediately. It was *don* Diego Cienfuegos, whom decades of public service had made a national hero. Clarisa's sons came out to greet him, and accompanied him in his laborious ascent to the second floor. When Clarisa saw him in the doorway, she became quite animated; the color returned to her cheeks and the shine to her eyes.

"Please, clear everyone out of the room and leave us alone," she whispered in my ear.

Twenty minutes later the door opened and *don* Diego Cienfuegos departed, feet dragging, eyes teary, bowed and crippled, but smiling. Clarisa's sons, who were waiting in the hall, again took his arms to steady him, and seeing them there together I confirmed something that had crossed my mind before. The three men had the same bearing, the same profile, the same deliberate assurance, the same wise eyes and firm hands.

I waited until they were downstairs, and went back to my friend's room. As I arranged her pillows, I saw that she, like her visitor, was weeping with a certain rejoicing.

"*Don* Diego was your grave sin, wasn't he?" I murmured.

"That wasn't a sin, child, just a little boost to help God balance the scales of destiny. You see how well it worked out, because my two weak children had two strong brothers to look after them."

Clarisa died that night, without suffering. Cancer, the doctor diagnosed, when he saw the buds of her wings; saintliness, proclaimed the throngs bearing candles and flowers; astonishment, say I, because I was with her when the Pope came to visit.

TOAD'S
MOUTH

TIMES were very hard in the south. Not in the south of this country, but the south of the world, where the seasons are reversed and winter does not come at Christmastime, as it does in civilized nations, but, as in barbaric lands, in the middle of the year. Stone, sedge, and ice; endless plains that toward Tierra del Fuego break up into a rosary of islands, peaks of a snowy cordillera closing off the distant horizon, and silence that dates from the birth of time, interrupted periodically by the subterranean sigh of glaciers slipping slowly toward the sea. It is a harsh land inhabited by rough men. Since there was nothing there at the beginning of the century the English could carry away, they obtained permits to raise sheep. After a few years the animals had multiplied in such numbers that from a distance they looked like clouds trapped against the ground; they ate all the vegetation and trampled the last altars of the indigenous cultures. This was where Hermelinda earned a living with her games of fantasy.

The large headquarters of Sheepbreeders, Ltd., rose up from the sterile plain like a forgotten cake; it was surrounded by an absurd lawn and defended against the depredations of the climate by the superintendent's wife, who could not resign herself to life outside the heart of the British Empire and continued to dress for solitary dinners with her husband, a phlegmatic gentleman buried beneath his pride in obsolete traditions. The native Spanish-speaking drovers lived in the camp barracks, separated from their English *patrones* by fences of thorny shrubs and wild roses planted in a vain attempt to limit the immensity of the pampas and create for the foreigners the illusion of a gentle English countryside.

Under surveillance of the management's guards, aching with cold without so much as a bowl of hot soup for months, the workers survived in misery, as neglected as the sheep they herded. In the evening, there was always someone who would pick up the guitar and fill the air with sentimental songs. They were so impoverished for love that despite the saltpeter the cook sprinkled over their food to cool their bodily ardor and the fires of memory the drovers lay with their sheep, even with a seal if they could get to the coast and catch one. The seals had large mammae, like a nursing mother's, and if they skinned the still living, warm, palpitating seal, a love-starved man could close his eyes and imagine he was embracing a siren. Even with such obstacles, the workers enjoyed themselves more than their employers, thanks to Hermelinda's illicit games.

Hermelinda was the only young woman in all the land—aside from the English lady who crossed through the rose fence with her shotgun only when in search of hares; even then, all the men could glimpse was a bit of veiled hat amid a cloud of dust and yelping English setters. Hermelinda, in contrast, was a female they could see and count on, one with a heady mixture of blood in her veins and a hearty taste for a good time. She was in the business of solace out of pure and simple vocation; she liked almost all the men in general, and many in particular. She reigned among them like a queen bee. She loved their smell of work and desire, their harsh voices, their unshaven cheeks, their bodies, so vigorous and at the same time so pliable in her hands, their pugnacious natures and naïve hearts. She knew the illusory strength and extreme vulnerability of her clients, but she never took advantage of those weaknesses; on the contrary, she was moved by both. Her rambunctious nature was tempered by traces of maternal tenderness, and night often found her sewing patches on a shirt, stewing a chicken for some sick drover, or writing love letters for distant sweethearts. She made her fortune on a mattress stuffed with raw wool under a leaky zinc roof that moaned like lutes and oboes when the wind blew. Hermelinda's flesh was firm and her skin blemished; she laughed with gusto and had grit to spare, far more than any terrified ewe or flayed seal could offer. In every embrace, however brief, she proved herself an enthusiastic and playful friend. Word of her firm horse-woman's legs and breasts without a trace of wear had spread across the six hundred kilometers of that wild province, and lovers traveled many miles to spend a while in her company. On Fridays, riders galloped frantically from such far reaches that as they arrived their foaming mounts dropped beneath them. The English *patrones* had outlawed the consumption of alcohol, but Hermelinda had found a way to distill a bootleg liquor that raised the spirits and ruined the liver of her guests. It also served to fuel the lamps at the hour of the entertainment. Bets began after the third round of drinks, when it was impossible for the men to focus their eyes or sharpen their wits.

Hermelinda had conceived a plan to turn a sure profit without cheating anyone. In addition to cards and dice, the men could try their hand at a number of games in which the prize was her person. The losers handed over their money to her, as did those who won, but the winners gained the right to dally briefly in her company, without pretext or preliminary—not because she was unwilling but because she lacked time to give each man special attention. The players in Blind Rooster removed their trousers but kept on their jackets, caps, and sheepskin-lined boots as protection against the antarctic cold whistling through the floorboards. Hermelinda blindfolded them and the chase began. At times they raised such a ruckus that their huffing and guffaws spread through the night beyond the roses to the ears of the impassive English couple who sat sipping a last cup of Ceylon tea before bed, pretending they heard nothing but the caprice of the wind across the pampas. The first man to lay a hand on Hermelinda blessed his good fortune as he trapped her in his arms and crowed a triumphant cock-a-doodle-doo. Swing was another of the games. Hermelinda would sit on a plank strung from the roof. Laughing before the men's hungry gazes, she would flex her legs so all could see she had nothing on beneath the yellow petticoats. The players, in an orderly line, had a single chance to possess her, and anyone who succeeded found himself clasped between the beauty's thighs, swept off his feet in a whirl of petticoats, rocked to his bone marrow, and lifted toward the sky. Very few reached the goal; most rolled to the floor amid the hoots of their companions.

A man could lose a month's pay in fifteen minutes playing the game of Toad's Mouth. Hermelinda would draw a chalk line on the floor and four steps away draw a large circle in which she lay down on her back, knees spread wide, legs golden in the light of the spirit lamps. The dark center of her body would be revealed as open as a fruit, as a merry toad's mouth, while the air in the room grew heavy and hot. The players took a position behind the chalk line and tossed their coins toward the target. Some were expert marksmen, with a hand so steady they could stop a panicked animal running at full speed by slinging two stone bolas between its legs, but Hermelinda had an evasive way of sliding her body, shifting it so that at the last instant the coin missed its mark. Those that landed inside the chalk circle belonged to her. If one chanced to enter the gate of heaven, it won for its owner a sultan's treasure: two hours alone with her behind the curtain in absolute ecstasy, seeking consolation for all past wants and dreams of the pleasures of paradise. They told, the men who had lived those two precious hours, that Hermelinda knew ancient love secrets and could lead a

63

man to the threshold of death and bring him back transformed into a wise man.

Until the day that an Asturian named Pablo appeared, very few had won that pair of wondrous hours, although several had enjoyed similar pleasure—but for half their salary, not a few coins. By then Hermelinda had accumulated a small fortune, but the idea of retiring to a more conventional life had never occurred to her; in fact, she took great pleasure in her work and was proud of the sparks of pleasure she afforded the drovers. This Pablo was a lean man with the bones of a bird and hands of a child, whose physical appearance contradicted his tremendous tenacity. Beside the opulent and jovial Hermelinda he looked like a peevish banty rooster, but anyone who thought he could enjoy a good laugh at El Asturiano's expense was in for a disagreeable surprise. The tiny foreigner tensed like a viper at the first provocation, ready to lash out at anyone who stood in his way, but the row was always settled before it began because Hermelinda's first rule was that no one fought beneath her roof. Once his dignity had been established, Pablo relaxed. He had a determined, rather funereal, expression; he spoke very little and when he did he revealed his European origins. He had left Spain one jump ahead of the police, and he earned his daily bread running contraband through the narrow Andean passes. He was known to be a surly, pugnacious loner who ridiculed the weather, the sheep, and the English. He had no fixed home and he admitted to no loves or obligations, but he was not getting any younger and solitude was seeping into his bones. Sometimes when he awoke at dawn on the icy ground, wrapped in his black Castilian cape and with his saddle for a pillow, every inch of his body ached. The pain was not the pain of stiff muscles but an accumulation of sorrow and neglect. He was tired of living like a lone wolf, but neither was he cut out for domestication. He had come south because he had heard the rumor that at the end of the world there was a woman who could change the way the wind blew, and he wanted to see her with his own eyes. The vast distance and the risks of the road had not dampened his determination, and when finally he found Hermelinda's saloon and had her in arm's reach, he could see she was forged of the same hard metal as he, and he decided that after such a long journey life would not be worth living without her. He settled into a corner of the room to study her and calculate his possibilities.

El Asturiano had guts of steel; even after several glasses of Hermelinda's liquor his eyes were still clear. He refused to remove his clothes for St. Michael's Patrol, or Mandandirun-dirun-dan, or other contests he found frankly infantile, but toward the end of the evening, when it was time for the crowning moment—The Toad—he shook off the fumes of the alcohol and joined the chorus of men around the chalk circle. To him, Hermelinda was as beautiful and wild as a puma. He felt the stirrings of his hunter's instinct, and the undefined pain of the alienation that had tormented him during his journey turned to tingling anticipation. He saw the feet shod in low boots, the woven stockings rolled below the knee, the long bones and tense muscles of those legs of gold in the froth of full petticoats, and he knew that he would have but one opportunity to win. He took his position, planting his feet on the floor and rocking back and forth until he found the true axis of his being; he transfixed Hermelinda with a knifelike gaze, forcing her to abandon her contortionist's tricks. Or that may not have been how it was; it may be that she chose him from among the others to honor with her company. Pablo squinted, exhaled a deep breath, and after a second or two of absolute concentration, tossed his coin. Everyone watched as it formed a perfect arc and entered cleanly in the slot. A salvo of applause and envious whistles celebrated the feat. Nonchalantly, the smuggler hitched up his pants, took three steps forward, seized Hermelinda's hand and pulled her to her feet, prepared to prove in his two hours that she could not do without him. He almost dragged her from the room; the men stood around drinking and checking their watches until the period of the reward had passed, but neither Hermelinda nor the foreigner appeared. Three hours went by, four, the whole night; morning dawned and the bells rang for work, and still the door did not open.

At noon the lovers emerged. Pablo, without a glance for anyone, went outside to saddle his horse, a horse for Hermelinda, and a mule to carry their belongings. Hermelinda was wearing riding pants and jacket, and a canvas bag filled with coins was tied to her waist. There was a new expression in her eyes and a satisfied swish to her memorable rump. Solemnly, they strapped their goods onto the mule, mounted their horses, and set off. Hermelinda made a vague wave of farewell to her desolate admirers, and followed El Asturiano across the barren plains without a backward glance. She never returned.

The dismay occasioned by Hermelinda's departure was so great that to divert the workmen the management of Sheepbreeders, Ltd., installed swings, bought a target for darts and arrows, and had an enormous open-mouthed ceramic toad imported from London so the drovers could refine their skill in coin tossing, but before a general indifference, those toys ended up on the superintendent's terrace, where as dusk falls the English still play with them to combat their boredom.

THE
GOLD OF
TOMÁS
VARGAS

BEFORE the monumental pandemonium of progress, anyone who had any savings buried them. That was the only way people knew to safeguard their money; it was only later they learned to have confidence in banks. Once the highway came through and it became easier to reach the town by bus, people exchanged their gold and silver coins for colored pieces of paper they kept in strongboxes, as if they were treasure. Tomás Vargas ridiculed these innocents because he never trusted the bank system. Time proved him right, and after the government of El Benefactor fell—it lasted some thirty years, they say—the bills had no value and many people ended up pasting them on the wall for decoration as an unpleasant reminder of their naïveté. While everyone else was writing letters to the new President and the newspapers were complaining of the general unworthiness of the new money, Tomás Vargas's gold nuggets were buried in a safe hiding place, although his good fortune did nothing to mitigate his miserliness or his scrounging. The man had no decency; he borrowed money with no intention of paying it back, and his children went hungry and his wife wore rags while he wore Panama hats and smoked expensive cigars. He even refused to pay the fees for his children's schooling; his six legitimate children were educated free, because the schoolteacher Inés was determined that as long as she had her wits about her and strength enough to work no child in her town would go without learning to read. Age did nothing to quell Vargas's bent for quarreling, carousing, and womanizing. He took great pride in being the most macho macho in the region, as he bellowed in the plaza every time he went off his head with drink and broadcast at the top of his lungs the names of all the girls he had seduced and all the bastards who carried his blood. If he were to be believed, he had sired at least three hundred, for with every fit he spouted different names. The police carried him off more than once, and the Lieutenant himself had given him a few well-placed kicks in the behind, hoping that would improve his character, but the Lieutenant's ministrations had no more effect than the priest's admonitions. In fact, the only person Vargas respected was Riad Halabí, the storekeeper. That is why the neighbors came to him when they suspected that Vargas was drunk and out of control, and was beating his wife or his children. When that happened, the Turk left his counter so fast he forgot to close the shop but raced, choked with righteous wrath, to set things right in the Vargas household. He never needed to say much; the minute Vargas saw him, he calmed down. Riad Halabí was the only person capable of shaming the brute.

Antonia Sierra, Vargas's wife, was twenty-six years younger than he. But she was an old woman by the time she was forty: she had hardly a tooth left in her head, and her once-audacious body had been ruined by work, births, and miscarriages; even so, she still displayed a trace of her past arrogance, a way of walking with her head held high and her body arched—an aftertaste of her old mulatto beauty—and a ferocious pride that arrested any overture of pity. For Antonia, there were not enough hours in the day, because besides caring for her children and looking after the garden and the hens, she earned a few pesos by cooking lunch for the police, taking in washing, and cleaning the school. There were times that her body was covered with black-and-blue marks; no one had to ask, all Agua Santa knew about the abuse she took from her husband. Only Riad Halabí and the schoolteacher Inés dared to give her something now and then, thinking up excuses to keep from offending her—a few clothes, a little food, notebooks and vitamins for the children.

Antonia had to put up with a lot from her husband, including his bringing his concubine into her house.

Concha Díaz arrived in Agua Santa on one of the National Petroleum trucks, as sad and mournful as a ghost. The driver had taken pity on her when he saw her walking barefoot down the road with one bundle over her shoulder and another in her belly. All the trucks stopped when they drove through town, so Riad Halabí was the first to hear the story. He saw the girl appear in his doorway, and by the way she plopped down her bundle before the counter, he immediately realized that she was not passing through; this girl had come to stay. She was very young, dark-skinned, and short, with a thick mop of sun-streaked curly hair that seemed not to have seen a comb for some time. As he always did with visitors, Riad Halabí offered Concha a chair and a cool pineapple drink, and prepared to listen to the account of her adventures or misfortunes. This girl, however, said very little; she just blew her nose with her fingers and kept her eyes on the floor, mumbling a string of laments as tears slowly trickled down her cheeks. Finally the Turk made out that she wanted to see Tomás Vargas, and he sent someone to fetch him from the tavern. He waited in the doorway, and as soon as he saw Vargas, he grabbed the old man by the arm and led him before the girl, not giving him time to recover from his fright.

"The girl says this is your baby," said Riad Halabí, in the mild tones he used when he was angry.

"No one can prove it, Turk. You always know who the mother is, but you can't be sure about the father," said Vargas, discomfited, but with still enough gall to try a raffish wink, which no one appreciated.

With that, the girl raised the pitch of her weeping, gulping out that she would never have come all this way if she hadn't known who the father was. Riad Halabí told Vargas that he should be ashamed, that he was old enough to be the girl's grandfather, and if he thought that people were going to forgive him his sins this time, he was mistaken, what could he have been thinking, but when the girl wailed even louder, he said what everyone knew he would say.

"There, there, child. It's all right. You can stay here in my house for a while, at least until the baby's born."

Concha Díaz began to sob even more wildly, and declared that she would not live anywhere except with Tomás Vargas; that was why she had come. The air congealed in the store; there was a long silence punctuated only by the sound of the ceiling fans and the woman's snuffling. No one had the nerve to tell the girl that the old man was married and had six children. Finally, Vargas picked up the girl's bundle and pulled her to her feet.

"All right, Conchita, if that's what you want, that's what it'll be. We'll go to my house right this minute."

That was how it happened that when Antonia Sierra got home from work she found another woman resting in her hammock, and for the first time in her life, her pride was not strong enough to conceal her feelings. Her insults could be heard all down the main street; they echoed in the plaza and penetrated every house; she screamed that Concha Díaz was a filthy sewer rat, and that Antonia Sierra would make her life so miserable that she would creep back to the gutter she never should have crawled out of, and that if she thought her children were going to live beneath the same roof with a bitch like her, she had another thing coming, because Antonia Sierra was no dumb yokel, and her husband had better watch his step, too, because she had swallowed all his deviltry and cheating for the sake of her children, poor innocents they were, but this was the last straw, they'd see who Antonia Sierra was. Her tantrum lasted a week, at the end of which her cries faded to an incessant muttering. She lost the last vestiges of her beauty, she even lost her way of walking, and dragged around like a whipped dog. Her neighbors tried to tell her that it was Vargas's fault, not Concha's, but she was in no mood to listen to advice to be kind or fair.

Life in that house had never been pleasant, but with the arrival of the concubine it became unrelenting hell. Antonia spent the nights huddled in her children's bed, spitting curses, while next to her snored her husband, cuddling the girl. With the first light of dawn Antonia had to get up, boil the coffee, stir up the cornmeal cakes, get the children off to school, tend the garden, cook for the police, and wash and iron. She performed all these chores like an automaton, while bitterness overflowed her heart. Since she refused to feed her husband, Concha took charge of that task after Antonia left, not wanting to meet her face to face over the cookstove. Antonia Sierra's hatred was so savage that there were those in the town who feared she would end up murdering her rival, and they went to Riad Halabí and the schoolteacher Inés to ask them to intervene before it was too late.

But that was not how things worked out. In two months, Concha's belly was the size of a watermelon, her legs were so swollen her veins seemed about to burst, and because she was lonely and afraid she never stopped crying. Tomás Vargas grew tired of all the tears and came home only to sleep. That meant the women no longer had to take turns cooking. Concha lost the last incentive to get up and get dressed, and lay in the hammock staring at the ceiling, without the energy even to boil a cup of coffee. Antonia ignored her all the first day, but by night had one of the children take her a bowl of soup and a glass of warm milk, so no one could say that she had let anyone die of hunger beneath her roof. The routine was repeated, and after a few days Concha got up to eat with the rest of them. Antonia pretended not to see her, but at least she stopped cursing every time the girl walked near her. Little by little, pity got the best of her. When she saw the girl growing thinner every day, a poor scarecrow with an enormous belly and deep circles under her eyes, she began to kill her hens one by one to make broth, and when all the chickens were gone, she did what she had never done before, she went to Riad Halabí for help.

"I've had six children, and some dead before they were born, but I've never seen anyone so sick from a pregnancy," she explained, blushing. "She's wasted down to her bones, Turk, the minute she swallows a bite of food she vomits it back up. It's not that I care, none of this is any of my affair, but what will I tell her mother if she dies on me? I don't want anyone coming round later asking for an accounting."

Riad Halabí put the sick girl in his truck and drove her to the hospital, and Antonia went with them. They returned with a variety of colored pills and a new dress for Concha, since she could not pull the one she was wearing down past her waist. The other woman's misery forced Antonia Sierra to relive portions of her youth, her first pregnancy, and similar outrages she

77

had lived through. In spite of herself, she wanted Concha Díaz's future to be less dismal than her own. She felt no anger toward her now, but a secret compassion, and she began to treat her like a daughter who had gone wrong, with a brusque authority that barely veiled her tenderness. The girl was terrified to see the pernicious transformations in her body: the ungovernable swelling, the shame of the constant need to urinate, the waddling like a goose, the uncontrollable nausea, the wishing she could die. Some days she woke up so sick she could not get out of her hammock; then Antonia left the children to take turns looking after her while she rushed through her work to get home early and care for Concha. Other days Concha woke with more spirit, and when Antonia returned home, exhausted, she found dinner waiting and the house cleaned. The girl would serve her a cup of coffee and stand by her side waiting for her to drink it, watching Antonia with the moist eyes of a grateful animal.

The baby was born in the hospital in the city, because he did not want to come into the world and they had to open up Concha Díaz to get him out. Antonia stayed with her a week, while the schoolteacher Inés looked after her own children. The two women returned in Halabí's supply truck, and all Agua Santa came out to welcome them back. The mother smiled while Antonia exhibited the baby with a grandmother's ebullience, proclaiming that he would be christened Riad Vargas Díaz in just tribute to the Turk, because without his help the mother would never have reached motherhood and, besides, the Turk had paid all the expenses when the father turned a deaf ear and pretended he was drunker than usual, to keep from digging up his gold.

Before two weeks had gone by, Tomás Vargas tried to coax Concha Díaz back to his hammock, despite the fact the woman had an unhealed scar and battlefield dressing across her belly. Antonia stepped up to him with her hands on her hips, determined for the first time in her life to keep the old vulture from getting his way. Her husband made a move to whip off his belt to give her the usual thrashing, but before he could complete the gesture, she started toward him with such ferocity that he stepped back in surprise. With that hesitation, he was lost, because she knew then who was the stronger. Meanwhile, Concha Díaz had set her baby in a corner and picked up a heavy clay pot, with the clear intention of breaking it across his skull. Vargas realized he was at a disadvantage, and left the house swearing and cursing. All Agua Santa learned what had happened, because he himself told the girls in the whorehouse, then they told everyone that Vargas couldn't cut the mustard anymore and that his bragging about being such a stud was pure swagger with nothing to back it up.

Things changed after that. Concha Díaz recovered rapidly, and while Antonia was out working she tended the children and the garden and the house. Tomás Vargas swallowed his pride and humbly returned to his hammock—without a companion. He made up for this affront by mistreating the children and telling in the tavern that, like mules, all women really understand is the stick, but at home he never tried to punish them again. When he was drunk he shouted the joys of bigamy to the four winds, and for several Sundays the priest would have to rebut that sacrilege from the pulpit, before the idea caught on and many years of preaching the Christian virtue of monogamy went down the drain.

In Agua Santa they could tolerate a man who mistreated his family, a man who was lazy and a troublemaker, who never paid back money he borrowed, but gambling debts were sacred. In the cockfights bills were folded and displayed between the fingers where everyone could see them, and in dominoes, darts, or cards, they were placed on the table to the player's left. Sometimes the National Petroleum truckdrivers stopped by for a few hands of poker, and although they never showed their money, they paid the last cent before they left. Saturdays the guards from Santa María Prison came to town to visit the whorehouse and gamble away their week's pay in the tavern. Not even they—twice as crooked as the prisoners they guarded—dared play if they couldn't pay. No one violated that rule.

Tomás Vargas never bet, but he liked to watch the players; he could spend hours observing a game of dominoes; he was the first to pick a spot at the cockfights; and he listened to the announcement of the lottery winners over the radio, even though he never bought a ticket. The magnitude of his greed had protected him from temptation. Nevertheless, when the steely complicity of Antonia Sierra and Concha Díaz nipped his manly impulses in the bud, he turned toward gambling. At first he made miserable little bets, and only the most down-and-out drunks would sit at the table with him, but he had more luck with cards than with his women, and before long he was bitten by the bug for easy money and began to change down to the marrow of his miserly bones. With the hope of getting rich at one lucky stroke and, in the process—using the illusory projection of that triumph—of mending his damaged reputation as a rake, he began to take bigger risks. Soon the boldest players were taking their measure against him, while the rest formed a circle around them to follow the turns of each encounter. Tomás Vargas did not spread his money on the table, as was the tradition, but he paid up when he lost. At home, things went from bad to worse, and Concha also had to go out and work. The children stayed home by themselves, and the schoolteacher Inés fed them to keep them from going into town to beg.

Tomás Vargas's real troubles began the day he accepted a challenge from the Lieutenant and after six hours of playing won two hundred pesos. The officer confiscated his subordinates' salaries to pay his debt. He was a stocky, dark-skinned man with a walrus mustache, who always left his jacket unbuttoned so the girls could appreciate his hairy chest and collection of gold chains. No one in Agua Santa liked him, because he was a man of unpredictable character and he granted himself authority to invent laws according to his whim and convenience. Before his arrival, the jail had been a couple of rooms where you spent the night after a brawl—there were never any serious crimes in Agua Santa and the only wrongdoers were prisoners being transported to Santa María Prison—but the Lieutenant made sure that no one left his jail without a sound beating first. Thanks to him, people learned to fear the law. He was furious about losing the two hundred pesos, but he handed over the money without a word, even with a certain elegant detachment, because not even he, with all the weight of his power, would have left the table without paying.

Tomás Vargas spent two days bragging about his triumph, until the Lieutenant advised him he would be waiting for his revenge the following Saturday. This time the bet would be a thousand pesos, he announced in such a peremptory tone that Vargas was reminded of the officer's boot in his rear and did not dare refuse. On Saturday afternoon the tavern was filled. It was so crowded and hot that no one could catch a breath, and they carried the table outside so that everyone could witness the game. Never had so much money been bet in Agua Santa, and Riad Halabí was appointed to ensure the fairness of the proceedings. He began by directing the public to stand two steps away, to prevent any cheating, and the Lieutenant and other policemen to leave their weapons at the jail.

"Before we begin, both players must place their money on the table," the arbiter declared.

"My word is good, Turk," replied the Lieutenant.

"In that case, my word's enough, too," added Tomás Vargas.

"How will you pay if you lose?" Riad Halabí wanted to know.

"I have a house in the capital; if I lose, Vargas will have the title tomorrow."

"Good. And you?"

"I will pay with my buried gold."

The game was the most exciting thing that had happened in the town in many years. Everyone in Agua Santa, from ancients to young children, gathered in the street to watch. Only Antonia Sierra and Concha Díaz were absent. Neither the Lieutenant nor Tomás Vargas inspired any sympathy, so no one cared who won; the entertainment consisted of speculating on the agonies of the two players and of the people wagering on one or the other. Tomás Vargas had on his side his string of good luck with cards, but the Lieutenant had the advantage of a cool head and his reputation as a hard man.

The game ended at seven and, according to the agreed terms, Riad Halabí declared the Lieutenant the winner. In his triumph, the policeman maintained the same calm he had shown the preceding week in defeat—no mocking smile, no sarcastic word—he merely sat in his chair picking his teeth with his little fingernail.

"All right, Vargas; the time has come to dig up your treasure," he said when the spectators' excitement had died down.

Tomás Vargas's skin was ashen, his shirt was soaked with sweat, and he gasped for air, which seemed to have stuck in his throat. Twice he tried to stand, but each time his knees buckled. Riad Halabí had to support him. Finally he gathered enough strength to start off in the direction of the highway, followed by the Lieutenant, the police, the Turk, the schoolteacher Inés, and, behind them, the whole town in a boisterous procession. They had walked a couple of miles when Vargas veered to the right, diving into the riot of gluttonous vegetation that surrounded Agua Santa. There was no path, but with little hesitation he made his way among gigantic trees and huge ferns until he came to the edge of a ravine barely visible through the impenetrable screen of the jungle. The crowd stopped there, while Vargas and the Lieutenant scrambled down the bank. The heat was humid and oppressive, even though it was almost sunset. Tomás Vargas signaled them not to come any farther; he got down on all fours, and crawled beneath some philodendrons with great fleshy leaves. A long minute went by before they heard his howl. The Lieutenant plunged into the foliage, grabbed him by the ankles, and jerked him out.

"What's the matter?"

"It isn't there, it isn't there!"

"What do you mean, 'it isn't there'?"

"I swear, Lieutenant, I don't know anything about this; they stole it, they stole my treasure!" and he burst out crying like a widow woman, so overcome he was oblivious to the Lieutenant's repeated kicks.

"Pig! I'll get my money. On your mother's grave, I'll get my money!"

Riad Halabí hurled himself down the slope of the ravine and removed Vargas from the Lieutenant's clutches before he kicked him to a pulp. He calmed the Lieutenant, arguing that blows would not resolve anything, and then helped the old man back up the ravine. Tomás Vargas was racked with fear; he was blubbering and staggering and swooning so that the Turk almost had to carry him to get him home. Antonia Sierra and Concha Díaz were sitting in the doorway in rush chairs, drinking coffee and watching it grow dark. They showed no sign of dismay when they learned what had happened, but continued sipping their coffee, unmoved.

For more than a week Tomás Vargas had a high temperature, during which he raved about gold nuggets and marked cards, but he was robust by nature, and instead of dying of grief as everyone expected, he regained his health. When he could get out of his hammock, he did not venture out for several days, but finally his habit of dissipation was stronger than his prudence, so he took his Panama hat and, still shaky and frightened, went down to the tavern. He did not return that night, and two days later someone brought the news that his mutilated body had been found in the very ravine where he had hidden his treasure. He had been quartered with a machete like a steer, the end everyone had known would be his sooner or later.

Antonia Sierra and Concha Díaz buried him without grief and with no funeral procession except Riad Halabí and the schoolteacher Inés, who had come to accompany them, not to pay posthumous tribute to a man they had never respected in life. The two women lived on together, happy to help each other in bringing up their children and in the many vicissitudes of life. Not long after the burial they bought hens, rabbits, and pigs; they rode the bus to the city and returned with clothes for all the family. That year they repaired the house with new lumber, they added two rooms, they painted the house blue, they installed a gas stove, and then began a cookery business in their home. Every noon they went out with all the children to deliver meals to the jail, the school, and the post office; and if there was any extra, they left it on the store counter for Riad Halabí to offer to the truckdrivers. And so they made their way out of poverty and started off down the road to prosperity.

IF YOU
TOUCHED
MY HEART

AMADEO Peralta was
raised in the midst of his father's gang and, like all the
men of his family, grew up to be a ruffian. His father
believed that school was for sissies; you don't need
books to get ahead in life, he always said, just balls and
quick wits, and that was why he trained his boys to be
rough and ready. With time, nevertheless, he realized
that the world was changing very rapidly and that his
business affairs needed to be more firmly anchored.
The era of undisguised plunder had been replaced by
one of corruption and bribery; it was time to administer
his wealth by using modern criteria, and to improve his
image. He called his sons together and assigned them
the task of establishing friendships with influential persons and of learning the legal tricks that would allow
them to continue to prosper without danger of losing
their impunity. He also encouraged them to find sweethearts among the old-line families and in this way see

whether they could cleanse the Peralta name of all its stains of mud and blood. By then Amadeo was thirty-two years old; the habit of seducing girls and then abandoning them was deeply ingrained; the idea of marriage was not at all to his liking but he did not dare disobey his father. He began to court the daughter of a wealthy landowner whose family had lived in the same place for six generations. Despite her suitor's murky reputation, the girl accepted, for she was not very attractive and was afraid of ending up an old maid. Then began one of those tedious provincial engagements. Wretched in a white linen suit and polished boots, Amadeo came every day to visit his fiancée beneath the hawklike eye of his future mother-in-law or some aunt, and while the young lady served coffee and guava sweets he would peek at his watch, calculating the earliest moment to make his departure.

A few weeks before the wedding, Amadeo Peralta had to make a business trip through the provinces and found himself in Agua Santa, one of those towns where nobody stays and whose name travelers rarely recall. He was walking down a narrow street at the hour of the siesta, cursing the heat and the oppressive, cloying odor of mango marmalade in the air, when he heard a crystalline sound like water purling between stones; it was coming from a modest house with paint flaked by the sun and rain like most of the houses in that town. Through the ornamental iron grille he glimpsed an entryway of dark paving stones and whitewashed walls, then a patio and, beyond, the surprising vision of a young girl sitting cross-legged on the ground and cra-

dling a blond wood psaltery on her knees. For a while
he stood and watched her.

"Come here, sweet thing," he called finally. She
looked up, and despite the distance he could see the
startled eyes and uncertain smile in a still childish face.
"Come with me," Amadeo asked—implored—in a
hoarse voice.

She hesitated. The last notes lingered like a question
in the air of the patio. Peralta called again. The girl
stood up and walked toward him; he slipped his hand
through the iron grille, shot the bolt, opened the gate,
and seized her hand, all the while reciting his entire
repertoire of seduction: he swore that he had seen her
in his dreams, that he had been looking for her all his
life, that he could not let her go, and that she was the
woman fate had meant for him—all of which he could
have omitted because the girl was simple and even
though she may have been enchanted by the tone of his
voice she did not understand the meaning of his words.
Hortensia was her name, and she had just turned
fifteen; her body was tuned for its first embrace, though
she was unable to put a name to the restlessness and
temblors that shook it. It was so easy for Peralta to
lead her to his car and drive to a nearby clearing that an
hour later he had completely forgotten her. He did not
recognize her even when a week later she suddenly
appeared at his house, one hundred and forty kilometers away, wearing a simple yellow cotton dress and
canvas espadrilles, her psaltery under her arm, and
inflamed with the fever of love.

Forty-seven years later, when Hortensia was rescued
from the pit in which she had been entombed, and

newspapermen traveled from every corner of the nation to photograph her, not even she could remember her name or how she had got there.

The reporters accosted Amadeo Peralta: "Why did you keep her locked up like a miserable beast?"

"Because I felt like it," he replied calmly. By then he was eighty, and as lucid as ever; he could not understand this belated outcry over something that had happened so long ago.

He was not inclined to offer explanations. He was a man of authority, a patriarch, a great-grandfather; no one dared look him in the eye; even priests greeted him with bowed head. During the course of his long life he had multiplied the fortune he inherited from his father; he had become owner of all the land from the ruins of the Spanish fort to the state line, and then had launched himself on a political career that made him the most powerful cacique in the territory. He had married the landowner's ugly daughter and sired nine legitimate descendants with her and an indefinite number of bastards with other women, none of whom he remembered since he had a heart hardened to love. The only woman he could not entirely discard was Hortensia; she stuck in his consciousness like a persistent nightmare. After the brief encounter in the tall grass of an empty lot, he had returned to his home, his work, and his insipid, well-bred fiancée. It was Hortensia who had searched until she found *him;* it was she who had planted herself before him and clung to his shirt with the terrifying submission of a slave. This is a fine kettle of fish, he had thought; here I am about to get married with all this hoopla and to-do, and now this idiot girl turns up on my doorstep. He wanted to be rid of her, and yet when he saw her in her yellow dress, with those entreating eyes, it seemed a waste not to take advantage of the opportunity, and he decided to hide her while he found a solution.

And so, by carelessness, really, Hortensia ended up in the cellar of an old sugar mill that belonged to the Peraltas, where she was to remain for a lifetime. It was a large room, dank and dark, suffocating in summer and in the dry season often cold at night, furnished with a few sticks of furniture and a straw pallet. Amadeo Peralta never took time to make her more comfortable, despite his occasionally feeding a fantasy of making the girl a concubine from an Oriental tale, clad in gauzy robes and surrounded with peacock feathers, brocade tented ceilings, stained-glass lamps, gilded furniture with spiral feet, and thick rugs where he could walk barefoot. He might actually have done it had Hortensia reminded him of his promises, but she was like a wild bird, one of those blind guacharos that live in the depths of caves: all she needed was a little food and water. The yellow dress rotted away and she was left naked.

"He loves me; he has always loved me," she declared when she was rescued by neighbors. After being locked up for so many years she had lost the use of words and her voice came out in spurts like the croak of a woman on her deathbed.

For a few weeks Amadeo had spent a lot of time in the cellar with her, satisfying an appetite he thought insatiable. Fearing that she would be discovered, and jealous even of his own eyes, he did not want to expose her to daylight and allowed only a pale ray to enter through the tiny hole that provided ventilation. In the darkness, they coupled frenziedly, their skin burning and their hearts impatient as carnivorous crabs. In that cavern all odors and tastes were heightened to the extreme. When they touched, each entered the other's being and sank into the other's most secret desires. There, voices resounded in repeated echoes; the walls returned amplified murmurs and kisses. The cellar became a sealed flask in which they wallowed like playful twins swimming in amniotic fluid, two swollen, stupefied fetuses. For days they were lost in an absolute intimacy they confused with love.

When Hortensia fell asleep, her lover went out to look for food and before she awakened returned with renewed energy to resume the cycle of caresses. They should have made love to each other until they died of desire; they should have devoured one another or flamed like mirrored torches, but that was not to be. What happened instead was more predictable and ordinary, much less grandiose. Before a month had passed, Amadeo Peralta tired of the games, which they were beginning to repeat; he sensed the dampness eating into his joints, and he began to feel the attraction of things outside the walls of that grotto. It was time to return to the world of the living and to pick up the reins of his destiny.

"You wait for me here. I'm going out and get very rich. I'll bring you gifts and dresses and jewels fit for a queen," he told her as he said goodbye.

"I want children," said Hortensia.

"Children, no; but you shall have dolls."

In the months that followed, Peralta forgot about the

dresses, the jewels, and the dolls. He visited Hortensia when he thought of her, not always to make love, sometimes merely to hear her play some old melody on her psaltery; he liked to watch her bent over the instrument, strumming chords. Sometimes he was in such a rush that he did not even speak; he filled her water jugs, left her a sack filled with provisions, and departed. Once he forgot about her for nine days, and found her on the verge of death; he realized then the need to find someone to help care for his prisoner, because his family, his travels, his business, and his social engagements occupied all his time. He chose a tight-mouthed Indian woman to fill that role. She kept the key to the padlock, and regularly came to clean the cell and scrape away the lichens growing on Hortensia's body like pale delicate flowers almost invisible to the naked eye and redolent of tilled soil and neglected things.

"Weren't you ever sorry for that poor woman?" they asked when they arrested her as well, charging her with complicity in the kidnapping. She refused to answer but stared straight ahead with expressionless eyes and spat a black stream of tobacco.

No, she had felt no pity for her; she believed the woman had a calling to be a slave and was happy being one, or else had been born an idiot and like others in her situation was better locked up then exposed to the jeers and perils of the street. Hortensia had done nothing to change her jailer's opinion; she never exhibited any curiosity about the world, she made no attempt to go outside for fresh air, and she complained about nothing. She never seemed bored; her mind had stopped at some moment in her childhood, and solitude in no way disturbed her. She was, in fact, turning into a subterranean creature. There in her tomb her senses grew sharp and she learned to see the invisible; she was surrounded by hallucinatory spirits who led her by the hand to other universes. She left behind a body huddled in a corner and traveled through starry space like a messenger particle, living in a dark land beyond reason. Had she had a mirror, she would have been terrified by her appearance; as she could not see herself, however, she was not witness to her deterioration: she was unaware of the scales sprouting from her skin, or the silkworms that had spun a nest in her long, tangled hair, or the lead-colored clouds covering eyes already dead from peering into shadows. She did not feel her ears growing to capture external sounds, even the faintest and most distant, like the laughter of children at school recess, the ice-cream vendor's bell, birds in flight, or the murmuring river. Nor did she realize that her legs, once graceful and firm, were growing twisted as they adjusted to moving in that confined space, to crawling, nor that her toenails were thickening like an animal's hooves, her bones changing into tubes of glass, her belly caving in, and a hump forming on her back. Only her hands, forever occupied with the psaltery, maintained their shape and size, although her fingers had forgotten the melodies they had once known and now extracted from the instrument the unvoiced sob trapped in her breast. From a distance, Hortensia resembled a tragic circus monkey; on closer view, she inspired infinite pity. She was totally ignorant of the malignant transformations taking place;

in her mind she held intact the image of herself as the young girl she had last seen reflected in the window of Amadeo Peralta's automobile the day he had driven her to this lair. She believed she was as pretty as ever, and continued to act as if she were; the memory of beauty crouched deep inside her and only if someone approached very close would he have glimpsed it beneath the external façade of a prehistoric dwarf.

All the while, Amadeo Peralta, rich and feared, cast the net of his power across the region. Every Sunday he sat at the head of a long table occupied by his sons and nephews, cronies and accomplices, and special guests such as politicians and generals whom he treated with a hearty cordiality tinged with sufficient arrogance to remind everyone who was master here. Behind his back, people whispered about his victims, about how many he had ruined or caused to disappear, about bribes to authorities; there was talk that he had made half his fortune from smuggling, but no one was disposed to seek the proof of his transgressions. It was also rumored that Peralta kept a woman prisoner in a cellar. That aspect of his black deeds was repeated with more conviction even than stories of his crooked dealings; in fact, many people knew about it, and with time it became an open secret.

One afternoon on a very hot day, three young boys played hooky from school to swim in the river. They spent a couple of hours splashing around on the muddy bank and then wandered off toward the old Peralta sugar mill that had been closed two generations earlier when cane ceased to be a profitable crop. The mill had the reputation of being haunted; people said you could hear sounds of devils, and many had seen a disheveled old witch invoking the spirits of dead slaves. Excited by their adventure, the boys crept onto the property and approached the mill. Soon they were daring enough to enter the ruins; they ran through large rooms with thick adobe walls and termite-riddled beams; they picked their way through weeds growing from the floor, mounds of rubbish and dog shit, rotted roof tiles, and snake nests. Making jokes to work up their courage, egging each other on, they came to the huge roofless room that contained the ruined sugar presses; here rain and sun had created an impossible garden, and the boys thought they could detect a lingering scent of sugar and sweat. Just as they were growing bolder they heard, clear as a bell, the notes of a monstrous song. Trembling, they almost retreated, but the lure of horror was stronger than their fear, and they huddled there, listening, as the last note drilled into their foreheads. Gradually, they were released from their paralysis; their fear evaporated and they began looking for the source of those weird sounds so different from any music they had ever known. They discovered a small trapdoor in the floor, closed with a lock they could not open. They rattled the wood planks that sealed the entrance and were struck in the face by an indescribable odor that reminded them of a caged beast. They called but no one answered; they heard only a hoarse panting on the other side. Finally they ran home to shout the news that they had discovered the door to hell.

The children's uproar could not be stilled, and thus the neighbors finally proved what they had suspected for decades. First the boys' mothers came to peer through the cracks in the trapdoor; they, too, heard the terrible notes of the psaltery, so different from the banal melody that had attracted Amadeo Peralta the day he had paused in a small alley in Agua Santa to dry sweat from his forehead. The mothers were followed by throngs of curious and, last of all, after a crowd had already gathered, came the police and firemen, who chopped open the door and descended into the hole with their lamps and equipment. In the cave they found a naked creature with flaccid skin hanging in pallid folds; this apparition had tangled gray hair that dragged the floor, and moaned in terror of the noise and light. It was Hortensia, glowing with a mother-of-pearl phosphorescence under the steady beams of the fire fighters' lanterns; she was nearly blind, her teeth had rotted away, and her legs were so weak she could barely stand. They only sign of her human origins was the ancient psaltery clasped to her breast.

The news stirred indignation throughout the country. Television screens and newspapers displayed pictures of the woman rescued from the hole where she had spent her life, now, at least, half clothed in a cloak someone had tossed around her shoulders. In only a few hours, the indifference that had surrounded the prisoner for almost half a century was converted into a passion to avenge and succor her. Neighbors improvised lynch parties for Amadeo Peralta; they stormed his house, dragged him out, and had the *guardia* not arrived in time, would have torn him limb from limb in the plaza. To assuage their guilt for having ignored Hortensia for so many years, everyone wanted to do something for her. They collected money to provide her a pension, they gathered tons of clothing and medicine she did not need, and several welfare organizations were given the task of scraping the filth from her body, cutting her hair, and outfitting her from head to toe, so she looked like an ordinary old lady. The nuns offered her a bed in a shelter for indigents, and for several months kept her tied up to prevent her from running back to her cellar, until finally she grew accustomed to daylight and resigned to living with other human beings.

Taking advantage of the public furor fanned by the press, Amadeo Peralta's numerous enemies finally gathered courage to launch an attack against him. Authorities who for years had overlooked his abuses fell upon him with the full fury of the law. The story occupied everyone's attention long enough to see the former caudillo in prison, and then faded and died away. Rejected by family and friends, a symbol of all that is abominable and abject, harassed by both jailers and companions-in-misfortune, Peralta spent the rest of his days in prison. He remained in his cell, never venturing into the courtyard with the other inmates. From there, he could hear the sounds from the street.

Every day at ten in the morning, Hortensia, with the faltering step of a madwoman, tottered down to the prison where she handed the guard at the gate a warm saucepan for the prisoner.

"He almost never left me hungry," she would tell the guard in an apologetic tone. Then she would sit in the street to play her psaltery, wresting from it moans of agony impossible to bear. In the hope of distracting her or silencing her, some passersby gave her money.

Crouched on the other side of the wall, Amadeo Peralta heard those sounds that seemed to issue from the depths of the earth and course through every nerve in his body. This daily castigation must mean something, but he could not remember what. From time to time he felt something like a stab of guilt, but immediately his memory failed and images of the past evaporated in a dense mist. He did not know why he was in that tomb, and gradually he forgot the world of light and lost himself in his misfortune.

GIFT
FOR A
SWEETHEART

HORACIO Fortunato was forty-six when the languid Jewish woman who was to change his roguish ways and deflate his fanfaronade entered his life. Fortunato came from a long line of circus people, the kind who are born with rubber bones and a natural gift for somersaults, people who at an age when other infants are crawling around like worms are hanging upside down from a trapeze and brushing the lion's teeth. Before his father made it into a serious enterprise, rather than the idle fancy it had been, the Fortunato Circus experienced more difficulty than glory. At different times of catastrophe and turmoil the company was reduced to two or three members of the clan who wandered the byways in a broken-down gypsy wagon with a threadbare tent they set up in godfor-saken little towns. For years Horacio's grandfather bore the sole responsibility for the spectacle: he walked the tightrope, juggled with lighted torches, swallowed Toledo swords, extracted oranges and serpents from a top hat, and danced a graceful minuet with his only companion, a female monkey decked out in ruffles and a plumed hat. His grandfather, however, managed somehow to survive bad times, and while many other circuses succumbed, obliterated by more modern diversions, he saved his circus and, at the end of his life, was able to retire to the south of the continent and cultivate his garden of asparagus and strawberries, leaving a debt-free enterprise to his son Fortunato II. The scion lacked his father's humility, nor was he disposed to perform a balancing act on a tightrope or do pirouettes with a chimpanzee; on the other hand, he was gifted with the unshakable prudence of a born businessman. Under his direction the circus grew in size and prestige until it was the largest in the nation. Three colossal striped tents replaced the modest tarp of the earlier hard times; various cages sheltered a traveling zoo of tamed wild animals; and other fanciful vehicles transported the artists, who included the only hermaphroditic and ventriloquist dwarf in history. An exact, wheeled replica of Christopher Columbus's caravel completed the Fortunato Family Famous International Circus. This enormous caravan no longer drifted aimlessly, as it had in his father's day, but steamed purposefully along the principal highways from the Rio Grande to the Straits of Magellan, stopping only in major cities, where it made an entrance with such a clamor of drums, elephants, and clowns—the caravel at the lead, like a miraculous reenactment of the Conquest—that no man, woman, or child could escape knowing the circus had come to town.

Fortunato II married a trapeze artist, and they had a son they named Horacio. But one day wife-and-mother stayed behind, determined to be independent of her husband and support herself through her somewhat precarious calling, leaving the boy in his father's care. Her son held a rather dim picture of her in his memory, never completely separating the image of his mother from that of the many acrobats he had known. When he was ten, his father married another circus artist, this time an equestrienne able to stand on her head on a galloping steed or leap from one croup to another with eyes blindfolded. She was very beautiful. No matter how much soap, water, and perfume she used, she could not erase the last trace of the essence of horse, a sharp aroma of sweat and effort. In her magnificent bosom the young Horacio, enveloped in that unique odor, found consolation for his mother's absence. But with time the horsewoman also decamped without a farewell. In the ripeness of his years, Fortunato II entered into matrimony, for the third and final time, with a Swiss woman he met on a tour bus in America. He was weary of his Bedouin-like existence and felt too old for new alarms, so when his Swiss bride requested it, he had not the slightest difficulty in giving up the circus for a sedentary life, and ended his days on a small farm in the Alps amid bucolic hills and woods. His son Horacio, who was a little over twenty, took charge of the family business.

Horacio had grown up with the instability of moving every few days, of sleeping on wheels and living beneath a canvas roof, but he was very content with his fate. He had never envied other little boys who wore gray uniforms to school and who had their destinies mapped out before they were born. By contrast, he felt powerful and free. He knew all the secrets of the circus, and with the same confidence and ease he mucked out the animal cages or balanced fifty meters above the ground dressed as a hussar and charming the audience with his dolphin smile. If at any moment he longed for stability, he did not admit it, even in his sleep. The experience of having been abandoned first by his mother and then by his stepmother had left him slightly insecure, especially with women, but it had not made him a cynic, because he had inherited his grandfather's sentimental heart. He had an enormous flair for the circus, but he was fascinated by the commercial aspect of the business even more than by the art. He had intended to be rich from the time he was a young boy, with the naïve conviction that money would bring the security he had not received from his family. He increased the number of tentacles spreading from the family enterprise by buying a chain of boxing arenas in several capital cities. From boxing he moved naturally to wrestling, and as he was a man of inventive imagination he transformed that gross sport into a dramatic spectacle. Among his initiatives were the Mummy, who appeared at ringside in an Egyptian sarcophagus; Tarzan, who covered his privates with a tiger skin so tiny that with every lunge the audience held its breath, expecting some major revelation; and the Angel, who every night bet his golden hair and lost it to the scissors of the ferocious Kuramoto— a Mapuche Indian disguised as a Samurai—but then appeared the following day with curls intact, irrefutable proof of his divine condition. These and other commercial ventures, along with public appearances with a pair of bodyguards whose role it was to intimidate his competitors and pique the ladies' curiosity, had earned him a reputation of being a shady character, a distinction he reveled in. He lived a good life, traveled through the world closing deals and looking for monsters, frequented clubs and casinos, owned a glass mansion in California and a retreat in the Yucatán, but lived most of the year in luxury hotels. He bought the temporary company of a series of blondes. He liked them soft, with ample bosoms, in homage to the memory of his stepmother, but he wasted very little energy on amorous affairs, and when his grandfather urged him to marry and bring sons into the world so the Fortunato name would not vanish without an heir, he replied that not even out of his mind would he ascend the matrimonial gallows. He was a dark-skinned, hefty man with thick hair slicked back with brilliantine, shrewd eyes, and an authoritative voice that accentuated his self-satisfied vulgarity. He was obsessed with elegance and he bought clothes befitting a duke—but his suits were a little too shiny, his ties verging on the audacious, the ruby in his ring too ostentatious, his cologne too penetrating. He had the heart of a lion tamer, and no English tailor alive would ever disguise that fact.

This man, who had spent a good part of his existence cutting a wide swath with his lavish life-style, met Patricia Zimmerman on a Tuesday in March, and on the spot lost both unpredictability of spirit and clarity of thought. He was sitting in the only restaurant in the city that still refused to serve blacks, with four cohorts and a diva whom he was planning to take to the

Bahamas for a week, when Patricia entered the room on her husband's arm, dressed in silk and adorned with some of the diamonds that had made the Zimmerman firm famous. Nothing could have been further from the unforgettable stepmother smelling of horses, or the complacent blondes, than this woman. He watched her advance, small, refined, her chest bones bared by her décolletage and her chestnut-colored hair drawn back into a severe bun, and he felt his knees grow heavy and an insufferable burning in his breast. He preferred uncomplicated women ready for a good time, whereas this was a woman who would have to be studied carefully if her worth was to be known, and even then her virtues would be visible only to an eye trained in appreciating subtleties—which had never been the case with Horacio Fortunato. If the fortune-teller in his circus had consulted her crystal ball and predicted that Fortunato would fall in love at first sight with a fortyish and haughty aristocrat, he would have had a good laugh. But that is exactly what happened as he watched Patricia walk toward him like the shade of a nineteenth-century widow-empress in her dark gown with the glitter of all those diamonds shooting fire at her neck. As Patricia walked past, she paused for an instant before that giant with the napkin tucked into his waistcoat and a trace of gravy at the corner of his mouth. Horacio Fortunato caught a whiff of her perfume and the full impact of her aquiline profile and completely forgot the diva, the bodyguards, his business affairs, everything that interested him in life, and decided with absolute seriousness to steal this woman from her jeweler and love her to the best of his ability. He turned his chair to one side and, ignoring his guests, measured the distance that separated her from him, while Patricia Zimmerman wondered whether that stranger was examining her jewels with some evil design.

That same night an extravagant bouquet of orchids was delivered to the Zimmerman residence. Patricia looked at the card, a sepia-colored rectangle with a name from a novel written in golden arabesques. What ghastly taste, she muttered, divining immediately it had come from the man with the plastered-down hair she had seen in the restaurant, and she ordered the gift to be tossed into the street, with the hope that the sender would be circling the house and thus learn the fate of his flowers. The following day a crystal box arrived bearing a single perfect rose, without a card. The majordomo also placed this offering in the trash. Different bouquets followed for the rest of the week: a basket of wild flowers on a bed of lavender, a pyramid of white carnations in a silver goblet, a dozen black tulips imported from Holland, and other varieties impossible to find in this hot climate. Each suffered the fate of the first, but this did not discourage the gallant, whose siege was becoming so unbearable that Patricia Zimmerman did not dare answer the telephone for fear of hearing his voice whispering indecent proposals, as had happened the previous Tuesday at two in the morning. She returned his letters unopened. She stopped going out, because she ran into Fortunato in the most unexpected places: observing her from the adjoining box at the opera; in the street, waiting to open the door of her car before the chauffeur could reach it; materializing like an illusion in an elevator or on some stairway. She was a prisoner in her own home, and frightened. He'll get over it, he'll get over it, she kept telling herself, but Fortunato did not evaporate like a bad dream; he was always there, on the other side of the wall, breathing heavily. She thought of calling the police, or telling her husband, but her horror of scandal prevented her. One morning she was attending to her correspondence when the majordomo announced the visit of the president of Fortunato and Sons.

"In my own house, how dare he!" Patricia muttered, her heart racing. She had to call on the implacable discipline she had acquired in years of small dramas played in salons to disguise the trembling of her hands and voice. For an instant she was tempted to confront this madman once and for all, but she realized that her strength would fail her; she felt defeated even before she saw him.

"Tell him I'm not in. Show him the door, and inform the servants that the gentleman is not welcome in this house," she ordered.

The next day there were no exotic flowers at breakfast, and Patricia thought with a sigh of relief, or dejection, that the man must finally have understood her message. That morning she felt free for the first time in a week, and she went out for a game of tennis and a trip to the beauty salon. She returned home at two in the afternoon with a new haircut and a bad headache. On the hall table she saw a royal purple velvet jewel box with the name Zimmerman printed in gold letters. She opened it rather absently, thinking that her husband had left it there, but found a necklace of emeralds accompanied by one of those pretentious sepia cards she had come to know and detest. Her headache turned to panic. This adventurer seemed prepared to ruin her life; as if it wasn't enough to buy a necklace from her own husband, he then had the gall to send it to her house. She could not throw this gift into the trash, as she had done with the flowers. With the case clutched to her bosom, she locked herself in her writing room. A half-hour later, she called the chauffeur and ordered him to deliver a package to the same address to which he had returned several letters. As she handed him the jewels she felt no relief; to the contrary, she had the impression that she was sinking into a quagmire.

At the same time, Fortunato was slogging through his own swamp, getting nowhere, feeling his way blindly. He had never spent so much money and time to court a woman, although it was true, he admitted, that all his women had been quite different from this one. For the first time in his life as a showman, he felt ridiculous. He could not go on this way; always strong as an ox, his health was suffering, he slept only a few hours at a time, he was short of breath, he had heart palpitations, he felt fire in his stomach and ringing in his temples. His business was similarly suffering the impact of his love fever; he was making hasty decisions, and losing money. Good Christ, I don't know who I am or what I'm doing here; damn it all, he grumbled, sweating, but not for a minute did he consider abandoning the chase.

Slumped in an armchair in the hotel where he was staying, the purple jewel box back in his hands, Fortunato remembered his grandfather. He rarely thought of his father, but his memory often dwelt on that formidable ancestor who at ninety-some years was still cultivating his garden. He picked up the telephone and asked for long distance.

The elder Fortunato was nearly deaf and, in addition, unable to adapt to the mechanism of that devilish apparatus that carried voices halfway around the planet, but the years had not affected his lucidity. He listened carefully to his grandson's sorrowful tale, speaking only at the end.

"So, the sly vixen is giving herself the luxury of snubbing my boy, is that it, eh?"

"She won't even look at me, Nono. She's rich, she's beautiful, she's classy. . . . She has everything."

"Ummm . . . including a husband."

"Yes, but that's not important. If I could only speak to her."

"Speak to her? What about? You have nothing to say to a woman like that, son."

"I gave her a necklace fit for a queen and she returned it without a word."

"Well, give her something she doesn't have."

"What, for example?"

"A good excuse to laugh, that always gets 'em." And his grandfather nodded off with the receiver in his hand, dreaming of the pretty things who had given him their hearts as he performed his death-defying acrobatics on the trapeze or danced with his monkey.

The next day in his office the jeweler Zimmerman received a splendid young woman, a manicurist by trade, she said; she had come, she explained, to sell back at half price the very emerald necklace he had sold only forty-eight hours before. The jeweler remembered the purchase very well; impossible to forget such a conceited boor.

"I need something that will crumble the defenses of a haughty lady," he had said.

Zimmerman had studied him a moment, and decided he must be one of those new oil or cocaine millionaires. He could not tolerate vulgarity; he was accustomed to a different class of customer. He rarely served clients himself, but this man had insisted on speaking to him and seemed prepared to spend an unlimited amount of money.

"What do you recommend?" the man had asked before the tray where the most valuable jewels sparkled.

"It depends upon the lady. Rubies and pearls look good on dark skin; emeralds on someone fairer; and diamonds are perfect for anyone."

"She has too many diamonds. Her husband gives them to her as if they were candy."

Zimmerman coughed. He disliked this kind of confidence. The man picked up a necklace, held it to the light with no respect, shook it like a sleigh bell, and the air filled with tinkling and green sparks as the jeweler's ulcer twitched within him.

"Do you think emeralds bring good luck?"

"I suppose that all precious stones fit that description, sir, but I am not superstitious."

"This is a very special woman. I don't want to make any mistake with the gift, you understand?"

"Perfectly."

But apparently that was precisely what had happened, Zimmerman told himself, unable to restrain a scornful smirk when the girl returned the necklace. No, there was nothing wrong with the jewels, the mistake was the girl. He had imagined a more refined woman, certainly not a manicurist carrying a plastic handbag and wearing a cheap blouse. He was, nonetheless, intrigued by the girl, there was something vulnerable and pathetic about her, poor child; she would not fare well in the hands of that bandit, he thought.

"Why don't you tell me the whole story, my dear," said Zimmerman finally.

The girl spun him the tale she had memorized, and an hour later left the shop with a light step. According to plan, the jeweler had not only bought back the necklace, he had invited her to dinner as well. It was plain to her that Zimmerman was one of those men who are astute and suspicious in business dealings but naïve in every other regard; she would have no difficulty distracting him the amount of time Horacio Fortunato needed and was prepared to pay for.

That was a memorable night for Zimmerman; he had planned on dinner but found himself in the grip of an unexpected passion. The next day he saw his new friend again and by the end of the week he was stammering to Patricia something about going to New York for a few days to attend a sale of Russian jewels saved from the massacre of Ekaterinburg. His wife was totally unmoved.

* * *

Alone in her house, too listless to go out and suffering that headache that came and went without respite, Patricia decided to devote her Saturday to recouping her strength. She settled on the terrace to leaf through some fashion magazines. It had not rained for a week and the air was still and hot. She read awhile, until the sun made her drowsy; her body grew heavy, her eyes closed, and the magazine slipped from her hands. At that moment she heard a sound from deep in the garden; she thought it must be the gardener, a head-strong old man who in less than a year had transformed her property into a tropical jungle, ripping out pots of chrysanthemums to make way for an efflorescence gone wild. She opened her eyes, stared half-seeing against the sun, and saw something unusually large moving in the top of the avocado tree. She removed her dark glasses and sat up. No doubt about it, a shadow was moving up there, and it was not part of the foliage.

Patricia Zimmerman rose from her chair and walked forward a step or two; then she saw it clearly: a ghostly blue-clad figure with a golden cape flew several meters over her head, turned a somersault in the air and, for an instant, seemed to freeze at the moment of waving to her from the sky. She choked back a scream, sure that the apparition would plummet like a stone and be pulverized on contact with the ground, but the cape filled with air and that gleaming coleopteran stretched out its arms and swung into a nearby medlar tree. Immediately, a second blue figure appeared, hanging by its legs in the top branches of another tree, swinging by the wrists a young girl wearing a flower crown. The

117

first gave a signal and the holder released the girl, who scattered a rain of paper butterflies before being caught by the ankles. Patricia did not dare move while those silent, gold-caped birds flew through the air.

Suddenly a whoop filled the garden, a long, barbaric yowl that tore Patricia's attention from the trapeze artists. She saw a thick rope fall from the rear wall of the property and, climbing down it, Tarzan, in person, the same Tarzan of the matinées and comic books of her childhood, with his skimpy loincloth and live monkey on his hip. The King of the Jungle leapt gracefully to earth, thumped his chest with his fists, and repeated the visceral bellow, attracting all the servants, who rushed out to the terrace. With a wave of the hand, Patricia gestured to them to stay where they were, while the voice of Tarzan gave way to a lugubrious drumroll announcing a retinue of four Egyptian dancers who advanced as if trapped in a frieze, head and feet at right angles to their bodies; they were followed by a hunchback wearing a striped hooded cape and leading a black panther at the end of a chain. Then came two monks carrying a sarcophagus and, behind them, an angel with long golden locks and then, bringing up the rear, an Indian disguised as a Japanese wearing a dressing gown and wooden clogs. All of them paused behind the swimming pool. The monks deposited the coffin on the grass and, while the Egyptian maidens chanted softly in some dead tongue and the Angel and Kuramoto rippled their prodigious muscles, the lid of the sarcophagus swung open and a nightmarish creature emerged from inside. Once revealed, swathed in gauze, it was obvious that this was a mummy in perfect health. At this moment, Tarzan yodeled another cry and, with absolutely no provocation, began hopping around the Egyptians, brandishing the simian. The Mummy lost its millenary patience, lifted one rigid arm and let it swing like a cudgel against the nape of the savage's neck, who fell to the ground, his face buried in the lawn. The monkey screamed and scrambled up a tree. Before the embalmed pharaoh could deliver a second blow, Tarzan leapt to his feet and fell upon the Mummy with a roar. Locked in legendary combat, their rolling and thrashing freed the panther; the characters in the parade ran to hide in the garden and all the servants flew back to the safety of the kitchen. Patricia was about to jump into the pool when, as if by magic, an individual in tails and a top hat appeared and with one snap of his whip stopped the cat, who fell to the ground purring like a pussycat, with all four paws in the air; the hunchback recaptured the chain, as the ringmaster swept off his hat and pulled from it a meringue torte that he carried to the terrace and deposited at the feet of the lady of the house.

This was the signal for the remainder of the cast to march in from the rear of the garden: musicians playing military marches, clowns assaulting one another with slapsticks, dwarfs from medieval courts, an equestrienne standing on her mount, a bearded lady, dogs on bicycles, an ostrich costumed as Columbine and, finally, a team of boxers in satin trunks and boxing gloves pushing a wheeled platform crowned by a painted cardboard arch. And there, on the dais of a stage-set emperor, sat Horacio Fortunato, his mane slicked down with brilliantine, grinning his irrepressible gallant's grin, pompous beneath his triumphal dome, surrounded by his outrageous circus, acclaimed by the trumpets and cymbals of his own orchestra, the most conceited, most lovesick, and most entertaining man in the world. Patricia laughed, and walked forward to meet him.

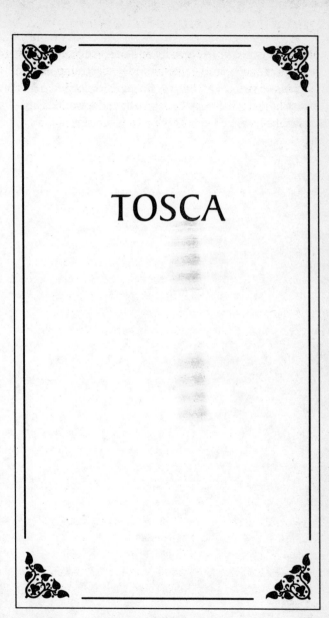

TOSCA

HER father first sat her down at the piano when she was five years old and, when she was ten, Maurizia Rugieri, dressed in pink organza and patent leather shoes, gave her first recital in the Club Garibaldi before a benevolent public composed principally of members of the Italian colony. At the end of the presentation they placed bouquets of flowers at her feet, and the president of the club gave her a commemorative plaque and a porcelain doll bedecked with ribbons and lace.

"We salute you, Maurizia Rugieri, as a precocious genius, a new Mozart. The great stages of the world await you," he declaimed.

The girl waited for the applause to die down and then, making her voice heard above the sound of her mother's proud sobs, she spoke with unexpected hauteur:

"This is the last time I ever play the piano," she

announced. "I want to be a singer." And she left the room, dragging the doll by one foot.

When he recovered from his embarrassment, her father enrolled her in voice classes with a severe maestro; for every false note he bestowed a rap on the knuckles but he did not succeed in killing the child's enthusiasm for the opera. As she emerged from adolescence it became clear that she had a small, birdlike voice barely strong enough to lull an infant in the cradle; despite all her efforts, she was forced to exchange her dreams of being an operatic soprano for a more banal fate. When she was nineteen, she married Ezio Longo, a first-generation immigrant, an architect without a degree and builder by trade who had proposed for himself the goal of founding an empire on cement and steel and, at thirty-five, had nearly achieved it.

Ezio Longo fell in love with Maurizia Rugieri with the same dedication that had made it possible for him to strew the capital with his buildings. He was short in stature, heavy-boned, with the neck of a draft animal and an expressive if somewhat brutal face with thick lips and black eyes. His work forced him to dress in rough clothing, and from being so much in the sun his skin was dark and crisscrossed with wrinkles, like tanned leather. He was good-natured and generous, he laughed easily, and he loved popular music and abundant, simple food. Under this rather common exterior hid a refined soul and a delicacy he did not know how to translate into deeds or words. When he gazed at Maurizia his eyes sometimes filled with tears and his chest contracted with a tenderness that shame caused him to disguise with a cuff or a smack. It was impossible for him to express his feelings for Maurizia, and he thought that by showering her with gifts and bearing with stoic patience her excessive mood swings and her imaginary ailments he would compensate for his failings as a lover. She provoked in him an urgent desire renewed each day with the ardor of their first encounters; frustrated, he would embrace her, hoping to bridge the abyss between them, but his passion dissipated on contact with the affectations of his wife, whose imagination was eternally fired by romantic novels and recordings of Verdi and Puccini. Ezio would fall asleep, conquered by the fatigue of the day, exhausted by nightmares of twisting walls and spiral staircases, but he awakened at dawn to sit on the edge of the bed and observe his sleeping wife with such attention that he learned to divine her dreams. He would have given his life to have her return his affection with equal intensity. He built for her a mammoth mansion supported by columns, in which the confusion of styles and profusion of adornment disoriented the senses, and where four servants worked constantly merely to burnish the bronzes, polish the floors, clean the crystal teardrops of the chandeliers, and beat the dust from the gold-footed furniture and imitation Persian rugs imported from Spain. The house had a small amphitheater in the garden with loudspeakers and stage lights where Maurizia Rugieri liked to sing for their guests. Ezio would never have admitted under threat of death that he was unable to appreciate those birdlike twitterings, not only to conceal his lack of culture but, especially, because of his respect for his wife's artistic inclinations. He was an optimistic man, and extremely self-confident, but when a weeping Maurizia announced that she was pregnant, he was overwhelmed by an ungovernable apprehension; he felt his heart would burst open like a watermelon, and that there was no place for such joy in this vale of tears. He feared that some violent catastrophe might wreak havoc on his precarious paradise, and he prepared to defend it against any attack.

The catastrophe came in the guise of a medical student Maurizia met on a streetcar. The child had been born by that time—an infant as vital as his father, who seemed immune to all harm, even the evil eye— and his mother had recovered her girlish waistline. The student sat down beside Maurizia en route to the city center, a slender, pale youth with the profile of a Roman statue. He was reading the score of *Tosca* and quietly whistling an aria from the third act. Maurizia felt that all the day's sunlight was captured on his cheekbones, and her bodice grew moist with sweet anticipation. Unable to restrain herself, she sang the words of the unfortunate Mario as he greeted the dawn before being led to the firing wall. And thus between two lines of the score, the romance began. The young man's name was Leonardo Gómez, and he was as mad about bel canto as Maurizia.

In the following months the student received his medical degree and Maurizia relived, one by one, all the tragedies from the operatic repertoire, and no few from romantic literature. She was killed successively by Don José, tuberculosis, an Egyptian tomb, a dagger, and poison; she was in love in Italian, French, and German; she was Aïda, Carmen, and Lucia di Lammermoor and, in every instance Leonardo Gómez was the object of her immortal passion. In real life they shared a chaste love, which she longed to consummate but did not dare initiate, and which he fought in his heart to preserve out of respect for Maurizia's married state. They met in public places, occasionally holding hands in a dark corner of some park. They exchanged notes signed Tosca and Mario; naturally, Scarpia was Ezio Longo, who was so grateful for his son, for his beautiful wife and all the blessings heaven had bestowed, and so busy working to provide for his family's security that, had a neighbor not come to repeat to him the gossip that his wife was riding the streetcar too often, he would never have learned what was going on behind his back.

Ezio Longo had prepared for the contingency of a business failure, and for any illness or accident that in his worst moments of superstitious terror he had imagined might befall his son, but it had never occurred to him that a honey-voiced student could steal his wife from beneath his nose. When he heard the story, he nearly laughed aloud, because of all misfortunes this seemed easiest to resolve. After his first reaction, however, his bile flowed with blind rage. He followed Maurizia to a discreet tearoom where he surprised her drinking chocolate with her beloved. He did not ask for explanations. He seized his rival by his lapels, lifted him off his feet, and threw him against the wall amid the crashing of broken china and shrieks of the clientele. Then he took his wife by the arm and led her to his car, one of the last of the Mercedes imported into the country before the Second World War had interrupted commercial relations with Germany. He locked Maurizia in the house and posted two of his bricklayers at the

127

doors. Maurizia lay two days in bed, weeping, without speaking or eating. During her silence, Ezio Longo had time to think things over, and his rage was transformed into a mute frustration that recalled the neglect of his infancy, the poverty of his youth, the loneliness of his existence—all that bottomless hunger for affection he had suffered before he met Maurizia Rugieri and had believed was resolved through love. On the third day he could bear no more, and he went into his wife's room.

"For our son's sake, Maurizia, you must get these fantasies out of your head. I know I am not very romantic, but if you help me, I can change. I'm not a man to wear the horns, and I love you too much to let you go. But if you give me the chance, I will make you happy, I promise."

Her only answer was to turn to the wall and prolong her fast for another two days, at the end of which her husband returned.

"Dammit, I would like to know what it is you don't have in this world; tell me, and I'll try to get it for you," he said, defeated.

"I don't have Leonardo. Without him, I will die."

"Very well. You can go off with that clown if you want, but you will never see our son again."

Maurizia packed her suitcases, put on a muslin dress and large veiled hat, and called a rented car. Before she left, she kissed the boy, sobbing, and whispered into his ear that very soon she would come back for him. Ezio Longo, who in a week's time had lost a dozen pounds and half his hair, tore the child from her arms.

Maurizia Rugieri arrived at her beloved's boarding-house to find that two days earlier he had left to work as a doctor in an oil field, in one of those hot provinces whose name evokes Indians and snakes. She could not believe that he had left without saying goodbye, but she attributed it to the drubbing he had received in the tearoom; she concluded that Leonardo was a poet, and that her husband's brutality had disrupted his behavior. She moved into a hotel, and for days sent telegrams to every conceivable place Leonardo Gómez might be. Finally she located him, and telegraphed him that for his sake she had given up her only son, defied her husband, society, and God Himself, and that her decision to follow him until death should them part was irrevocable.

The journey was a wearing expedition by train, bus, and, in some places, riverboat. Maurizia had never been alone outside a radius of some thirty blocks surrounding her home, but neither the grandeur of the landscape nor the incalculable distances held any terror for her. Along the way she lost two suitcases, and her muslin dress became limp and yellow with dust, but finally she reached the river landing where Leonardo was to meet her. When she descended from her conveyance she saw a pirogue at the dock and ran toward it with tattered veil and escaping curls flying. Instead of Mario, however, she found a black man in a pith helmet, and two melancholy Indian oarsmen. It was too late to turn back. She accepted the explanation that Doctor Gómez had been detained by an emergency, and climbed into the boat with the remnants of her battered luggage, praying that these men were neither bandits nor cannibals. Fortunately they were not, and they bore her safely through a huge expanse of precipitous, savage territory to the place where her lover awaited her. There were two small settlements, one of large dormitories where the workers lived, and another for staff consisting of the company offices, twenty-five prefabricated houses brought by airplane from the United States, an absurd golf course, and a stagnant green swimming pool filled each morning with gigantic frogs, all enclosed within a metal fence with a gate guarded by two sentinels. It was an encampment of transient men; life turned around that dark ooze that poured from the bowels of the earth like inexhaustible dragon vomit. In these solitudes there were no women but a few suffering companions of the workers; the gringos and bosses all journeyed to the city every three months to visit their families. The arrival of Doctor Gómez's wife, as they called her, upset the routine for a few days, until everyone grew used to seeing her pass by with her veils, her parasol, and her dancing slippers, like a character escaped from some tale.

Maurizia Rugieri did not allow the roughness of the men or the unrelenting heat to vanquish her; she intended to live out her destiny with grandeur, and she very nearly succeeded. She had converted Leonardo Gómez into the hero of her personal opera, investing him with utopian virtues, and exalting to the point of mania the quality of his love, never pausing to measure her lover's response, or gauge whether he was keeping pace with her in their grand passion. If Leonardo Gómez showed signs of lagging behind, she attributed it to his timid character and the poor health made worse by the accursed climate. In truth, he seemed so fragile that she cured herself once and for all of her imagined ills and devoted herself to caring for him. She accompanied him to his primitive hospital, and learned the duties of a nurse in order to assist him. Attending victims of malaria and treating the terrible accidents from the wells seemed better to her than lying in the house beneath a ceiling fan reading for the hundredth time the same old magazines and romantic novels.

Among the syringes and bandages she could imagine herself as Florence Nightingale, one of those brave heroines she sometimes saw in the films shown in the camp clubhouse. She refused with suicidal determination to acknowledge any diminution of her reality; she insisted on embellishing every moment with words, though in fact she now had no other alternative. She spoke of Leonardo Gómez—whom she continued to call Mario—as a saint dedicated to the service of mankind, and set herself the task of demonstrating to the world that they were the protagonists of an exceptional love—which served at least to discourage any company employee who might have been stirred by the only white woman around. Maurizia called the rusticity of the camp "contact with nature," ignoring mosquitoes, poisonous insects, iguanas, the hellish heat of the day, the breathless nights, and the fact that she could not venture alone beyond the gate. She referred to her loneliness, her boredom, her natural love of the city, her desire to dress in the latest fashions, to visit her friends and attend the theater, as a vague "nostalgia." The only thing she could not give a different name to was the animal pain that sank its claws in her every time she thought of her son—so she chose never to mention his name.

Leonardo Gómez worked as a camp doctor for more than ten years, until tropical fevers and climate destroyed his health. He had lived so long within the protective fence of the National Petroleum Company that he lacked the spirit to make a new beginning in a more competitive atmosphere; in addition, he had never forgotten Ezio Longo's fury as he threw him against the wall, and thus never considered the possibility of returning to the capital. He sought a post in an out-of-the-way corner where he could continue his low-key existence, and in this way one day found himself in Agua Santa with his wife, his medical instruments, and his opera recordings. It was the decade of the fifties, and Maurizia Rugieri descended from the bus dressed in the latest style, a tight polka-dotted dress and enormous black straw hat she had ordered from a catalogue in New York, a vision like none ever seen in Agua Santa. They were, at any rate, welcomed with typical small-town hospitality, and in less than twenty-four hours everyone knew the legend of the exceptional love between the new arrivals. They called them Tosca and Mario, without the least idea of who those people were, though Maurizia soon made it her business to instruct them. She gave up her nursing duties at Leonardo's side, formed a parish choir, and offered the first voice recitals held in that village. Mute with amazement, the citizens of Agua Santa saw Maurizia on an improvised stage in the schoolhouse, transformed into Madame Butterfly, decked out in an outlandish bathrobe, with knitting needles in her hair, two plastic flowers over her ears, and her face painted plaster white, trilling away in her little bird voice. No one understood a single word of the song, but when she knelt and pulled out a kitchen knife, threatening to plunge it into her stomach, the audience cried out with horror and a spectator rushed to the stage to dissuade her, grabbing the weapon from her hands and pulling her to her feet. Immediately following the performance there was a long discussion about the reasons for the Japanese lady's tragic decision, and everyone agreed that the North American sailor who had abandoned her was a soulless brute, and that he was not worth dying for since life goes on and there are many men in the world. The evening ended with general merrymaking when an improvised band played *cumbias* and everyone began to dance. That memorable night was followed by others: song, death, explication of the opera's plot by the soprano, public discussion, and closing party.

Doctor Mario and señora Tosca were select members of the community; he was in charge of everyone's health, and she was responsible for their cultural life and news of changes in fashion. The couple lived in a cool, pleasant house, half of which was occupied by his consulting room. In their patio they kept a blue and yellow macaw that flew overhead when they went out for a stroll in the plaza. You could always tell where the doctor or his wife were, because the bird accompanied them, gliding silently some two meters above their heads on large brightly colored wings. The couple lived in Agua Santa many years, well respected by the citizenry, who pointed to them as exemplars of perfect love.

During one of his attacks, the doctor lost his way among the byways of fever, and did not return. The town was moved by his death. They feared that his wife might do herself harm, as she had in the roles she played, and they arranged to keep her company day and night in the following weeks. Maurizia Rugieri dressed in mourning from head to toe, painted all her furniture black, and carried her sorrow around like a tenacious shadow that incised two deep furrows at the corners of her mouth. She did not, nevertheless, attempt to put an end to her life. Perhaps in the privacy of her room, when she lay alone in her bed, she felt a profound relief; now she would not have to bear the heavy load of her dreams; it was no longer necessary to keep alive the character she had invented to represent herself, nor constantly juggle facts to mask the weakness of a lover who had never lived up to her illusions. But the habit of theater was too deeply ingrained. With the same infinite patience with which she had created for herself an image of the romantic heroine, in her widowhood she constructed the legend of her despair. She remained in Agua Santa, always in black—although mourning had been out of mode for many years—and refused to sing again, despite the pleas of her friends who believed that the opera would be a consolation. The town closed about her in a circle, like a strong embrace, to make her life bearable and help her retain her dreams. With the town's complicity, Doctor Gómez's memory grew in popular imagination. After two years, people took up a collection and commissioned a bronze bust to be installed on a column in the plaza facing the stone statue of the Liberator.

That was the year the main highway came through Agua Santa, which altered forever the look and spirit of the town. At first, people had opposed the project; they believed it would mean that the inmates of Santa María Prison would be brought in shackles to cut down trees and crush stone; that was how their grandfathers said the road had been built during the time of El Benefactor's dictatorship. Soon, however, engineers arrived from the city with the news that modern machines, not prisoners, would do the work. Behind the engineers came surveyors, followed by crews of workers in orange helmets and jackets that glowed in the dark. The machines turned out to be enormous steel beasts that the schoolteacher calculated to be roughly the size of dinosaurs; on their flanks they bore the name of their owners, Ezio Longo and Son. That very Friday, the father and son came to Agua Santa to inspect the work and pay the workmen.

When Maurizia Rugieri saw the signs and machines bearing the name of her former husband, she hid in her house with doors and shutters locked, in the unrealistic hope that she could somehow escape the past. But for twenty-eight years the recollection of her son had been a pain buried deep in her heart, and when she heard that the owners of the construction company were in Agua Santa having lunch in the tavern, she could not help yielding to her instinct. She examined herself in the mirror. She was fifty-one years old, aged by the tropical sun and the effort of feigning a chimerical happiness, but her features still bore the nobility of pride. She brushed her hair and combed it into a high bun, not attempting to hide the gray; she put on her best black dress and her wedding pearls, saved through her many adventures, and with a gesture of timid coquetry drew a line of black on her eyelids and touched crimson to cheeks and lips. She left her house under the protection of Leonardo Gómez's umbrella. Sweat ran down her back, but she did not tremble.

At that hour the tavern shutters were closed against the midday heat, so Maurizia had to stand a moment while her eyes adjusted to the darkness before she recognized Ezio Longo and the young man who must be her son at one of the rear tables. Her husband had changed much less than she, probably because he had always seemed ageless. The same leonine neck and shoulders, the same solid build, the same rather coarse features and deep-set eyes—softened now by a fan of good-humored laugh lines. Bent over his plate, he chewed enthusiastically, listening to his son's conversation. Maurizia observed them from a distance. Her son must be nearly thirty. Although he had her long bones and delicate skin, his gestures were those of his father; he ate with the same pleasure, pounded the table to emphasize his words, and laughed heartily. He was a vital and energetic man with an uncompromising sense of his own worth, a man ready for any struggle. Maurizia looked at Ezio Longo through new eyes, and for the first time appreciated his solid masculine virtues. She stepped forward, touched, breathless, seeing herself from a new dimension, as if she were on a stage playing out the most dramatic moment of the long theater of her life, with the names of her husband and her son on her lips, and with warm hopes of being forgiven for all her years of neglect. But in those few instants, too, she saw the minute gears of the trap in which she had enmeshed herself for thirty hallucinatory years. She realized that the true hero of the drama was Ezio Longo, and she wanted to believe that he had continued to desire her and wait for her during all that time, with the persistent and impassioned love that Leonardo Gómez could never give because it was not in his nature.

At that moment, when she was only inches from stepping from the shadow and being exposed, the young man leaned forward, grasped his father's wrist, and said something with a sympathetic wink. Both burst out laughing, clapped each other on the shoulder, and ruffled each other's hair with a virile tenderness and staunch complicity that excluded Maurizia Rugieri and the rest of the world. She hesitated for an infinite moment on the borderline between reality and dream, then stepped back, left the tavern, opened her black umbrella, and walked home with the macaw flying above her head like a bizarre archangel from a book of days.

WALIMAI

THE name given me by my father is Walimai, which in the tongue of our brothers in the north means "wind." I can tell it to you, since now you are like my own daughter and you have my permission to call my name, although only when we are among family. The names of persons and living creatures demand respect, because when we speak them we touch their heart and become a part of their life force. This is how we blood kinsmen greet each other. I cannot understand the ease with which the white ones call each others' names, with no fear; not only does it show a lack of respect, it can also lead to grave danger. I have noted that these persons speak unthinkingly, not realizing that to speak is also to be. Word and gesture are man's thought. We should not speak without reason; this I have taught my sons and daughters, but they do not always listen to my counsel. Long ago, taboos and traditions were respected. My grandfathers, and the grandfathers of my grandfathers, received all necessary knowledge from their grandfathers. Nothing changed. A man with a good memory could recall every teaching he had received and thus knew what to do in any situation. But then came the white ones speaking against the wisdom of the grandfathers, and pushing us off our land. We move always deeper into the jungle, but always they overtake us; sometimes years pass, but finally they come again, and we must destroy our planted fields, put our children on our back, bind our animals, and depart. So it has been as long as I have memory: leave everything, and run away like mice—not like the mighty warriors and gods who inhabited these lands in days of old. Some of our young are curious about the whites, and while we travel deeper into the forest to continue to live as our ancestors did, others undertake a different path. We think of those who leave as if they were dead, because very few return, and those who do have changed so that we cannot recognize them as kinsmen.

They tell that in the years before I came into the world not enough women were born to our people, and thus my father had to travel long roads to seek a wife from a different tribe. He journeyed through the forests, following the marks of others who had traveled that route before him and for the same purpose and returned with women not of our blood. After much traveling, when my father had begun to lose hope of finding a life companion, he saw a girl standing by a tall waterfall, a river that fell from the sky. Staying some distance away, in order not to frighten her, he spoke to her in the tone that hunters use to calm their prey, and explained his need to marry her. She made signs that he might come near, studied him openly, and must have been pleased by the face of the traveler, because she decided that the idea of marriage was not a rash one. My father had to work for his father-in-law until he paid for the woman's value. After they had fulfilled the rituals of marriage, they made the return journey to our village.

I grew up with my brothers and sisters beneath the canopies of tall trees, never seeing the sun. Sometimes a wounded tree would fall, leaving an opening in the thick dome of the forest; at those times we saw the blue eye of the sky. My father and mother told me stories; they sang songs to me, and taught me what a man must know to survive alone, with nothing but his bow and his arrows. I was free. We, the Children of the Moon, cannot live unless we are free. When we are closed inside walls or bars we collapse inward; we become blind and deaf, and in a few days our spirit detaches itself from the bones of our chest and abandons us. At those times we become like miserable beasts and, almost always, we prefer to die. That is why our houses have no walls, only a sloped roof to stop the wind and shed the rain; beneath it we hang our hammocks close together, because we like to listen to the dreams of the women and the children and feel the breath of the monkeys and dogs and pigs that sleep beneath the same shelter. In the earliest times we lived in the jungles without knowing that there was a world beyond the cliffs and rivers. Friends came to visit from other tribes, and told us rumors of Boa Vista and El Plantanal, of the white ones and their customs, but we believed these were only stories to make us laugh. I reached manhood, and my turn came to find a wife, but I decided to wait, because I liked being with the bachelors; we were happy, and lived well. Even so, I could not devote myself solely to games and resting as the others did, because my family is very large: brothers and sisters, cousins, nieces and nephews, many mouths to feed, and much work for a hunter.

One day a group of the pale men came to our village. They hunted with powder, from far away, without skill or courage; they could not climb a tree or spear a fish in the water; they moved clumsily through the jungle, they were always getting tangled in their packs, their weapons, even their own feet. They did not clothe themselves in air, as we do, but wore wet and stinking clothing; they were dirty and they did not know the laws of decency, but they insisted on telling us of their knowledge and their gods. We compared them with what we had been told about the white men, and we verified the truth of that gossip. Soon we realized that these men were not missionaries, or soldiers or rubber collectors: they were mad. They wanted the land; they wanted to carry away the wood; they were also searching for stones. We explained that the jungle is not something to be tossed over your shoulder and transported like a dead bird, but they did not want to hear our arguments. They made camp near our village. Each one of them was like a wind of catastrophe; he destroyed everything he touched; he left a trail of waste behind him; he disturbed animals and people. At first we obeyed the laws of courtesy, and pleased them, because they were our guests; but they were never

satisfied, they wanted always more, until, weary of
their games, we declared war with all traditional ceremonies. They are not good warriors; they are easily
frightened and their fragile skullbones could not withstand the clubbing we gave them. Afterward we abandoned our village and we journeyed to the east where
the forest is impenetrable, traveling for long stretches
through the tops of the trees so their companions could
not find us. We had been told that they are vengeful,
and that for each one of them who dies, even in fair
battle, they are capable of eliminating an entire tribe,
including the children. We discovered a place to establish a new village. It was not as good—the women had
to walk hours to find clean water—but we stayed there
because we believed that no one would come so far to
search for us. A year later I was far from our village
following the track of a puma, when I approached too
near a camp of soldiers. I was tired, and had not eaten
in several days; for this reason, I used poor judgment.
Instead of turning back when I glimpsed the strangers,
I lay down to rest. The soldiers caught me. They did
not mention the men we had clubbed to death. In fact,
they asked me nothing; perhaps they did not know
those men or did not know that I am Walimai. They
pressed me into work with the rubber collectors, with
many men from other tribes, men they had dressed in
trousers and driven to work with no thought for their
wishes. The rubber demands much care, and there
were not enough people to do the work; that was why
they forced us. That was a time without freedom, and
I do not want to speak of it. I stayed only to see
whether I could learn anything, but from the beginning

I knew I would return to my people. Nothing can long hold a warrior against his will.

We worked from sun to sun, some bleeding the trees to drain their life drop by drop, others cooking the liquid to thicken it and form it into great balls. The air outdoors was sick with the stench of the burned sap, and the air indoors in the sleeping quarters foul with the sweat of the men. No one could draw a deep breath in that place. They gave us maize to eat, and bananas, and the strange contents of some cans, which I never tasted, because nothing good for humans can grow in tins. At one end of the camp they had built a large hut where they kept the women. After two weeks of working with the raw rubber, the boss handed me a slip of paper and sent me where the women were. He also gave me a cup of liquor, which I turned out on the ground, because I have seen how that water destroys a man's good sense. I stood in line with the others. I was the last, and when it came my turn to enter the hut, the sun had gone down and night begun, with its clamor of frogs and parrots.

She was of the tribe of the Ila, the people of gentle heart, from which the most delicate girls come. Some men travel months on end to find the Ila; they take them gifts and hunt for them in the hope of obtaining one of their women. She looked like a lizard lying there, but I recognized her because my mother, too, was an Ila woman. She lay naked on her straw mat, tied by one ankle to a chain staked in the ground, sluggish, as if she had breathed in the *yopo* of the acacia; she had the smell of sick dogs, and she was wet with the dew of all the men who had covered her before me. She was the size of a young boy, and her bones clicked like small stones in the river. The Ila women remove all their bodily hair, even their eyelashes; they adorn their ears with feathers and flowers; they thrust polished sticks through their cheeks and nose; they paint designs over all their body in the reds of the annatto, the deep purple of the palm, and the black of carbon. But she had none of that. I placed my machete on the ground, and greeted her as a sister, imitating some songbirds and the sound of rivers. She did not respond. I pounded her chest, to see whether her spirit still resonated in her rib cage, but there was no echo; her soul was very weak and could not answer me. Kneeling beside her, I gave her water to drink and spoke to her in my mother's tongue. She opened her eyes, and stared at me a long time. I understood.

First of all, I washed myself without wasting the clean water. I took a good draft into my mouth and sprinkled it in small streams onto my hands, which I rubbed carefully and then wet to clean my face. I did the same with her, to cleanse the men's dew from her body. I removed the trousers the boss had given me. From a cord at my waist hung my sticks for making fire, the tips of arrows, my roll of tobacco, my wooden knife with a rat's tooth in the point, and a bag of strong leather in which I carried a small amount of curare. I spread a bit of that paste on the point of my knife, bent over the woman and, with the poisoned instrument, opened a small cut in her neck. Life is a gift from the gods. The hunter kills to feed his family; he tries not to eat the flesh of his prey but prefers to eat what another hunter offers him. At times, tragically, a man kills another in war, but he never harms a woman or a child. She looked at me with large eyes yellow as honey, and I thought she tried to smile, gratefully. For her I had violated the first taboo of the Children of the Moon, and I would have to pay for my shame with many labors of expiation. I held my ear to her mouth, and she murmured her name. I repeated it twice in my mind to be very sure, but did not speak it aloud; it is not good to mention the dead or disturb their peace, and she was already dead even though her heart still beat. Soon I saw the muscles of her belly, her chest, her arms stiffen with paralysis; she stopped breathing, and changed color. A sigh escaped her, and her body died without a struggle, as small creatures die.

Immediately, I felt her spirit leave through her nostrils and enter mine, anchoring itself to my breastbone. All her weight fell upon me, and I had to struggle to get to my feet. I moved very slowly, as if I were under water. I arranged her body in the position of the last rest, with her knees touching her chin. I bound her with fibers from the mat, then made a mound with the rest of the straw and used my sticks to make fire. When I saw that the fire was blazing intensely, I left the hut slowly, laboriously climbed the camp fence—because she kept dragging me down—and walked into the forest. I had reached the first trees when I heard the alarm bells.

I walked all the first day without stopping. On the second day I fashioned a bow and arrows so I could hunt for her, and for myself as well. The warrior who bears the weight of another human life must fast for ten days; in this way the spirit of the dead one grows weak; finally it lets go and journeys to the land of souls. If the warrior does not do this, the spirit grows fat on the food it is fed and grows inside the man until it suffocates him. I have seen men of great courage die this way. But before I fulfilled those conditions, I had to lead the spirit of the Ila woman into the thickest jungle where she would never be found. I ate very little, barely enough not to kill her a second time. Each mouthful tasted like spoiled meat, and every sip of water was bitter, but I forced myself to swallow, to nourish the two of us. For one complete cycle of the moon I traveled deep into the jungle, carrying inside me the soul of the woman who weighed more each day. We spoke often. The tongue of the Ila is uninhibited and resounds beneath the trees with a long echo. We communicated singing, with our body, with our eyes, our waist, our feet. I repeated to her the legends I had learned from my mother and my father; I told her my past, and she told me of the first part of her life, when she was a happy girl playing with her brothers and sisters, rolling in the mud and swinging from the high branches. Out of courtesy, she did not mention her recent past of misfortune and humiliation. I caught a white bird; I plucked the finest feathers and made adornments for her ears. At night I kept a small fire burning so she would not be cold, and so jaguars or serpents would not disturb her sleep. I bathed her in the river with care, rubbing her with ash and crushed flowers, to take away her bad memories.

Finally one day we reached the perfect spot, and had no further excuse to continue walking. There the jungle was so dense that in places I had to open a path by slashing the undergrowth with my machete, even my teeth, and we had to speak in a low voice not to alter the silence of time. I chose a place near a thread of water; I put up a roof of leaves and made a hammock for her from three long strips of bark. With my knife I shaved my head and began my fast.

During the time we had walked together the woman and I had come to love one another so much that we did not want to part; but man does not control life, not even his own, and so I had to fulfill my obligation. For many days, I took nothing in my mouth except a few sips of water. As I grew weak, she slipped from my embrace, and her spirit, ever more ethereal, did not weigh upon me as before. After five days, while I dozed, she took her first steps, but she was not ready to continue her journey alone, and she returned to me. She repeated those brief travels on several occasions, each time venturing a little farther. The sorrow of her parting was as terrible as a deep burn, and I had to call on all the courage I had learned from my father not to call her name aloud and bring her back to me forever. After twelve days I dreamed that she was flying like a toucan above the treetops, and I awakened feeling very light, and wanting to weep. She was gone. I picked up my weapons and walked for many hours until I reached a branch of the river. I walked into the water up to my waist; I speared a small fish with a sharp stick and swallowed it whole, scales, tail, and all. I immediately vomited it up with a little blood; it was as it should be. I was not sad now. I had learned that sometimes death is more powerful than love. Then I went to hunt, so I would not return to my village with empty hands.

ESTER
LUCERO

T HEY bore Ester Lucero away on an improvised stretcher, bleeding like a stuck pig, her dark eyes wide with terror. When Doctor Angel Sánchez saw her, he lost his proverbial calm for the first time in memory—and not without reason, for he had been in love with her from the first day he saw her. Then she was still a little girl playing with dolls; he, in contrast, was returning from the last Glorious Campaign, aged a thousand years. He had come riding into town at the head of his column, sitting on the roof of a truck with his rifle across his knees, several months' growth of beard, and a bullet permanently lodged in his groin, but happier than ever before, or after, in his life. In the middle of the throng cheering the liberators, he had spied a little girl waving a red paper flag. He was thirty years old, and she was not yet twelve, but from the firm alabaster bones and the depths in the child's gaze, Angel Sánchez divined the

153

beauty that was secretly germinating within her. From his vantage atop the truck roof, he had stared at her until she was out of sight, convinced that she was a vision brought on by swamp fever and the elation of victory; but as that night, when it came his turn, he found no consolation in the arms of a bride-for-the-moment, he realized he would have to search for that girl, if for no other reason than to determine whether she was a mirage. The following day, when the tumult of celebration had died down in the streets and the task of restoring order to the world and sweeping clean the debris of the dictatorship had begun, Sánchez set out to scour the town. His first plan was to visit all the schools, but he found that they had been closed during the final battle, and he was forced to knock on doors, one by one. After several days of this patient pilgrimage, just when he was thinking that the girl had indeed been a trick of a vulnerable heart, he came to a tiny blue-painted house; the front was riddled with bullet-holes, and the only window opened onto the street with nothing but flowered curtains for protection. He called several times without receiving an answer, then decided to go in. Inside was a single scantly furnished room, cool and shadowed. He walked through this cubicle, opened a second door, and found himself in a large patio blighted by piles of castoffs and assorted junk; there was a hammock strung beneath a mango tree, a trough for doing laundry, a chicken coop in the rear, and a profusion of old tins and crocks sprouting herbs, vegetables, and flowers. There, finally, he found the person he thought he had dreamed. Ester Lucero—bright as the morning star of her name, barefoot, wearing a dress of cheap cotton, her luxuriant hair tied at the neck with a shoestring—was helping her grandmother hang out the wash to dry. When they saw him, both took an instinctive step backward, because they had learned to distrust anyone who wore boots.

"Don't be afraid," he bowed, greasy beret in hand. "I'm a *compañero*."

From that day on, Angel Sánchez confined himself to desiring Ester Lucero in silence, shamed by his unseemly passion for a child who still had not reached puberty. Because of her, he declined the opportunity to go to the capital when the spoils of power were divided, but chose instead to stay on as director of the only hospital in that godforsaken town. He had no hope of ever consummating his love outside the sphere of his imagination. He lived for infinitesimal satisfactions: watching her walk by on her way to school; attending her when she caught the measles; providing her with vitamins during the years when there were enough milk, eggs, and meat for only the very youngest, and the rest had to content themselves with plantains and corn; taking a chair in her patio and, beneath her grandmother's vigilant eye, teaching Ester the multiplication tables. Ester Lucero came to call him "Uncle," for want of a more appropriate name, and the old grandmother accepted his presence as yet one more of the inexplicable mysteries of the Revolution.

"What do you think an educated man like him, a doctor, the head of the hospital and hero of the nation, gets from the chatter of an old woman and the silence of her granddaughter?" the town gossips used to ask each other.

With the years, the girl blossomed, as almost always happens, but Angel Sánchez believed that in her case it was a kind of marvel and only he could see the hidden beauty ripening beneath the schoolgirl dresses her grandmother stitched on her sewing machine. He was sure, at the same time, that when she walked by she stirred the senses of all who saw her, as she stirred his, and he was dumbfounded not to find a whirl of suitors around Ester Lucero. He lived a torment of overpowering emotions: specific jealousy of any and all men; a perennial melancholy—the fruit of despair—and the hellfire that bedeviled him at the hour of the siesta, when he would imagine the girl, naked and moist, summoning him with lewd gestures from the shadows of the room. No one ever knew his tormented state of mind. He gained a reputation as a kind and gentle man. Eventually the wives of the town tired of their match-making attempts and accepted the fact that their doctor was simply a little strange.

"You'd never take him for one of *those*," they muttered. "But maybe the malaria or that bullet he has there in his crotch rid him forever of a taste for women."

Angel Sánchez cursed the mother who had brought him into the world twenty years too soon, and a destiny that had left body and soul raked with scars. He prayed that some caprice of nature would upset the harmony and eclipse the glow of Ester Lucero, so that no man could ever suspect that she was the most beautiful woman in this world, or any other. That is why, on the fateful Thursday when they carried her into the hospital on a stretcher, with her grandmother leading the way and a procession of curious bringing up the rear, the doctor reacted with a visceral cry. When he turned back the sheet and saw the gaping wound that perforated her body, he felt he had provoked the catastrophe by wishing so hard that she would never belong to another man.

"She climbed the mango in the patio, slipped, and fell on the stake where we tie the goose," the grandmother explained.

"Poor little thing, it was like someone had tried to kill a vampire," added a neighbor man who had helped carry the stretcher. "We had a terrible time working her free."

Ester Lucero closed her eyes and moaned quietly.

From that instant, Angel Sánchez entered into a personal duel with death. He called on all his powers to save the girl. He operated, he gave her injections, he transfused her with his own blood, he shot her full of antibiotics, but after forty-eight hours it was obvious that life was flowing from her wound like a torrent that could not be dammed. Sitting on the chair beside the dying girl's bed, consumed with tension and grief, he rested his head on the foot of her bed, and for a few minutes slept like a newborn babe. While he dreamed of gigantic flies, she was wandering lost in the nightmares of her agony, and so they met in a no man's land, and in their shared dream she clung to his hand and begged him not to let death claim her, never to abandon her. Angel Sánchez awakened, startled by the clear recollection of one Negro Rivas and the absurd miracle that had given him back his life. He rushed from the room and in the corridor passed the grandmother, who was submersed in a murmur of uninterrupted prayers.

"Keep praying. I'll be back in fifteen minutes," he shouted as he ran by.

Ten years earlier, when Angel Sánchez and his comrades were marching through the jungle in knee-high undergrowth amid the irremediable torture of mosquitoes and heat, crisscrossing the country to ambush the soldiers of the dictatorship; when they were but a handful of mad visionaries, surrounded, their belts stuffed with bullets, their knapsacks with poems, and their heads with ideals; when they had been months without even the scent of a woman or soap on their bodies; when hunger and fear were a second skin, and the only thing that kept them on the move was desperation; when they saw enemies everywhere and mistrusted even their own shadows, that was when Negro Rivas had fallen into a ravine and plunged almost twenty feet toward the bottom of the abyss, hurtling down noiselessly, like a bag of rags. It took his comrades, using ropes, twenty minutes to make their way to him through sharp-edged rocks and twisted treetrunks to where he lay buried in dense vegetation, and almost two hours to bring him up, soaked in blood.

This Negro Rivas was a huge man, cheerful and brave, always ready with a song, and more than willing to sling a weaker companion over his shoulder. But now he was split open like a ripe pomegranate, and the deep slash that began in the middle of his back and ended at mid-chest had laid bare his ribs. Sánchez carried an emergency medical kit, but this injury was far beyond his modest resources. With no illusions, he sutured the wound, bound it with strips of cloth, and administered what medicines he had at hand. They placed Rivas on a piece of canvas fastened to two poles and carried him, in shifts, until it was obvious that every jolt meant one minute less of life. Negro Rivas was bubbling blood like a spring and raving about iguanas with women's breasts, and hurricanes of salt.

They were just planning to make camp, in order to allow the man to die in peace, when one of them noticed two Indians squatting by a black water hole, amiably grooming each other for lice. Slightly behind them, lost in the thick jungle mist, lay their village. They were a tribe frozen in remote time, whose only contact with this century had been a daring missionary who had, unsuccessfully, come to preach to them of the laws of God. Even more grave: these Indians had never heard of the Revolution, nor the cry "Liberty or Death!" Despite these vast differences, and the barrier of language, the Indians understood that those exhausted men represented no serious danger to them, and they offered them a timid welcome. The rebels pointed to the dying man. The Indian whom they took to be the chief led them to a hut shadowed in eternal darkness and permeated with the stench of mud and urine. There they lay Negro Rivas on a rush mat, surrounded by his comrades and the members of the tribe. Shortly thereafter the witch doctor appeared in all his ceremonial garb. The Comandante was intimidated by the necklaces of peonies, the fanatic's eyes, and the layers of filth that caked his body, but Angel Sánchez pointed out that there was almost nothing to be done for the wounded man, and anything the witch doctor accomplished—even if it were only to help him die—would be better than nothing. The Comandante ordered his men to lower their weapons, and not interrupt, so that this strange, half-naked healer could perform his offices without distraction.

Two hours later the fever was gone and Negro Rivas was able to swallow water. By nightfall the sick man was sitting up eating cornmeal mush, and two days later he was attempting his first steps outside the hut, his wound already in full process of healing. While the other guerrillas kept an eye on the convalescent's progress, Angel Sánchez followed the witch doctor through the jungle, collecting plants in a bag. Years later in the capital, Negro Rivas was made Chief of Police, and the only time he remembered being at the point of death was when he took off his shirt to make love to a new woman, who invariably asked about the long scar that split him in half.

"If a naked Indian saved Negro Rivas, I will save Ester Lucero, even if it means making a pact with the devil," Angel Sánchez swore as he turned his house upside down searching for the herbs he had kept all those years but until that instant completely forgotten. He found them, dry and brittle, wrapped in newspaper at the bottom of a beat-up trunk, along with his notebook of poems, his beret, and other mementoes of the war.

The doctor ran back to the hospital as if pursued, beneath a sun so hot it melted the asphalt. He ran up the stairs two at a time, and burst into Ester Lucero's room, dripping with sweat. The grandmother and the nurse on duty saw him race by, and followed as far as the door to peer in. They watched as he removed his white coat, cotton shirt, dark trousers, the blackmarket socks and gum-soled shoes he always wore. Horrified, they then saw him remove his undershorts to stand as stark naked as a recruit.

"Holy Mary, Mother of God," breathed the grand-mother.

Through the little window in the door they could just see the doctor as he moved the bed to the center of the room, placed both hands for several seconds on Ester Lucero's head, and then began a frenetic dance around the sick girl. He lifted his knees so high they touched his chest, he swooped low, he waved his arms and made grotesque faces, without for an instant losing the internal beat that set wings to his feet. For half an hour he danced like a madman, never pausing, dodging oxygen tanks and intravenous solutions. Then he ex-tracted a few dried leaves from the pocket of his white coat, placed them in a tin basin, crushed them with his fist until they were a coarse powder, spit upon them repeatedly, stirred everything together to form a kind of paste, and walked toward the dying girl. The two women watched as he removed the bandages and then, as the nurse dutifully noted in her report, he smeared the revolting mixture on the wound, unmindful of the first laws of asepsis, as well as the fact that his private parts were shamefully exposed to the girl. When the treatment was complete, the doctor slumped to the floor, totally drained, but illuminated by a beatific smile.

If Doctor Angel Sánchez had not been the hospital's director and an undisputed Hero of the Revolution, they would have strapped him in a straitjacket and packed him off to the mental hospital, forthwith. But there was no one who dared break down the door he had bolted, and by the time the mayor took responsibility for doing so, with the help of local firemen, fourteen hours had gone by, and Ester Lucero was sitting up in bed, bright-eyed, amusedly watching her Uncle Angel, who had again removed his clothes and begun the second phase of treatment with new ritual dances. Two days later, when the commission from the Ministry of Health arrived, specially dispatched from the capital, the patient was walking down the corridor on her grandmother's arm. The whole town paraded through the third floor in hopes of catching a glimpse of the resuscitated girl and of the impeccably attired Hospital Director, at his desk, ready to receive his colleagues. The commission refrained from asking details concerning the doctor's extraordinary dance but instead concentrated its inquiry on the witch doctor's wondrous plants.

Several years have gone by since Ester Lucero fell from the mango tree. She married an Atmospheric Inspector and went to live in the capital, where she gave birth to a baby girl with alabaster bones and dark eyes. From time to time she sends her Uncle Angel nostalgic postcards sprinkled with horrific spelling errors. The Ministry of Health has organized four expeditions in quest of the phenomenal herbs, without a trace of success. The jungle has sallowed up the Indian village and, with it, hopes for a scientific cure for fatal accidents.

Doctor Angel Sánchez is still alone, his only company the image of Ester Lucero, who visits him in his room at the hour of the siesta, setting his soul aflame in a never-ending bacchanal. His prestige as a medical man continues to grow throughout the region, because he is often heard to speak with the stars in aboriginal tongues.

SIMPLE
MARÍA

SIMPLE María believed in love. That was what made her a living legend. All her neighbors came to her funeral, even the police and the blind man from the kiosk who almost never abandoned his business. Calle República was vacated and, as a sign of mourning, black ribbons hung from balconies and the red lights turned off in the houses. Every person has his or her story, and in this barrio they were almost always sad, stories of poverty and accumulated injustice, of every form of violence, of children dead before term and lovers who had run away, but María's story was different; it had a glow of elegance that gave wing to the imagination. She had been able to ply her trade independently, discreetly looking after her own affairs without hindrance. She never had the least curiosity about alcohol or drugs; she was not even interested in the five-peso consolations sold by the neighborhood fortune-tellers and seers. She seemed beyond the torment of hope, protected by the armor of her invented love. She was a small, inoffensive woman, short, with refined features and manner, but if some pimp tried to enlist her he found himself facing a rabid beast, all claws and fangs, ready to return blow for blow, even if it meant her life. They learned to leave her alone. While the other women spent half their lives hiding bruises under thick layers of cheap makeup, María grew old with respect, with something of the air of a queen in rags. She was not aware of the renown of her name, nor of the legend that had been created around her. She was an old prostitute with the soul of a girl.

In her memories a murderous trunk and a dark-skinned man who smelled of the sea figured prominently: one by one, her friends uncovered scraps of information about her life and pieced them together patiently, filling in the blank spaces with fantasy, until they had reconstructed a past for her. She was not, it goes without saying, like the other women in that place. She had come from a distant world where skin is fair and Spanish is spoken with hard consonants and echoes of Spain. María was born to be a great lady; this was what the other women deduced from her aristocratic manner of speaking and her unique behavior, and, if any doubt remained, it was dissipated at her death. She died with her dignity intact. She suffered no recognizable illness; she was not frightened, nor did she breathe through her ears as ordinary people do when they are dying; she merely announced that she could no longer bear the tedium of living, put on her best dress, painted her lips bright red, and opened the plastic curtains that gave access to her room, so that everyone could be with her.

"My time has come to die" was her only comment.

She lay back in her bed, supported by three pillows whose cases had been starched for the occasion, and drank the contents of a large jug of thick chocolate at one swallow. The other women laughed at her, but when four hours later they were unable to wake her they realized that her decision was categorical and they ran to spread the word through the barrio. Some people came only out of curiosity, but most were truly distressed and stayed to be near her. Her friends brewed coffee to offer the visitors, because it seemed in bad taste to serve liquor; they did not want the wake to be confused with a celebration. About six in the evening, María shuddered, opened her eyes, looked around without seeing the faces, and immediately gave up the ghost. That was all. Someone suggested that she might have swallowed poison with the chocolate, in which case they would all be guilty for not having taken her to the hospital in time, but no one paid much attention to such slanderous remarks.

"If María decided to leave this world, she was within her rights, because she had no children or parents to look after" was the judgment of the madam of the house.

María's friends did not want to see her in a funeral parlor, because the tranquil premeditation of her death was a solemn occurrence for Calle República and it was only right that her last hours before being lowered into the ground should be spent in the place where she had lived and not like some stranger whom no one cares to mourn. There were various opinions about whether holding a wake in the house would bring bad luck to the soul of the departed or to those of the clients, and whether just in case, they should break a mirror and lay the pieces around the coffin or bring holy water from the chapel of the Seminario to sprinkle in the corners. No one worked that night; there was no music and no laughter, but neither were there tears. They set the casket on a table in the lounge; the neighbors all lent chairs, and that was where the visitors made themselves comfortable and drank coffee and talked in low voices. In the center lay María, her head resting on a satin cushion, her hands crossed, and the photo of the dead child upon her bosom. During the course of the night her skin changed color until it was as dark as the chocolate she had drunk.

I learned about María's story during the long hours we were sitting around her coffin. Her fellow workers told me that she had been born around the time of the Great War, in a southern province where the trees lose their leaves in the middle of the year and the cold seeps into your bones. She was the daughter of a proud family of Spanish emigrés. When they went through her room they had found some brittle, yellow papers in a biscuit tin; among them were a birth certificate and some photographs and letters. Her father had owned a hacienda and, according to a newspaper clipping stained with time, before she was married her mother had been a pianist. When María was twelve, she had been struck by a freight train as she was absentmindedly crossing the railroad track. She was picked up from between the rails, seemingly unharmed; she had only a few scratches and she had lost her hat. It was soon clear, nevertheless, that the impact had transported the girl into a state of innocence from which she would never return. She forgot even the most rudimentary schooling from before the accident; she could barely remember her piano lessons or how to use her embroidery needle, and when anyone spoke to her it was as if she were not there. In contrast, what she never forgot was the civility that she retained intact until her dying day.

After being struck by the locomotive, María was incapable of reasoning; she was inattentive and devoid of animosity. She was, in fact, well equipped to be happy, but happiness was not to be her fate. When she was sixteen her parents, eager to transfer to another the burden of their somewhat retarded daughter, decided to marry her off before her beauty faded. They chose for the purpose a Doctor Guevara, a retiring man little suited for marriage, but one who owed them money and could not refuse when they suggested the union. That same year the wedding was celebrated in private, as befitted a lunatic bride and a groom many decades her senior.

María came to the marriage bed with the mind of a babe, although her body had matured and was that of a woman. The train had obliterated her natural curiosity but had not destroyed the impatience of her senses. All she knew was what she had observed of the animals on her parents' hacienda; she knew that cold water is good for separating dogs who are unable to disengage after coupling, and that the rooster fluffs his feathers and crows when he wants to cover a hen, but she had not found any useful purpose for those facts. On her wedding night she watched a trembling old man walk toward her, his flannel bathrobe flapping, with something un- anticipated below his navel. Surprise brought on a state of constipation she was too inhibited to discuss, and when she began to swell up like a balloon she drank a whole bottle of Agua de la Margarita, an anti-scrofula tonic that in large quantities served as a purge, and then spent twenty-two days seated on a chamber pot, so undone that she nearly lost several vital organs. Not even that ordeal, however, had the effect of deflating her. Soon she could not button her clothing and, in due time, she gave birth to a blond baby boy. After a month in bed drinking chicken broth and two liters of milk a day, she arose stronger and more lucid than she had ever been in her life. She seemed cured of her perennial somnambulism, and even had the spunk to buy herself some elegant clothes. She was not, however, to have the opportunity to show off her new wardrobe, because her doctor husband suffered a sudden stroke and died in the dining room, soupspoon in hand. María resigned herself to wearing mourning and veiled hats, feeling as if she were buried in a tomb of cloth. She spent two years in black, knitting vests for the poor, playing with her lap dogs and her son, whom she dressed as a little girl with long curls—as evidenced in one of the photo- graphs found in the biscuit tin, where he is seen sitting on a bearskin rug beneath a supernatural beam of light.

For the widow, time had frozen in an eternal instant; the air of her room seemed unchanged, still heavy with her husband's musty odor. She continued to live in the same house, looked after by faithful servants and closely watched by her parents and brothers, who took turns visiting her daily in order to supervise her expenses and make even the most minor decisions for her. The seasons rolled by; the leaves fell from the trees in the garden and the hummingbirds of summer appeared once again with no change in her routine. At times she wondered about the reasons for her black clothing, because she had completely forgotten the decrepit husband who once or twice had feebly embraced her between the linen sheets, then, full of remorse for his lust, had thrown himself at the feet of the Madonna and lashed himself with a horsewhip. From time to time she opened her armoire to shake out her beautiful dresses; she could not resist the temptation to remove her inky clothing and secretly try on the jewel-embroidered gowns, the fur stoles, the satin slippers, the kid gloves. She regarded herself in the three leaves of the mirror and greeted a woman dressed for a ball, a woman in whom she found it very difficult to recognize herself.

After two years of solitude, the sound of the blood racing through her body became unbearable. On Sundays, at the door of the church, she would hang back to watch the men pass, attracted by the harsh sound of their voices, their fresh-shaved cheeks, and the smell of tobacco. Furtively, she would lift her veil and smile. It was not long before her father and brothers noticed this behavior and, convinced that American soil had corrupted the decency even of widows, they decided in a family council to send María to live with an aunt and uncle in Spain; there, doubtless, protected by the solid traditions and power of the Church, she would be safe from frivolous temptations. And so began the voyage that was to change the destiny of simple María.

Her mother and father saw her off on a transatlantic steamer, accompanied by her son, a servant, and her lap dogs. Her mountains of baggage included, in addition to her bedroom furniture and her piano, a cow that traveled in the hold to provide fresh milk for the baby. Among her many suitcases and hatboxes she had also brought an enormous brass-trimmed and studded trunk containing the ball gowns she had rescued from mothballs. The family did not believe that in her aunt and uncle's house María would have any opportunity to wear them, but they had not wanted to gainsay her. The first three days, she did not lift her head from her berth, overcome by seasickness, but then she became accustomed to the pitching of the ship and managed to get out of bed. She called her servant to help her unpack her clothes for the long crossing.

María's life was marked by sudden misfortunes, like the train that had claimed her mind and flung her back into an irreversible childhood. She was arranging her dresses in the stateroom closet when her son peered into the opened trunk. At that moment the ship lurched and the heavy metal-edged lid slammed shut, breaking the child's neck. It took three strong sailors to tear the mother away from the accursed trunk and a dose of laudanum strong enough to fell an athlete to prevent her from tearing out her hair and clawing her face raw. She howled for hours, and then fell into a crepuscular coma, rocking from side to side as she had done in the days when she earned the reputation of being an idiot. The ship's captain announced the unfortunate news over the loudspeaker, read a brief prayer for the dead, and then ordered the small corpse to be wrapped in a flag and slipped over the side, because they were in mid-ocean and there was no way to preserve the body until they reached the next port.

Several days after the tragedy, María emerged with unsteady step to take the air on the deck for the first time. It was a warm night, and an unsettling odor of seaweed, shellfish, and sunken ships rose from the ocean, entered her nostrils, and raced through her veins with the effect of an earthquake. She found herself staring at the horizon, her mind a blank and her skin tingling from her heels to the base of her neck, when she heard an insistent whistle; she half-turned and beheld two decks below a dark shadow in the moonlight, signaling to her. She descended the ladder in a trance, walked to the dark-skinned man who had beckoned to her, submissively allowed him to remove her black veils and voluminous clothing, and followed him behind a large coil of rope. Battered by an impact not unlike that of the train, she learned in less than three minutes the difference between an aged husband stifled by the fear of God and an insatiable Greek sailor afire from the craving born of several weeks of oceanic chastity. Dazed, María discovered her own potential; she dried her tears, and asked for more. They spent a good part of the night getting to know one another, and parted only when they heard the ship's emergency horn, a terrible blast for "man overboard" that transmuted the silence of the fish. Thinking that the inconsolable mother had thrown herself into the sea, the servant had spread the alarm, and all the crew, with the exception of the Greek sailor, were searching for her.

María joined her lover behind the coils of rope every night until the ship sailed near Caribbean shores, where the sweet perfume of flowers and fruit borne on the breeze was a final assault on her senses. She accepted her lover's proposition that they leave the ship where the ghost of her dead child wandered and where they were the target of so many spying eyes; she stuffed the expense money for the voyage into her petticoats and said goodbye to a respectable past. They lowered a lifeboat and disappeared at dawn, leaving behind the servant, the dogs, the cow, and the murderous trunk. The man rowed with his burly sailor's arms toward a stupendous port that rose before their eyes in the dawn light like a vision from another world: huts, palm trees, and brightly colored birds. The two fugitives settled in to stay for as long as their reserves lasted.

The sailor, it turned out, was a brawler and a drunk. He spoke a lingo incomprehensible to either María or the local inhabitants, but he managed to communicate through grimaces and smiles. María was fully alert only when he showed up to practice with her the acrobatics he had learned in whorehouses from Singapore to Valparaíso; the rest of the time she lay numbed by a mortal lassitude. Bathed in tropical sweat, the woman invented love without her companion, venturing alone into hallucinatory lands with the audacity of one who does not know the risks. The Greek lacked sufficient intuition to appreciate that he had opened a floodgate, that he himself was but the instrument of revelation, or that he was incapable of valuing the gift this woman offered to him. He had by his side a creature caught in the limbo of an invulnerable innocence, a woman dedicated to exploring her own senses with all the playfulness of a cub, but he did not know how to follow her in her games. Before him, she had never known the diversion of pleasure; she had not even imagined it, although it had always been there in her blood like the germ of a raging fever. When she discovered that pleasure, she believed it was the blessing from heaven that the nuns in her school had promised good girls in the Beyond. She knew almost nothing of the world, and she was incapable of studying a map to learn her whereabouts on the planet, but when she saw the hibiscus and the parrots she was sure she was in Paradise, and she prepared to enjoy it. No one there knew her; she felt comfortable for the first time, far from her home, from the inescapable guardianship of her parents and brothers, free of social pressures and veils at mass, free finally to savor the torrent of emotions that originated on her skin and sank through every pore to her innermost grottoes, where she was tossed and tumbled in roaring cataracts that left her exhausted and happy.

After a time, however, María's lack of malice, her imperviousness to sin or humiliation, terrified the sailor. The periods between love-making grew longer, the man's absences more frequent, and a silence swelled between them. The Greek longed to escape from that moist, tumid, inflamed woman with the face of a child who called him incessantly, convinced that the widow he had seduced on the high seas had become a perverse spider who would devour him like a defenseless fly in the tumult of their bed. In vain he sought alleviation for his threatened virility by cavorting with prostitutes, fighting knife and fist with pimps, and betting on cockfights anything he had left from his sprees. When he found himself with empty pockets, he seized the excuse to disappear completely. For several weeks María waited patiently. On the radio, from time to time, she would hear that a French sailor who had deserted from a British ship, or a Dutchman who had fled a Portuguese vessel, had been stabbed to death in the rough barrios around the port; she listened impassively, because she was waiting for a Greek who had jumped ship from an Italian cruiser. When the heat in her bones and anxiety in her soul had become too much to bear, she went out to seek consolation with the first man who passed by. She took the man's hand, and asked him in the most genteel and educated way whether he would do her the favor of taking off his clothes for her. The stranger hesitated a moment, disoriented by this young woman who in no way resembled the neighborhood professionals but whose proposal, despite the unusual way it was phrased, was very clear. He reckoned that he could divert himself with her for ten minutes, and followed her, never suspecting that he would find himself submersed in the whirlpool of a sincere passion. Amazed and moved, he left some money on María's table and went to tell everyone he knew. Soon other men came, drawn by the gossip that there was a woman who was able, even if briefly, to sell the illusion of love. All her clients were satisfied. And so María became the most famous prostitute in the port; sailors tattooed her name on their arm and told her story on other seas, until the legend had circled the globe.

Time, poverty, and the strain of fending off disillusion destroyed María's freshness. Her complexion grew drab, she was nothing but skin and bones, and for greater convenience she had cut her hair short like a prisoner's, but she retained her elegant manners and her enthusiasm for each new encounter with a man; she never saw them as anonymous objects, only the reflection of herself in the arms of her imaginary lover. Confronted with reality, she was blind to the sordid urgency of her temporary partner, because to each one she gave herself with the same uncompromising love, anticipating, like a daring bride, the other's desires. Her memory deteriorated with age, she sometimes spoke nonsense, and by the time she moved to the capital and set up shop in Calle República, she no longer remembered that once she had been the muse for verses improvised by sailors of all races, and she was puzzled when someone traveled from the port to the city just to verify whether the woman he had heard of someplace in Asia was still alive. When he found himself standing before that tiny grasshopper, that pile of pathetic bones, that little nobody, and when he saw the legend reduced to ashes, many a man turned and walked away, deeply saddened, but some remained out of pity. Those who did received an unexpected prize. When María closed her plastic curtain the atmosphere in the room immediately changed. Later, the stunned man would leave, carrying with him the image of a mythic girl, not the pitiful old whore he thought he had seen when he arrived.

María's past was gradually fading—her only clear memory was a fear of trains and trunks—and had it not been for the persistence of the other whores, no one would ever have known her story. She lived in expectation of the moment that the curtain to her room would open and reveal a Greek sailor, or some other ghost born of her fancy, who would encircle her in the safe haven of his arms and rekindle the delight shared on the deck of a ship on the high seas. She sought that ancient illusion in every passing man, illuminated by an imagined love, holding back the shadows with fleeting embraces, with sparks that were consumed before they blazed, and when she grew weary of waiting in vain and felt that her soul was covered with scales, she decided that it would be better to leave this world. That was when, with the same delicacy and consideration she lent to all her actions, she picked up her jug of warm chocolate.

OUR
SECRET

SHE let herself be caressed, drops of sweat in the small of her back, her body exuding the scent of burnt sugar, silent, as if she divined that a single sound could nudge its way into memory and destroy everything, reducing to dust this instant in which he was a person like any other, a casual lover she had met that morning, another man without a past attracted to her wheat-colored hair, her freckled skin, the jangle of her gypsy bracelets, just a man who had spoken to her in the street and begun to walk with her, aimlessly, commenting on the weather and the traffic, watching the crowd, with the slightly forced confidence of her countrymen in this foreign land, a man without sorrow or anger, without guilt, pure as ice, who merely wanted to spend the day with her, wandering through bookstores and parks, drinking coffee, celebrating the chance of having met, talking of old nostalgias, of how life had been when both were growing up in the same city, in the same barrio, when they were fourteen, you remember, winters of shoes soggy from frost, and paraffin stoves, summers of peach trees, there in the now forbidden country. Perhaps she was feeling a little lonely, or this seemed an opportunity to make love without complications, but, for whatever reason, at the end of the day, when they had run out of pretexts to walk any longer, she had taken his hand and led him to her house. She shared with other exiles a sordid apartment in a yellow building at the end of an alley filled with garbage cans. Her room was tiny: a mattress on the floor covered with a striped blanket, bookshelves improvised from boards stacked on two rows of bricks, books, posters, clothing on a chair, a suitcase in the corner. She had removed her clothes without preamble, with the attitude of a little girl eager to please. He tried to make love to her. He stroked her body patiently, slipping over her hills and valleys, discovering her secret routes, kneading her, soft clay upon the sheets, until she yielded, and opened to him. Then he retreated, mute, reserved. She gathered herself, and sought him, her head on his belly, her face hidden, as if constrained by modesty, as she fondled him, licked him, spurred him. He tried to lose himself; he closed his eyes and for a while let her do as she was doing, until he was defeated by sadness, or shame, and pushed her away. They lighted another cigarette. There was no complicity now; the urgent anticipation that had united them during the day was lost, and all that was left were two vulnerable people lying on a mattress, without memory, floating in the terrible vacuum of unspoken words. When they had met that morning they had had no extraordinary expectations, they had had no particular plan, only companionship, and a little pleasure, that was all, but at the hour of their coming together they had been engulfed by melancholy. We're tired, she smiled, seeking excuses for the desolation that had settled over them. In a last attempt to buy time, he took her face in his hands and kissed her eyelids. They lay down side by side, holding hands, and talked about their lives in this country where they had met by chance, a green and generous land in which, nevertheless, they would forever be foreigners. He thought of putting on his clothes and saying goodbye, before the tarantula of his nightmares poisoned the air, but she looked so young and defenseless, and he wanted to be her friend. Her friend, he thought, not her lover; her friend, to share quiet moments, without demands or commitments; her friend, someone to be with, to help ward off fear. He did not leave, or let go her hand. A warm, tender feeling, an enormous compassion for himself and for her, made his eyes sting. The curtain puffed out like a sail, and she got up to close the window, thinking that darkness would help them recapture their desire to be together, to make love. But darkness was not good; he needed the rectangle of light from the street, because without it he felt trapped again in the abyss of the timeless ninety centimeters of his cell, fermenting in his own excrement, delirious. Leave the curtain open, I want to look at you, he lied, because he did not dare confide his night terrors to her, the wracking thirst, the bandage pressing upon his head like a crown of nails, the visions of caverns, the assault of so many ghosts. He could not talk to her about that, because one thing leads to another, and he would end up saying things that had never been spoken. She returned to the mattress, stroked him absently, ran her fingers over the small lines, exploring them. Don't worry, it's nothing contagious, they're just scars, he laughed, almost with a sob. The girl perceived his anguish and stopped, the gesture suspended, alert. At that moment he should have told her that this was not the beginning of a new love, not even of a passing affair; it was merely an instant of truce, a brief moment of innocence, and soon, when she fell asleep, he would go; he should have told her that there was no future for them, no secret gestures, that they would not stroll hand in hand through the streets again, nor share lovers' games, but he could not speak, his voice was buried somewhere in his gut, like a claw. He knew he was sinking. He tried to cling to the reality that was slipping away from him, to anchor his mind on anything, on the jumble of clothing on the chair, on the books piled on the floor, on the poster of Chile on the wall, on the coolness of this Caribbean night, on the distant street noises; he tried to concentrate on this body that had been offered him, think only of the girl's luxuriant hair, the caramel scent of her skin. He begged her voicelessly to help him save those seconds, while she observed him from the far edge of the bed, sitting cross-legged like a fakir, her pale breasts and the eye of her navel also observing him, registering his trembling, the chattering of his teeth, his moan. He thought he could hear the silence growing within him; he knew that he was coming apart, as he had so often before, and he gave up the struggle, releasing his last hold on the present, letting himself plunge down the endless precipice. He felt the crusted straps on his ankles and wrists, the brutal charge, the torn tendons, the insulting voices demanding names, the unforgettable screams of Ana, tortured beside him, and of the others, hanging by their arms in the courtyard.

What's the matter? For God's sake, what's wrong? Ana's voice was asking from far away. No, Ana was still bogged in the quicksands to the south. He thought he could make out a naked girl, shaking him and calling his name, but he could not get free of the shadows with their snaking whips and rippling flags. Hunched over, he tried to control the nausea. He began to weep for Ana and for all the others. What is it, what's the matter? Again the girl, calling him from somewhere. Nothing! Hold me! he begged, and she moved toward him timidly, and took him in her arms, lulled him like a baby, kissed his forehead, said, Go ahead, cry, cry all you want; she laid him flat on his back on the mattress and then, crucified, stretched out upon him.

For a thousand years they lay like that, together, until slowly the hallucinations faded and he returned to the room to find himself alive in spite of everything, breathing, pulsing, the girl's weight on his body, her head resting on his chest, her arms and legs atop his: two frightened orphans. And at that moment, as if she knew everything, she said to him, Fear is stronger than desire, than love or hatred or guilt or rage, stronger than loyalty. Fear is all-consuming . . . , and he felt her tears rolling down his neck. Everything stopped: she had touched his most deeply hidden wound. He had a presentiment that she was not just a girl willing to make love for the sake of pity but that she knew the thing that crouched beyond the silence, beyond absolute solitude, beyond the sealed box where he had hidden from the Colonel and his own treachery, beyond the memory of Ana Díaz and the other betrayed *compañeros* being led in one by one with their eyes blindfolded. How could she know all that?

She sat up. As she groped for the switch, her slender arm was silhouetted against the pale haze of the window. She turned on the light and, one by one, removed her metal bracelets, dropping them noiselessly on the mattress. Her hair was half covering her face when she held out her hands to him. White scars circled her wrists, too. For a timeless instant he stared at them, unmoving, until he understood everything, love, and saw her strapped to the electric grid, and then they could embrace, and weep, hungry for pacts and confidences, for forbidden words, for promises of tomorrow, shared, finally, the most hidden secret.

THE LITTLE
HEIDELBERG

EL Capitán and the woman
niña Eloísa had danced together so many years that
they had achieved perfection. Each could sense the
other's next movement, divine the exact instant of the
next turn, interpret the most subtle hand pressure or
deviation of a foot. They had not missed a step once in
forty years; they moved with the precision of a couple
used to making love and sleeping in a close embrace.
This was what made it so difficult to believe that they
had never exchanged a single word.

The Little Heidelberg is a tavern a certain distance
from the capital and located on a hill surrounded by
banana groves; there, besides good music and invigor-
ating air, they offer a unique aphrodisiac stew made
heady with a combination of spices, too heavy for the
fiery climate of the region but in perfect harmony with
the traditions that activate the proprietor *don* Rupert.
Before the oil crisis, when there was still an illusion of

plenty and fruits were imported from other latitudes, the specialty of the house had been apple strudel, but now that nothing is left from the petroleum but a mountain of indestructible refuse and a memory of better times, they make the strudel with guavas and with mangoes. The tables, arranged in a large circle that leaves an open space in the middle for dancing, are covered with green-and-white-checked cloths, and the walls display bucolic scenes of country life in the Alps: shepherdesses with golden braids, strapping youths, and immaculate bovines. The musicians—dressed in lederhosen, woolen knee socks, Tyrolean suspenders, and felt hats that with the sweat of years have lost their dash and from a distance resemble greenish wigs—sit on a platform crowned by a stuffed eagle that according to *don* Rupert sprouts new feathers from time to time. One plays the accordion, another the saxophone, and the third, through some feat of agility involving all his extremities, simultaneously manipulates bass drum, snares, and top hat. The accordion player is a master of his instrument, and he also sings in a warm tenor voice that vaguely suggests Andalusia. Despite his foolish Swiss publican's garb, he is the favorite of the female faithful, and several of these *señoras* secretly nurture the fantasy of being trapped with him in some mortal adventure—a landslide, say, or bombing—in which they would happily draw their last breath folded in the strong arms capable of tearing such heartrending sobs from the accordion. The fact that the median age of these ladies is nearly seventy does not diminish the sensuality stirred by the tenor; it merely adds the gentle breath of death to their enchantment. The orchestra begins playing shortly after sunset and ends at midnight, except on Saturdays and Sundays, when the place is filled with tourists and the trio must keep playing until near dawn when the last customer leaves. They play only polkas, mazurkas, waltzes, and European folk dances, as if instead of being firmly established in the Caribbean, The Little Heidelberg were located on the shores of the Rhine.

Doña Burgel, *don* Rupert's wife, reigns in the kitchen, a formidable matron whom few know because she spends her days amid stewpots and mounds of vegetables; lost in the task of preparing foreign dishes with local ingredients. It was she who invented the strudel with tropical fruits, and the aphrodisiac stew capable of restoring dash to the most disheartened. The landlords' two daughters wait on the tables, a pair of sturdy women smelling of cinnamon, clove, vanilla, and lemon, along with a few local girls, all with rosy cheeks. The clientele is composed of European emigrés who reached these shores escaping poverty or some war or other, businessmen, farmers, and tradesmen, a pleasant and uncomplicated group of people who may not always have been so but who with the passing of time have eased into the benevolent courtesy of healthy old people. The men wear bow ties and jackets, but as the exertion of the dancing and abundance of beer warms their souls, they shed superfluous garments and end up in their shirt-sleeves. The women wear bright colors in antiquated styles, as if their dresses have been rescued from bridal trunks brought with them from their homeland. From time to time a gang of aggressive teenagers stops by; their presence is preceded by the thundering roar of motorcycles and the rattle of boots, keys, and chains, and they come with the sole purpose of making fun of the old people, but the event never goes any further than a skirmish, because the drummer and the saxophonist are prepared to roll up their sleeves and restore order.

On Saturdays, about nine, when all present have enjoyed their servings of the aphrodisiac stew and abandoned themselves to the pleasure of the dance, La Mexicana arrives and sits alone. She is a provocative fiftyish woman with the body of a galleon—proud bow, rounded keel, ample stern, and face like a carved figurehead—who displays a mature but still firm décolletage and a flower over one ear. She is not, of course, the only woman dressed like a flamenco dancer, but on her it looks more natural than on ladies with white hair and resigned waistlines who do not even speak proper Spanish. La Mexicana dancing the polka is a ship adrift on a storm-tossed sea, but to the rhythm of the waltz she seems to breast calm waters. This is how El Capitán sometimes espies her in his dreams, and awakens with the nearly forgotten restiveness of adolescence. They say that this captain sailed with a Nordic line whose name no one could decipher. He was an expert on old ships and sea lanes, but all that knowledge lay buried in the depths of his mind, with no possible application in a land where the sea is a placid aquarium of green, crystalline waters unsuited to the intrepid vessels of the North Sea. El Capitán is a leafless tree, a tall, lean man with straight back and still firm neck muscles, a relic clothed in a gold-buttoned jacket and the tragic aura of retired sailors. No one has ever heard a word of Spanish from his lips, nor any other recognizable language. Thirty years ago *don* Rupert argued that El Capitán must be Finnish because of the icy color of his eyes and the unremitting justice of his gaze; as no one could contradict him everyone came to accept his opinion. Anyway, language is secondary at The Little Heidelberg, for no one comes there to talk.

A few of the standard rules of conduct have been modified for the comfort and convenience of all. Anyone can go onto the dance floor alone, or invite someone from another table; if they wish to, the women can take the initiative and ask the men. This is a fair solution for unaccompanied widows. No one asks La Mexicana to dance because it is understood that she considers it offensive; the men must wait, trembling with anticipation, until she makes the request. She deposits her cigarette in the ashtray, uncrosses the daunting columns of her legs, tugs at her bodice, marches toward the chosen one, and stops before him without a glance. She changes partners with every dance, but always reserves at least four numbers for El Capitán. He places a firm helmsman's hand at her waist and pilots her about the floor without allowing his years to curtail his inspiration.

The oldest client of The Little Heidelberg, one who in half a century has never missed a Saturday, is *niña* Eloísa, a tiny lady, meek and gentle, with rice-paper skin and a corona of baby-fine hair. She has earned a living for so many years making bonbons in her kitchen that she is permeated with the scent of chocolate, and always smells of birthday parties. Despite her age, she has retained some of her girlish mannerisms and she still has the strength to spend the entire evening whirling around the dance floor without disturbing a curl of her topknot or skipping a heartbeat. She came to this country at the turn of the century from a village in the south of Russia, accompanied by her mother, who was then a raving beauty. They lived together for years, making their chocolates, completely indifferent to the rigors of the climate, the century, or loneliness, without husbands, family, or major alarms, their sole diversion The Little Heidelberg every weekend. When her mother died, *niña* Eloísa came alone. *Don* Rupert always received her at the door with great deference and showed her to her table as the orchestra welcomed her with the first chords of her favorite waltz. At some tables, mugs of beer were raised to greet her, because she was the oldest person there and undoubtedly the most beloved. She was shy; she had never dared invite a man to dance, but in all those years she had never needed to do so; everyone considered it a privilege to take her hand, place his arm—delicately, so as not to break a crystal bone—about her waist, and lead her to the dance floor. She was a graceful dancer and, besides, she had that sweet fragrance that recalled to any who smelled it his happiest childhood memories.

El Capitán always sat alone, and always at the same table; he drank in moderation and showed no enthusiasm for *doña* Burgel's aphrodisiac stew. He tapped his toe in time with the music, and when *niña* Eloísa was unengaged he would invite her to dance, stopping smartly before her with a discreet click of his heels and a slight bow. They never spoke, they merely looked at each other and smiled between the gallops, skips, and obliques of some old-time dance.

One December Saturday less humid than others, a tourist couple came into The Little Heidelberg. These were not the disciplined Japanese they had been seeing recently but tall Scandinavians with tanned skin and pale eyes; they took a table and watched the dancers with fascination. They were merry and noisy; they clinked their mugs of beer, laughed heartily, and chatted in loud voices. The strangers' words reached the ears of El Capitán at his table and, from a long way away, from another time and another world, came the sound of his own language, as whole and fresh as if it had just been invented, words he had not heard for several decades but retained intact in his memory. An unfamiliar expression softened the features of this ancient mariner and he wavered several minutes between the absolute reserve in which he felt comfortable and the almost forgotten delight of losing himself in conversation. Finally he rose and walked toward the strangers. Behind the bar, *don* Rupert observed El Capitán as he leaned forward slightly, hands clasped behind his back, and spoke to the new arrivals. Soon the other customers, the waitresses, and the musicians realized that the man was speaking for the first time since they had known him, and they, too, fell silent in order to hear him better. He had a voice like a greatgrandfather, reedy and deliberate, but he uttered every phrase with clear determination. When he had poured out the contents of his heart, the room was so silent that *doña* Burgel hurried from the kitchen to find out whether someone had died. Finally, after a long pause, one of the tourists emerged from his astonishment, summoned *don* Rupert, and asked him in rudimentary English to help translate the capitain's words. The Nordic couple followed the elderly seaman to the table where *niña* Eloísa sat, and *don* Rupert trailed along, removing his apron on the way, with the intuition that a solemn event was about to occur. El Capitán spoke a few words in his language, one of the strangers translated it into English, and *don* Rupert, his ears pink and his mustache trembling, repeated it in his hind-to-fore Spanish.

"Niña Eloísa, asks El Capitán will you marry him."

The fragile old lady sat there, her eyes round with surprise and her mouth hidden behind her batiste handkerchief, while all waited, holding their breath, until she was able to find her voice.

"Don't you think this is a little sudden?" she whispered.

Her words were repeated by the tavernkeeper and then the tourist, and the answer traveled the same route in reverse.

"El Capitán says he has waited forty years to ask you, and that he could not wait until again comes someone who speaks his language. He says please to do him the favor of answering now."

"All right," *niña* Eloísa whispered faintly, and it was not necessary to translate her answer because everyone understood.

A euphoric *don* Rupert threw his arms in the air and announced the engagement; El Capitán kissed the cheeks of his fiancée, the tourists shook everyone's hand, the musicians struck up a ringing triumphal march, and the guests formed a circle around the couple. The women wiped away tears, the men offered sentimental toasts, *don* Rupert sat down at the bar and buried his head in his arms, shaken with emotion, while *doña* Burgel and her two daughters uncorked bottles of their best rum. The trio began to play *The Blue Danube* waltz and the dance floor emptied.

El Capitán took the hand of the gentle lady he had wordlessly loved for so many years and walked with her to the center of the room, where they began to dance with the grace of two herons in their courtship dance. El Capitán held *niña* Eloísa in his arms with the same loving care with which in his youth he had caught the wind in the sails of an ethereal sailing ship, gliding with her around the floor as if they were skimming the calm waves of a bay, while he told her in the language of blizzards and forests all the things his heart had held silent until that moment. Dancing, dancing, El Capitán felt as if time were flowing backward, as if they were growing younger, as if with every step they were happier and lighter on their feet. Turn after turn, the chords of the music grew more vibrant, their feet more rapid, her waist more slender, the weight of her tiny hand fainter in his, her presence less substantial. El Capitán danced on as *niña* Eloísa turned to lace, to froth, to mist, until she was but a shadow, then, finally, nothing but air, and he found himself whirling, whirling, with empty arms, his only companion a faint aroma of chocolate.

The tenor indicated to the musicians that they should continue playing the same waltz, because he realized that with the last note the captain would wake from his reverie and the memory of *niña* Eloísa would disappear forever. Deeply moved, the elderly customers of The Little Heidelberg sat motionless in their chairs until finally La Mexicana, her arrogance transformed into affection and tenderness, stood and walked quietly toward the trembling hands of El Capitán, to dance with him.

THE
JUDGE'S
WIFE

Nicolás Vidal had always
known that a woman would cost him his life. That had
been prophesied on the day he was born, and confirmed
by the proprietress of the general store on the one
occasion he had permitted her to read his fortune in the
coffee dregs; he could never have imagined, however,
that the woman would be Casilda, the wife of Judge
Hidalgo. The first time he had seen her was the day
she arrived in town to be married. He did not find her
attractive; he preferred females who were brazen and
brunette, and this translucent young girl in her traveling
suit, with bashful eyes and delicate fingers useless for
pleasuring a man, seemed as insubstantial to him as a
handful of ashes. Knowing his fate so well, he was
cautious about women, and throughout his life he fled
from any sentimental attachments, hardening his heart
to love and limiting himself to hasty encounters aimed
at outwitting loneliness. Casilda seemed so insignificant

and remote to him that he took no precautions against her and, when the moment came, he lost sight of the prediction that had always governed his decisions. From the roof of the building where he was crouched with two of his men, he observed the young *señorita* from the capital as she descended from her car on her wedding day. She had arrived in the company of a half dozen of her family members, all as pale and delicate as she, who had sat through the ceremony fanning themselves with a frank air of consternation and then departed, never to return.

Like all the town's residents, Vidal was sure the bride would never survive the climate and that soon the old women would be laying her out for her funeral. In the unlikely event she did endure the heat and dust that blew through the skin and settled in the heart, she would without question succumb before the foul humor and bachelor manias of her husband. Judge Hidalgo was several times her age, and had slept alone for so many years that he did not know how to begin to please a wife. His severity and stubbornness in carrying out the law—even at the cost of justice—was feared in every corner of the province. In the exercise of his duties he ignored any rationale for humaneness, punishing with equal firmness the theft of a hen and premeditated murder. He dressed in rigorous black, so that everyone would be reminded of the dignity of his responsibilities, and despite the inescapable dust clouds of this town without dreams his high-topped shoes always gleamed with a beeswax shine. A man like that is not made to be wed, the gossips would say; their dire prophecies about the marriage, however, were not fulfilled. To the contrary, Casilda survived three pregnancies in a row, and seemed content. On Sundays, with her husband, she attended twelve o'clock mass, imperturbable beneath her Spanish mantilla, untouched by the inclemency of the never-ending summer, as colorless and silent as a shadow. No one ever heard anything more than a timid hello from her, nor witnessed gestures more bold than a nod of the head or a fleeting smile; she seemed weightless, on the verge of dematerializing in a moment of carelessness. She gave the impression of not being there, and that was why everyone was so surprised by the influence she exerted on the Judge, who underwent striking changes.

Although Hidalgo maintained the same appearance—funereal and sour-faced—his decisions in court took a strange turn. Before a stupefied public he let off a boy who had stolen from his employer, folllowing the logic that for three years his *patrón* had underpaid him, and the money he had pilfered was a form of compensation. He similarly refused to punish an adulterous wife, arguing that the husband had no moral authority to demand rectitude from her when he himself kept a concubine. Gossiping tongues had it that Judge Hidalgo turned inside out like a glove when he crossed the threshold of his front door, that he removed his sepulchral clothing, played with the children, laughed, and dandled Casilda on his knees, but those rumors were never substantiated. Whatever the case, his wife was given credit for his new benevolence, and his reputation improved. Nicolás Vidal, however, was indifferent to all of this because he was outside the law, and he was sure that there would be no mercy for him the day he was led in shackles before the Judge. He ignored the gossip about *doña* Casilda; the few times he had seen her from a distance confirmed the first impression of a blurred ectoplasm.

Vidal had been born thirty years earlier in a window-less room of the only bordello in town, the son of Juana la Triste and an unknown father. He had no business in this world, and his sad mother knew it; that was why she had tried to tear him from her womb by means of herbs, candle stubs, lye douches, and other brutal methods, but the tiny creature had stubbornly hung on. Years later, Juana la Triste, pondering why her son was so different from others, realized that her drastic mea-sures to eradicate him had, instead of dispatching him, tempered him, body and soul, to the hardness of iron. As soon as he was born, the midwife had held him up to the light of the kerosene lamp to examine him and had immediately noticed that he had four nipples.

"Poor mite, a woman will cost him his life," she had prophesied, guided by long experience in such matters.

Those words weighed on the boy like a deformity. With a woman's love, his life might have been less miserable. To compensate for the numerous attempts to eliminate him before he was born, his mother chose for him a noble-sounding first name and a solid surname selected at random. Even that princely appellation had not been enough to exorcise the fatal omens, and before he was ten the boy's face was scarred from knife fights, and very soon thereafter he had begun his life as a fugitive. At twenty, he was the leader of a gang of desperados. The habit of violence had developed the strength of his muscles, the street had made him merciless, and the solitude to which he had been condemned by fear of dying over love had determined the expression in his eyes. Anyone in the town could swear on seeing him that he was Juana la Triste's son because, just like hers, his eyes were always filled with unshed tears. Anytime a misdeed was committed anywhere in the region, the *guardia,* to silence the protests of the citizenry, went out with dogs to hunt down Nicolás Vidal, but after a few runs through the hills, they returned empty-handed. In fact they did not want to find him, because they did not want to chance a fight. His gang solidified his bad name to the point that small towns and large haciendas paid him to stay away. With those "donations" his men could have led a sedentary life, but Nicolás Vidal kept them riding, in a whirlwind of death and devastation, to prevent the men from losing their taste for a fight or their infamous reputation from dwindling. There was no one who dared stand up to them. On one or two occasions Judge Hidalgo had asked the government to send Army troops to reinforce his deputies, but after a few futile excursions the soldiers had returned to their barracks and the renegades to their old tricks.

Only once was Nicolás Vidal close to falling into the traps of justice; he was saved by his inability to feel emotion. Frustrated by seeing Vidal run roughshod over the law, Judge Hidalgo decided to put aside scruples and set a trap for the outlaw. He realized that in the name of justice he was going to commit a heinous act, but of two evils, he chose the lesser. The only bait he had been able to think of was Juana la Triste, because Vidal had no other family, nor known lovers. The Judge collected Juana from the whorehouse where she was scrubbing floors and cleaning latrines for want of clients willing to pay for her miserable services, and threw her into a made-to-measure cage he then placed in the very center of the Plaza de Armas, with a jug of water as her only comfort.

"When her water runs out, she'll begin to scream. Then her son will come, and I will be waiting with the soldiers," said the Judge.

Word of this torture, outdated since the time of runaway slaves, reached the ears of Nicolás Vidal shortly before his mother drank the last drop from her pitcher. His men watched as he received the news in silence: no flicker of emotion crossed the impassive, loner's mask of his face; he never lost a stroke in the calm rhythm of stropping his knife. He had not seen Juana la Triste for many years and had not a single happy memory of his childhood; this, however, was not a question of sentiment, it was a matter of honor. No man can tolerate such an offense, the outlaws thought, and they readied their weapons and mounts, willing to ride into the ambush and give up their lives if that was what it took. But their leader showed no signs of haste.

As the hours went by, tension heightened among the men. They exchanged glances, dripping with sweat, not daring to comment, impatient from waiting, hands on the butts of their revolvers, the manes of their horses, the coil of their lariats. Night came, and the only person in the whole camp who slept was Nicolás Vidal. At dawn the men's opinions were divided; some had decided that Vidal was much more heartless than they had ever imagined; others believed that their leader was planning a spectacular manner of rescuing his mother. The one thing no one thought was that he might lack courage, because he had too often demonstrated that—in spades. By noon they could bear the uncertainty no longer, and they went to ask him what he was going to do.

"Nothing," he said.

"But what about your mother?"

"We'll see who has more balls, the Judge or me," Nicolás Vidal replied, unperturbed.

By the third day Juana la Triste was no longer pleading or begging for water; her tongue was parched and her words died in her throat. She lay curled up like a fetus on the floor of her cage, her eyes expressionless, her lips swollen and cracked, moaning like an animal in moments of lucidity and dreaming of hell the remainder of the time. Four armed men guarded the prisoner to prevent townspeople from giving her water. Her wails spread through all the town; they filtered through closed shutters, the wind carried them through the chinks of doors, they clung to the corners of rooms, dogs caught them up and repeated them in their howling, they infected newborn babies, and grated on the nerves of any who heard them. The Judge could not prevent the parade of people through the plaza, commiserating with the old woman, nor stop the sympathy strike of the prostitutes, which coincided with the miners' payday. On Saturdays, the streets were taken over by these roughnecks from the mines, eager to spend their savings before returning to their caverns, but this week the town offered no diversion apart from the cage and the moan of pain carried from mouth to mouth, from the river to the coast highway. The priest headed a group of parishioners who presented themselves before Judge Hidalgo to remind him of Christian charity and to entreat him to release that poor innocent woman from her martyr's death; the magistrate shot the bolt to his office door and refused to hear them, wagering that Juana la Triste would last one more day and that her son would fall into his trap. That is when the town leaders decided to appeal to *doña* Casilda.

The Judge's wife received them in the darkened parlor of their home and listened to their arguments silently, eyes lowered, as was her custom. Her husband had been away from home for three days, locked in his office, waiting for Nicolás Vidal with senseless determination. Even without going to the window, she had known everything happening outside: the sound of that long torment had also invaded the vast rooms of their home. *Doña* Casilda waited until the visitors had retired, then dressed her children in their Sunday best and with them headed in the direction of the plaza. She carried a basket of food and a jug of fresh water for Juana la Triste. The guards saw her as she turned the corner, and guessed her intentions, but they had precise orders, and they crossed rifles before her, and when she tried to walk by them—watched by an expectant crowd—they took her arms to prevent her from passing. The children began to cry.

Judge Hidalgo was in his office on the plaza. He was the only person in town who had not put wax plugs in his ears, because all his attention was focused on the ambush: he was waiting for the sound of Nicolás Vidal's horses. For three days and nights he had withstood the sobs of the victim and the insults of the people crowded outside the building, but when he heard the voices of his children he realized he had reached the limits of his endurance. He left the Court of Justice wearing the beard that had been growing since Wednesday, totally exhausted, red-eyed from waiting, and with the weight of defeat on his shoulders. He crossed the street, stepped onto the square of the plaza, and walked toward his wife. They gazed at each other sorrowfully. It was the first time in seven years that she had confronted him, and she had chosen to do so before the whole town. Judge Hidalgo took the basket and water jug from *doña* Casilda's hands, and himself opened the cage to minister to his prisoner.

"I told you, he hasn't got the balls I have," laughed Nicolás Vidal when he heard what had happened.

But his guffaws turned sour the following day when he was told that Juana la Triste had hanged herself on the lamppost of the whorehouse where she had spent her life, because she could not bear the shame of having been abandoned by her son in that cage in the center of the Plaza de Armas.

"Now it's the Judge's turn!" swore Vidal.

His plan was to ride into town at nightfall, take the Judge by surprise, kill him in some spectacular fashion, and stuff him in the damned cage; at dawn the next day his humiliated remains would be waiting for the whole world to see. He learned, however, that the Hidalgo family had left for a spa on the coast, hoping to wash away the bad taste of defeat.

The news that a revenge-bent Vidal and his men were on their trail overtook Judge Hidalgo in mid-route at an inn where they had stopped to rest. Without a detachment of the *guardia*, the place could not offer sufficient protection, but the Judge and his family had several hours' advantage and their car was faster than Vidal's horses. He calculated that he would be able to reach the next town and get help. He ordered his wife and children into the car, pressed the pedal to the floor, and sped off down the road. He should have reached the town with an ample margin of safety, but it was written that this was the day Nicolás Vidal would meet the woman from whom he had been fleeing all his life.

Weakened by sleepless nights, by the townspeople's hostility, by the embarrassment he had suffered, and by the tension of the race to save his family, Judge Hidalgo's heart gave a great leap and burst without a sound. The driverless car ran off the road, bumped along the shoulder, and finally rolled to a stop. It was a minute or two before *doña* Casilda realized what had happened. Since her husband was practically ancient she had often thought what it would be like to be widowed, but she had never imagined that he would leave her at the mercy of his enemies. She did not pause to mull that over, however, because she knew that she must act quickly if she was to save her children. Hurriedly she looked around for help; she nearly burst into hopeless tears: in all those sun-baked, barren reaches there was no trace of human life, only the wild hills and burning white sky. At second glance, however, she spied in the distance the shadow of a cave, and it was there she ran, carrying two babies in her arms with a third clinging to her skirttails.

Three times Casilda scaled the slope to the cave, carrying her children, one by one. It was a natural cave, like many others in those hills. She searched the interior, to be sure she had not happened into the den of some animal, settled the children in the rear, and kissed them without shedding a tear.

"In a few hours the *guardia* will come looking for you. Until then, don't come out for any reason, even if you hear me scream. Do you understand?" she instructed.

The tots hugged each other in terror, and with a last farewell glance the mother ran down the hill. She reached the car, closed her husband's eyelids, brushed her clothes, straightened her hair, and sat down to wait. She did not know how many men were in Nicolás Vidal's band, but she prayed there were many; the more there were, the more time would be spent in taking their pleasure of her. She gathered her strength, wondering how long it would take to die if she concentrated on expiring inch by inch. She wished she were voluptuous and robust, that she could bear up longer and win more time for her children.

She did not have long to wait. She soon saw a dust cloud on the horizon and heard galloping hoofs; she gritted her teeth. Confused, she watched as with drawn pistol a single rider reined in his horse a few meters from her. By the knife scar on his face she recognized Nicolás Vidal, who had decided to pursue Judge Hidalgo alone: this was a private matter to be settled between the two of them. She understood then that she must do something much more difficult than die slowly.

With one glance the bandit realized that his enemy, sleeping his death in peace, was beyond any punishment; but there was his wife, floating in the reverberating light. He leapt from his horse and strode toward her. She did not look away, or flinch, and he stopped short; for the first time in his life someone was defying him without a hint of fear. For several seconds they took each other's measure in silence, calculating the other's strength, estimating their own tenacity, and accepting the fact they were facing a formidable adversary. Nicolás Vidal put away his revolver, and Casilda smiled.

The Judge's wife earned every instant of the next hours. She employed all the seductive tricks recorded since the dawn of human knowledge, and improvised others out of her need to gratify the man's every dream. She not only played on his body like a skilled performer, strumming every chord in the pursuit of pleasure, she also called upon the wiles of her own refinement. Both realized that the stakes of this game were their lives, and that awareness lent the ultimate intensity to their encounter. Nicolás Vidal had fled from love since the day of his birth; he had never known intimacy, tenderness, secret laughter, the celebration of the senses, a lover's joyful pleasure. With every minute the *guardia* were riding closer and closer, and, with them, the firing wall; but he was also closer, ever closer, to this stupendous woman, and he gladly traded *guardia* and wall for the gifts she was offering him. Casilda was a modest and shy woman; she had been married to an austere old man who had never seen her naked. She did not forget for one instant throughout that memorable afternoon that her objective was to gain time, but at some point she let herself go, marveling at her own sensuality, and somehow grateful to Vidal. That was why when she heard the distant sound of the troops, she begged him to flee and hide in the hills. Nicolás Vidal preferred to hold her in his arms and kiss her for the last time, thus fulfilling the prophecy that had shaped his destiny.

THE
ROAD
NORTH

IT took Claveles Picero and
her grandfather Jesús Dionisio Picero thirty-eight days
to walk the seventy kilometers between their village
and the capital. On foot they had traveled through
lowlands where the vegetation simmered in an eternal
broth of mud and sweat, climbed and descended hills
past motionless iguanas and drooping palm trees,
crossed coffee plantations while avoiding foremen, lizards, and snakes, and made their way beneath tobacco
leaves among phosphorescent mosquitoes and sidereal
butterflies. They had headed directly toward the city,
following the highway, but once or twice had made long
detours in order to avoid encampments of soldiers.
Occasionally, truckdrivers slowed as they passed,
drawn by the girl's mestizo-queen backside and long
black hair, but the look on the old man's face immediately dissuaded them from any thought of annoying her.
The grandfather and granddaughter had no money, and

did not know how to beg. When their basket of provisions was exhausted, they continued on sheer courage. At night they wrapped themselves in their rebozos and slept beneath the trees, with a prayer on their lips and their mind on the boy, to avoid thinking of pumas and venomous predators. They awakened covered with blue beetles. At the first light of dawn, when the landscape was still wreathed in the last mists of dream and neither man nor beast had yet begun the day's tasks, they started off, taking advantage of the coolness. They entered the capital city by way of the Camino de los Españoles, asking everyone they met in the street where they might find the Department of Welfare. By that time Dionisio's bones were clicking and the colors had faded from Claveles's dress; she wore the bewitched expression of a sleep-walker, and a century of fatigue had fallen over the splendor of her youth.

Jesús Dionisio Picero was the best-known artist in the province; in a long life he had won a fame he never boasted of because he believed that his talent was a gift in God's service and that he was but the trustee. He had begun as a potter, and still made small clay animals, but the basis of his true renown were the wooden saints and small sculptures in bottles bought by *campesinos* for their home altars and by tourists in the capital. His was a slow labor, a matter of eye, time, and heart, as he would explain to the small boys who crowded round to watch as he worked. With long-necked tweezers he would insert a small painted stick into the bottle, with a dot of glue on the areas that needed bonding, and wait patiently for them to dry before adding the next piece. His specialty were the *Calvarios,* consisting of a large central cross complete with the figure of the crucified Christ, His nails, His crown of thorns, and a gold-paper aureole, and two more simple crosses for the thieves of Golgotha. On Christmas he carved crèches for the Baby Jesus, with doves representing the Holy Spirit and stars and flowers to symbolize the Glory. He did not know how to read or sign his name, because when he was a boy there had been no school, but he could copy Latin phrases from the missal to decorate the pedestals of his saints. He always said that his mother and father had taught him to respect the laws of Church and man, and that was worth more than having gone to school. He did not make enough with his carving to support his family, so he rounded out his income by breeding gamecocks. Each rooster demanded assiduous attention; he handfed them a pap of ground grains and fresh blood he obtained from the slaughterhouse; he groomed them for mites, ventilated their feathers, polished their spurs, and worked with them every day so they would not lack for valor when the chips were down. Sometimes he traveled to other villages to watch the birds fight, but he never bet, because in his view any money won without sweat and hard labor was the work of the devil. On Saturday nights he and his granddaughter Claveles cleaned the church for Sunday service. The priest, who made the rounds of the villages on his bicycle, did not always get there, but good Christians gathered anyway to pray and sing. Jesús Dionisio was

221

also responsible for taking and safeguarding the collection used for the upkeep of the temple and the priest.

Picero and his wife, Amparo Medina, had thirteen children, of whom five had survived the epidemics and accidents of infancy. Just when the couple thought they were through with children, because all theirs were grown and out of the house, their youngest son returned on a military pass, carrying a ragged bundle that he placed in Amparo's lap. When it was opened, they found a newborn baby girl, half dead from want of maternal milk and being bounced on the journey.

"Where did you get this, son?" asked Jesús Dionisio Picero.

"It seems she's mine," the youth replied, worrying his uniform cap with sweating fingers, not daring to meet his father's eyes.

"And, if it is not too much to ask, where is the mother?"

"I don't know. She left the baby at the barracks door with a piece of paper saying I'm the father. The sergeant told me to take her to the nuns; he says there's no way to prove she's mine. But I'd feel bad about that; I don't want her to be an orphan . . ."

"Who ever heard of a mother leaving her baby on someone's doorstep?"

"That's how they do in the city."

"So, that's the way it is, then. And what is the little thing's name?"

"Whatever name you give her, Papa, but if you're asking me, I like Claveles; carnations were her mother's favorite flower."

Jesús Dionisio went out to find the she-goat to milk,

while Amparo bathed the infant carefully with oil and prayed to the Virgin of the Grotto to give her the strength to care for another child. Once he saw that the baby was in good hands, their youngest son thanked them, said goodbye, threw his pack over his shoulder, and marched back to the barracks to serve out his sentence.

Claveles was raised by her grandparents. She was a stubborn, rebellious child impossible to discipline either with reasoning or exercise of authority, but she yielded immediately if someone played on her emotions. She got up every day at dawn and walked five miles to a shed set in the middle of some field, where a teacher assembled the local children to administer their basic schooling. Claveles helped her grandmother in the house and her grandfather in the workshop; she went to the hill to look for clay and she washed his brushes, but she was never interested in any other aspect of his art. When Claveles was nine, Amparo Medina, who had been shrinking until she was no bigger than a six-year-old, died cold in her bed, worn out by so many births and so many years of hard work. Her husband traded his best rooster for some planks and built her a coffin he decorated with Biblical scenes. Her granddaughter dressed her for her burial in the white tunic and celestial blue cord of Saint Bernadette, the one she herself had worn for First Communion and which fit perfectly her grandmother's emaciated body. Jesús Dionisio and Claveles set out for the cemetery pulling a small cart carrying the paper-flower-decorated pine box. Along the way they were joined by friends, men and shawl-draped women who walked beside them in silence.

Then the elderly wood-carver and his granddaughter were alone in the house. As a sign of mourning they painted a large cross on the door and for years both wore a black ribbon sewed to their sleeve. The grandfather tried to replace his wife in the practical details around the house, but nothing was ever again the same. The absence of Amparo Medina pervaded him like a malignant illness; he felt that his blood was turning to water, his bones to cotton, his memories fading, his mind swimming with doubts. For the first time in his life he rebelled against fate, asking himself why Amparo had been taken without him. After her death he was unable to carve manger scenes; from his hands came only *Calvarios* and martyred saints, all in mourning, to which Claveles pasted legends bearing pathetic messages to Divine Providence her grandfather dictated to her. Those figures did not sell well among the city tourists, who preferred the riotous colors they erroneously attributed to the Indian temperament, nor were they popular among the *campesinos,* who needed to adore joyful deities, because the only consolation for the sorrows of this world was to imagine that in heaven there was eternal celebration. It became almost impossible for Jesús Dionisio Picero to sell his crafts, but he continued to carve them, because in that occupation the hours passed effortlessly, as if it were always early morning. Even so, neither his work nor the company of his granddaughter could console him, and he began to drink, secretly, so that no one would be aware of his shame. Drunk, he would call out to his wife, and sometimes he would see her beside the kitchen hearth. Without Amparo Medina's diligent care, the house deteriorated, the hens stopped laying, he had to sell the she-goat, he neglected the garden, and soon they were the poorest family in the region. Not long thereafter, Claveles left to get a job in town. At fourteen she had reached her full growth, and as she did not have the coppery skin or prominent cheeks of the rest of the family, Jesús Dionisio Picero concluded that her mother must have been white—which would explain the inconceivable act of having left her baby at the barracks door.

A year and a half later, Claveles Picero returned home with a blemished face and prominent belly. She found her grandfather with no company but a pack of hungry dogs and a couple of bedraggled roosters in the patio. He was talking to himself, empty-eyed, and he showed signs of not having bathed for quite some time. He was surrounded by chaos. He had given up on his little bit of land and spent his days carving saints with demented haste, but with little of his former talent. His sculptures were deformed, lugubrious creatures unfit for either devotions or sale that had piled up in the corners of the house like stacks of firewood. Jesús Dionisio Picero had changed so much that he did not even favor his granddaughter with a diatribe on the evils of bringing children into the world without a father; in fact, he seemed unmindful of the signs of her pregnancy. He merely hugged her, trembling, calling her Amparo.

"Look at me, Grandfather, look carefully," the girl said. "I am Claveles, and I've come home to stay, because there's a lot to be done around here." And she went inside to light the kitchen fire to boil some potatoes and heat water to bathe the old man.

During the course of the following months, the old man seemed to come back to life; he stopped drinking, he began working his small garden, busying himself with his gamecocks, and cleaning the church. He still talked to the shade of his wife, and sometimes confused granddaughter for grandmother, but he recovered the gift of laughter. The companionship of Claveles and the hope that soon there would be another living creature in the house renewed his love of color, and gradually he stopped painting his saints pitch black and arrayed them in robes more appropriate for an altar. Claveles's baby emerged from his mother's belly one evening at six and was received into the callused hands of his great-grandfather, who had long experience in such matters, having assisted at the birth of his thirteen children.

"We'll call him Juan," the makeshift midwife declared as soon as he had cut the cord and wrapped his descendant in a clean swaddling cloth.

"Why Juan? There's no Juan in our family, Grandfather."

"Well, because Juan was Jesus's best friend, and this boy will be mine. And what was his father's name?"

"You can see he doesn't have a father."

"Picero, then. Juan Picero."

Two weeks after the birth of his great-grandson, Jesús Dionisio began to carve the pieces for a crèche, the first he had made since the death of Amparo Medina.

Claveles and her grandfather soon realized that the boy was not normal. He was alert, and he kicked and waved his arms like any baby, but he did not react when they spoke to him, and would lie awake for hours, not

226

fussing. They took the infant to the hospital, and there the doctor confirmed that he was deaf and, because he was deaf, that he would also be mute. The doctor added that there was not much hope for him unless they were lucky enough to place him in an institution in the city, where he would be taught good behavior and, later, trained for a trade that would enable him to earn a decent living and not always be a burden for others.

"Never. Juan stays with us," Jesús Dionisio Picero replied, without even glancing at Claveles, who was weeping in a corner, her head covered with her shawl.

"What are we going to do, Grandfather?" she asked as they left.

"Why, bring him up."

"How?"

"With patience, the way you train fighting cocks, or build *Calvarios* in bottles. It's a thing of eye, time, and heart."

And that was what they did. Ignoring the fact that the baby could not hear them, they spoke to him constantly, sang to him, and placed him beside a radio turned to full volume. The great-grandfather would take the baby's hand and press it firmly to his chest, so the boy would feel the vibration of his voice when he spoke; he made him make sounds and then celebrated his grunts with exaggerated reactions. As soon as the boy could sit up, Jesús Dionisio installed him in a box by his side; he gave him sticks, nuts, bones, bits of cloth, and small stones to play with, and as soon as the child learned not to put it in his mouth, he would hand him a ball of clay to model. Each time she got work, Claveles went into town, leaving her son with Jesús Dionisio.

Wherever the old man went, the baby followed like a shadow; they were rarely apart. A camaraderie developed between the two that obliterated the vast difference in ages and the obstacle of silence. By watching his great-grandfather's gestures and expressions, Juan learned to decipher his intentions, with such good results that by the time he had learned to walk he could read his great-grandfather's thoughts. For his part, Jesús Dionisio looked after Juan like a mother. While his hands were occupied in their painstaking work, he instinctively followed the boy's footsteps, attentive to any danger, but he intervened only in extreme cases. He did not run to console him when he fell, or help him out of difficult situations; he trained him to look out for himself. At an age when other boys were still staggering around like puppies, Juan Picero could dress, wash, and eat by himself, feed the chickens, and go to the well for water; he knew how to carve the most elementary parts of the saints, mix colors, and prepare the bottles for the *Calvarios*.

"We'll have to send the boy to school so he doesn't end up ignorant like me," said Jesús Dionisio Picero as the boy's seventh birthday approached.

Claveles made some inquiries, but she was told that her son could not attend a normal class, because no teacher was prepared to venture into the abyss of solitude in which he had settled.

"It doesn't matter, Grandfather; he can earn a living carving saints, like you."

"Carving won't put food on the table."

"Not everyone can go to school, Grandfather."

"Juan can't talk, but he's not stupid. He's bright. He

can get away from here; life in the country is too hard
for him."

Claveles was convinced that her grandfather had lost
his reason, or that his love for the boy was blinding him
to his limitations. She bought a primer and tried to pass
on her meager knowledge, but she could not make her
son understand that those squiggles represented
sounds, and she finally lost patience.

It was at that juncture that *señora* Dermoth's volunteers appeared. They were young men from the city
who were traveling through the most remote regions of
the country on behalf of a humanitarian project aimed at
helping the poor. They explained how in some places
too many children are born and their parents cannot
feed them, while in others there are couples who have
no children. Their organization was intent on alleviating
that imbalance. They showed the Piceros a map of
North America and color brochures containing photographs of dark-skinned children with blond parents, in
luxurious surroundings of blazing fireplaces, huge,
woolly dogs, pine trees decorated with silvery frost and
Christmas ornaments. After making a rapid inventory
of the Piceros' poverty, they told them all about *señora*
Dermoth's charitable mission: locating the most neglected and afflicted children and then placing them for
adoption by wealthy families, to rescue them from a life
of misery. Unlike similar institutions, this good lady was
interested only in children with birth defects or those
handicapped through accident or illness. Up North there
were couples—good Catholics, it went without saying—
waiting to adopt these children. And they had the
resources to take care of them. There in the North

there were clinics and schools where they worked miracles for deaf-mutes; for example, they taught them to lip-read and talk, and then they sent them to special schools where they received a thorough education, and some went on to the university and graduated as lawyers or doctors. The organization had aided many children; the Piceros had only to look at the photographs. See how happy they look, how healthy; see all those toys, and the expensive houses. The volunteers could not promise anything, but they would do everything they could to arrange for one of those couples to take Juan and give him all the opportunities his mother could not provide for him.

"You never give up your children, no matter what," said Jesús Dionisio Picero, clasping the boy's head to his chest so he would not see the visitors' faces and understand the subject of their conversation.

"Don't be selfish now, Grandfather; think of what's best for the boy. Don't you see that he would have everything up there? You don't have the money to pay for his treatment; you can't send him to school. What will become of him? The poor kid doesn't even have a father."

"But he has a mother and a great-grandfather!" was the old man's rejoinder.

The visitors departed, leaving *señora* Dermoth's brochures on the table. In the days that followed, Claveles often found herself looking at them and comparing those large, well-decorated homes with her own bare boards, straw roof, and tamped-down dirt floor; those pleasant, well-dressed parents with herself, dog-weary and barefoot; those children surrounded by toys and her own playing with clay dirt.

A week later Claveles ran into one of the volunteers in the market where she had gone to sell some of her grandfather's sculptures, and again she listened to the same arguments: that an opportunity like this would not come a second time, that people adopt healthy off-spring, not those with defects; that those people up North had noble sentiments, and she should think it over carefully, because for the rest of her life she would regret having denied her son such advantages and condemned him to a life of suffering and poverty.

"But why do they want only sick children?" Claveles asked.

"Because these gringos are near saints. Our organization is concerned only with the most distressing cases. It would be easy for us to place normal children, but we're trying to help the ones who most need assistance."

Claveles Picero kept seeing the volunteers. They showed up whenever her grandfather was out of the house. Toward the end of November they showed her a picture of a middle-aged couple standing before the door of a white house set in the middle of a park, and told her that *señora* Dermoth had found the ideal parents for her son. They pointed out to her on the map the precise spot the couple lived; they explained that there was snow in the winter and that children built big dolls from the snow and ice-skated and skied, and that in the autumn the woods looked like gold and in the summertime you could swim in the lake. The couple was so thrilled at the possibility of adopting the young lad that they had already bought him a bicycle. They also showed her the picture of the bicycle. And all this did not even take into account the fact they were offering two hundred and fifty dollars to Claveles; she could live for a year on that money, until she married again and had healthy children. It would be madness to miss this opportunity.

Two days later, when Jesús Dionisio had gone to clean the church, Claveles Picero dressed her son in his best pants, put his saint's medal around his neck, and explained in the sign language his great-grandfather had invented for him that they would not see each other for a long time, maybe never, but it was all for his good; he was going to a place where he would have plenty to eat every day, and presents on his birthday. She took him to the location the volunteers had indicated, signed a paper transferring custody of Juan to *señora* Dermoth, and quickly ran away so her son would not see her tears and begin crying, too.

When Jesús Dionisio Picero learned what she had done he was struck speechless and breathless; he flailed about wildly, destroying everything in reach, including the saints in bottles, and then set upon Claveles, punching her with a strength unexpected in someone as old and mild-mannered as he. When he could speak, he accused her of being just like her mother, a woman capable of giving away her own son, something not even beasts in the wild do, and he called on the ghost of Amparo Medina to wreak vengeance on her depraved granddaughter. In the following months he refused to speak a word to Claveles; he opened his mouth only to eat and to mutter curses all the while his hands were busy with his carving tools. Grandfather and granddaughter grew used to living in stony silence, each absorbed in his or her own tasks. She cooked and set his plate on the table; he ate with eyes fixed on the food. Together they tended the garden and animals, each going through the motions of the daily routine in perfect coordination with the other, but never touching. On local fair days, Claveles collected the bottles and wooden saints, took them to market to sell, returned with provisions, and put any remaining coins in a tin can. On Sundays they went to church, separately, like strangers.

They might have spent the rest of their lives without speaking if sometime in mid-February *señora* Dermoth's name had not been in the news. The grandfather heard about it on the radio, while Claveles was washing clothes in the patio: first the announcer's commentary and then a personal confirmation by the Department of Welfare. With his heart in his mouth, Jesús Dionisio ran to the door and shouted for Claveles. She turned, and when she saw his distorted face she ran to catch him, thinking he was dying.

"They've killed him," the old man moaned, dropping to his knees. "Oh, God, I know they've killed him!"

"Killed who, Grandfather?"

"Juan," and through his sobs he repeated the words of the Secretary of Welfare: a criminal organization headed by a *señora* Dermoth had been discovered selling Indian children. They chose children who were ill or from very poor families, with the promise that they would be put up for adoption. They kept the children for a while to fatten them, and when they were in better shape took them to a secret clinic where they performed operations on them. Dozens of innocents had been sacrificed like living organ banks, their eyes, kidneys, liver, and other body parts removed and sent to be used as transplants in the North. He added that in one of these fattening houses they had found twenty-eight youngsters waiting their turn. The police had intervened, and the government was continuing its investigations in order to exterminate such an abominable trafficking.

Thus had begun the long journey of Claveles and Jesús Dionisio Picero to the capital to talk with the Secretary of Welfare. They wanted to ask him, with all due deference, whether their boy was among the children rescued, and whether possibly they could have him back. There was very little left of the money they had been given, but they would work like slaves for this *señora* Dermoth however long it took to pay her back the last cent of her two hundred and fifty dollars.

THE
SCHOOL-
TEACHER'S
GUEST

THE schoolteacher Inés entered The Pearl of the Orient, deserted at this hour, walked to the counter where Riad Halabí was rolling up a bolt of bright-flowered cloth, and announced to him that she had just cut off the head of a guest in her boardinghouse. The merchant took out his white handkerchief and clapped it to his mouth.

"What did you say, Inés?"

"Exactly what you heard, Turk."

"Is he dead?"

"Of course."

"And now what are you going to do?"

"That's what I came to ask *you*," she replied, tucking back a stray lock of hair.

"I think I'd better close the store," sighed Riad Halabí.

The two had known each other so long that neither could remember the exact number of years, although both recalled every detail of the day their friendship had begun. At the time, Halabí had been one of those salesmen who wander the byways offering their wares, a commercial pilgrim without compass or fixed course, an Arab immigrant with a false Turkish passport, lonely, weary, with a palate split like a rabbit's and a subsequent longing to sit in the shadows. She had been a still-young woman with firm hips and proud shoulders, the town's only schoolteacher, and the mother of a twelve-year-old son born of a fleeting love affair. The boy was the center of the schoolteacher's life; she cared for him with unwavering devotion but, barely masking her inclination to indulge him, applied to him the same norms of discipline she demanded of the other schoolchildren. She did not want anyone to be able to say she had brought him up badly; at the same time, she hoped to negate the father's legacy of waywardness and instead form her son to be of clear mind and generous heart. The very evening on which Riad Halabí had driven into Agua Santa from one side of town, from the other a group of boys had carried in the body of schoolteacher Inés's son on an improvised stretcher. He had walked onto someone's property to pick up a fallen mango, and the owner, an outsider whom no one really knew, had fired a blast from his rifle meaning to scare the boy away but drilling a black hole in the middle of his forehead through which his life rapidly escaped. At that moment, the salesman had discovered his vocation for leadership and, without knowing how, had found himself at the center of things, consoling the mother, organizing the funeral as if he were a member of the family, and calming the people to prevent them from tearing the perpetrator limb from limb. Meanwhile, the murderer, realizing that his life would be worth very little if he remained there, had fled, meaning never to return.

It was Riad Halabí who the following morning was at the head of the crowd that marched from the cemetery to the place where the boy had fallen. All the inhabitants of Agua Santa had spent that day hauling mangoes, which they threw through the windows until the house was filled from floor to ceiling. After a few weeks, the sun had fermented the fruit, which burst open, spilling a viscous juice and impregnating the walls with a golden blood, a sweetish pus, that transformed the dwelling into a fossil of prehistoric dimensions, an enormous beast in process of putrefaction, tormented by the infinite diligence of the larvae and mosquitoes of decomposition.

The death of the boy, the role Riad Halabí had played during those days, and the welcome he had received in Agua Santa, had determined the course of his life. He forgot his nomadic ancestry and remained in the village. There he opened a business, The Pearl of the Orient. He married, was widowed, married a second time, and continued his trade, while his reputation for being a just man steadily increased. Inés, in turn, educated several generations of children with the tenacious affection she would have bestowed upon her son, until her energies were spent; then she stepped aside for teachers who arrived from the city with new primers, and retired. After leaving the schoolroom, she felt as if she had aged suddenly, as if time were accelerating; the days passed so quickly that she could not remember where the hours had gone.

"I go around in a daze, Turk. I'm dying and don't even know it," she commented.

"You're as healthy as you ever were, Inés," replied Riad Halabí. "The problem is that you're bored. You should not be idle." And he suggested she add a few rooms to her house and take in guests: "We don't have a hotel in this town."

"We don't have tourists, either," she added.

"A clean bed and warm breakfast are a blessing for travelers."

And so they had been, primarily for the truckdrivers for National Petroleum, who stayed the night in her boardinghouse when the fatigue and tedium of the road had filled their heads with hallucinations.

The schoolteacher Inés was the most respected matron in all Agua Santa. She had taught the town's children for several decades, which granted her the authority to intervene in all their lives and take them by the ear when she felt it necessary. Girls brought their boyfriends for her approval, husbands and wives came to her with their marital disagreements; she was counselor, arbiter, and judge in all the town's problems. Her authority, in fact, was mightier than that of the priest, the doctor, or the police. No one stopped her from the exercise of that power. On one occasion she had stalked into the jail, passed the Lieutenant without speaking, snatched the keys from a nail on the wall, and removed from a cell one of her students who had been jailed after a drunken spree. The officer had tried to stand in her way, but she had shoved him aside and marched the boy outside by the back of his collar. Once in the street, she had given him a couple of smacks and assured him that the next time this happened she would lower his pants and give him a spanking he would never forget. The day that Inés came to tell Riad Halabí she had killed one of her clients, he did not doubt for a moment that she was serious, because he knew her too well. He took her arm and walked with her the two blocks that separated The Pearl of the Orient from her house. It was one of the grandest buildings in town, adobe and wood, with a wide veranda where hammocks were hung during the hottest siestas, and ceiling fans in every room. At that hour the house seemed to be empty; only one guest sat in the parlor drinking beer, mesmerized by the television.

"Where is he?" whispered the Arab merchant.

"In one of the back rooms," Inés replied, not even lowering her voice.

She led him to the row of rooms she rented—all joined by an arcade with purple morning-glories climbing the columns and pots of ferns hanging from the beams—bordering a patio planted with medlar and banana trees. Inés opened the last door and Riad Halabí entered a room in deep shadow. The shutters were closed, and it was a moment before he saw on the bed the corpse of an inoffensive-looking old man, a decrepit stranger swimming in the puddle of his own death, his trousers stained with excrement, his head hanging by a strip of ashen flesh, and wearing a terrible expression of distress, as if apologizing for all the disturbance and blood, and for the uncommon bother of having allowed himself to be murdered. Riad Halabí sat down on the room's only chair, his eyes on the floor, trying to control the lurch of his stomach. Inés remained standing, arms across her chest, calculating that it would take her two days to wash up the stains and at least two more to rid the room of its odor of feces and fear.

"How did you do it?" Riad Halabí asked finally, wiping the sweat from his forehead.

"With the machete for harvesting coconuts. I came up behind him and lopped off his head with one swing. He never knew what hit him, poor man."

"Why?"

"I had to do it. It was fate. This old man had very bad luck. He never meant to stop in Agua Santa; he was driving through town and a rock shattered his windshield. He came to pass a few hours here while the Italian down at the garage found another windshield. He's changed a lot—we've all grown older, I guess—but I recognized him instantly. I've been waiting all these years; I knew he would come sooner or later. He's the man with the mangoes."

"May Allah protect us," murmured Riad Halabí.

"Do you think we should call the Lieutenant?"

"Not on your life; why do you say that?"

"I'm in the right. He killed my boy."

"The Lieutenant wouldn't understand that, Inés."

"An eye for an eye and a tooth for a tooth, Turk. Isn't that what your religion teaches?"

"But that's not how the law works, Inés."

"Well, then, we can fix him up a little and say he committed suicide."

"Don't touch him. How many guests do you have in the house?"

"Just that truckdriver. He'll be on his way as soon as it's cool; he has to drive to the capital."

"Good. Don't take in any more guests. Lock the door to this room and wait for me. I'll be back tonight."

"What are you going to do?"

"I'll take care of this in my own way."

Riad Halabí was sixty-five years old, but he had conserved his youthful vigor and the same spirit that had positioned him at the head of the throng the day he arrived in Agua Santa. He left the schoolteacher's house and walked rapidly to the first of several visits he was to make that afternoon. Soon after, a persistent murmur began to spread through the town. The inhabitants of Agua Santa wakened from the lethargy of years, excited by the unbelievable news that was being repeated from house to house, an insuppressible buzzing, information that strained to be uttered in shouts, gossip that by the very need to be held to a murmur was conferred special status. Before sunset you could sense in the air the restless elation that for several years would be a characteristic of the town, one incomprehensible to strangers passing through, who could find nothing extraordinary in this town that had the appearance of being an insignificant backwater like so many others on the edge of the jungle. Early in the evening, men began arriving at the tavern; women carried their kitchen chairs out to the sidewalk and sat down to enjoy the cool air; young people gathered en masse in the plaza, as if it were Sunday. The Lieutenant and his men casually made their rounds and then accepted the invitation of the girls at the whorehouse who were celebrating a birthday, they said. By nightfall there were more people in the street than on All Saints' Day; all of them were so studiously occupied in their activities that they seemed to be practicing a part in a movie: some were playing dominoes, others were drinking rum and smoking on the street corners, some couples were out for a stroll, hand in hand, mothers were running after their children, grandmothers peering nosily from open doorways. The priest lighted the lamps in the parish church and rang the bells signaling a novena to Saint Isidro Martyr, but no one was in the mood for that kind of devotion.

At nine-thirty there was a meeting in the house of schoolteacher Inés: the Turk, the town doctor, and four young men she had taught from the first grade and who were now hefty veterans back from military service. Riad Halabí led them to the back room, where they found the cadaver covered with insects: the window had been left open and it was the hour of the mosquitoes. They stuffed the victim in a canvas sack, wrestled it out to the street, and unceremoniously threw it into the back of Riad Halabí's truck. They drove through the town, right down the main street, waving, as usual, to anyone they happened to see. Some neighbors returned their salutation with more than ordinary enthusiasm, while others pretended not to notice them, furtively giggling, like children surprised at some mischief. Beneath brilliant moonlight the men drove to the spot where many years before the son of the schoolteacher Inés had stooped down for the last time to pick up a mango. The overgrown property sat amid the malign weeds of neglect, decayed by time and bad memories, a tangled hill where mangoes had grown

244

wild, where fruit had dropped from the trees and taken root in the ground, giving birth to new clumps that had in turn engendered others, until an impenetrable jungle had been created that had swallowed up fences, path, even the ruins of the house, of which only a lingering trace of the odor of marmalade remained. The men lighted their kerosene lanterns and plunged into the dense growth, hacking a path with their machetes. When they felt they had gone far enough, one of them pointed to a spot and there, at the foot of a gigantic tree weighed down with fruit, they dug a deep hole in which they deposited the canvas sack. Before shoveling back the dirt, Riad Halabí spoke a brief Muslim prayer, because he knew no other. When they got back to town at midnight, they found that no one had gone to bed; lights were blazing in every window, and people were circulating through the streets.

Meanwhile, the schoolteacher Inés had scrubbed the walls and furniture in the back room with soap and water; she had burned the bedclothing, aired the house, and was waiting for her friends with a fine dinner and a pitcher of rum and pineapple juice. The meal was eaten to the accompaniment of merry chatter about the latest cockfights—a barbaric sport according to the schoolteacher, but less barbaric, the men alleged, than the bullfights in which a Colombian matador had just lost his liver. Riad Halabí was the last to say goodbye. That night, for the first time in his life, he felt old. At the door, the schoolteacher Inés took his hands and for a moment held them in hers.

"Thank you, Turk," she said.

"Why did you come to see me, Inés?"

"Because you are the person I love most in this world, and because you should have been the father of my son."

The next day the inhabitants of Agua Santa returned to their usual chores exalted by a magnificent complicity, by a secret kept by good neighbors, one they would guard with absolute zeal and pass down for many years as a legend of justice, until the death of the schoolteacher Inés freed us, and now I can tell the story.

THE
PROPER
RESPECT

THEY were a pair of scoundrels. He had the face of a pirate, and he dyed his hair and mustache jet black; with time, he changed his style and left the gray, which softened his expression and lent him a more circumspect air. She was fleshy, with the milky skin of reddish blondes, the kind of skin that in youth reflects light with opalescent brush strokes, but with age becomes crinkled paper. The years she had spent in the oil workers' camps and tiny towns on the frontier had not drained her vigor, the heritage of her Scots ancestors. Neither mosquitoes nor heat nor abuse had spoiled her body or diminished her desire for dominance. At fourteen she had run away from her father, a Protestant pastor who preached the Bible deep in the jungle; his was a totally futile labor, since no one understood his English palaver and, furthermore, in those latitudes words, even the word of God, were lost in the jabbering of the birds. At fourteen the girl had reached her full growth and was in absolute command of her person. She was not sentimental. She rejected one after another of the men who, attracted by the incandescent flame of her hair, so rare in the tropics, had offered her their protection. She had never heard love spoken of, and it was not in her nature to invent it; on the other hand, she knew how to make the most of the only commodity she possessed, and by the time she was twenty-five she had a handful of diamonds sewed into the hem of her petticoat. She handed them over without hesitation to Domingo Toro, the bull of a man who had managed to tame her, an adventurer who trekked through the region hunting alligators and trafficked in arms and bootleg whiskey. He was an unscrupulous rogue, the perfect companion for Abigail McGovern.

In their first years together, the couple had fabricated bizarre schemes for accumulating capital. With her diamonds, his alligator hides, funds he had obtained dealing contraband, and chicanery at the gaming tables, Domingo had purchased chips at the casino he knew were identical to those used on the other side of the border where the value of the currency was much stronger. He filled a suitcase with chips, made a brief trip, and traded them for good hard cash. He was able to repeat the operation twice more before the authorities became suspicious, and even when they did they could not accuse him of anything illegal. In the meantime, Abigail had been selling clay pots and bowls she bought from the Goajiros and sold as archeological treasures to the gringos who worked with National Petroleum—with such success that soon she branched out into fake Colonial paintings produced by a student in his cubbyhole behind the cathedral and preternaturally aged with sea water, soot, and cat urine. By then Abigail, who had outgrown her roughneck manners and speech, had cut her hair and now dressed in expensive clothes. Although her taste was a little extreme and her effort to appear elegant a little too obvious, she could pass as a lady, which facilitated social relationships and contributed to the success of her business affairs. She entertained clients in the drawing rooms of the Hotel Inglés and, as she served them tea with the measured gestures she had learned by imitation, she would natter on about big-game hunting and tennis tournaments in hypothetical places with British-sounding names that no one could locate on a map. After the third cup she would broach in a confidential tone the subject of the meeting. She would show her guests photographs of the purported antiquities, making it clear that her proposal was to save those treasures from local neglect. The government did not have the resources to preserve these extraordinary objects, she would say, and to slip them out of the country, even though it was against the law, constituted an act of archeological conscience.

Once the Toros had laid the foundations for a small fortune, Abigail's next plan was to found a dynasty, and she tried to convince Domingo of the need to have a good name.

"What's wrong with ours?"

"No one is called Toro, that's a barroom name," Abigail argued.

"It was my father's name, and I don't intend to change it."

"In that case, we will have to convince the world that we are wealthy."

She suggested that they buy land and plant bananas or coffee, as social snobs had done before them; but he did not like the idea of moving to the interior, a wild land fraught with the danger of bands of thieves, the army, guerrillas, snakes, and all the diseases known to man. To him it seemed insane to head off into the jungle in search of a future when a fortune was theirs for the taking right in the capital; it would be less risky to dedicate themselves to commerce, like the thousands of Syrians and Jews who had debarked with nothing but misery in the packs slung over their backs, but who within a few years were living in the lap of luxury.

"No small-time stuff!" objected Abigail. "What I want is a respectable family; I want them to call us *don* and *doña* and not dare speak to us without removing their hats."

But Domingo was adamant, and finally she accepted his decision. She nearly always did, because anytime she opposed her husband, he punished her by withdrawing communication and sexual favors. He would disappear from the house for days at a time, return hollow-eyed from his clandestine mischief, change his clothes, and go out again, leaving Abigail at first furious and then terrified at the idea of losing him. She was a practical person totally devoid of romantic notions, and if once there had been a seed of tenderness in her, the years she had spent on her back had destroyed it. Domingo, nevertheless, was the only man she could bear to live with, and she was not about to let him get away. The minute Abigail gave in, Domingo would come home and sleep in his own bed. There were no noisy reconciliations; they merely resumed the rhythm of their routines and returned to the complicity of their questionable dealings. Domingo Toro set up a chain of shops in poor neighborhoods, where he sold goods at low prices but in huge quantities. The stores served as a screen for other, less legal, activities. Money continued to pile up, and they could afford the extravagances of the very wealthy, but Abigail was not satisfied: she had learned that it is one thing to have all the comforts but something very different to be accepted in society.

"If you had paid attention to me, they wouldn't be thinking of us as Arab shopkeepers. Why did you have to act like a ragpicker?" she protested to her husband.

"I don't know why you're complaining; we have everything."

"Go ahead and sell that trash, if that's what you want, but I'm going to buy racehorses."

"Horses? What do you know about horses, woman?"

"I know that they're classy. Everyone who is anyone has horses."

"You'll be the ruin of us."

For once Abigail had her way, and in a very short time had proved that her idea was not a bad one. Their stallions gave them an excuse to mingle with the old horse-breeding families and, in addition, were extremely profitable, but although the Toros appeared frequently in the racing section, their names were never in the society pages. Disheartened, Abigail compensated with even more vulgar ostentation. She bought a china service with her hand-painted portrait on every piece, cut-glass goblets, and furniture with raging gargoyles carved on the feet. Her prize, however, was a threadbare armchair she passed off as a Colonial relic, telling everyone it had belonged to El Libertador, which was why she had tied a red cord across the arms, so no one would place his unworthy buttocks where the Father of the Nation had sat. She hired a German governess for her children, and a Dutch vagabond who affected an admiral's uniform as custodian of the family yacht. The only vestiges of their past life were Domingo's buccaneer's tattoos and an old injury to Abigail's back, a consequence of spread-legged contortions during her oil-field days; but long sleeves covered his tattoos, and she had a silk-padded iron corset made to prevent pain from infringing upon her dignity. By then she was obese, laden with jewels, the spit and image of Nero. Greed had wrought the physical havoc her jungle adventures had not imposed upon her.

For the purpose of attracting the most select members of society, every year the Toros hosted a masked ball at Carnival time: the Court of Baghdad with the elephant and camels from the zoo and an army of waiters dressed as Bedouins; a Bal de Versailles at which guests in brocade gowns and powdered wigs danced the minuet amid beveled mirrors; and other scandalous revels that became a part of local legend and gave rise to violent diatribes in leftist newspapers. The Toros had to post guards before the house to prevent students—outraged by such extravagance—from painting slogans on the columns and throwing excrement through the windows, alleging that the newly rich filled their bathtubs with champagne, while to eat, the newly poor hunted cats on the rooftops. Such lavish displays

had afforded the Toros a degree of respectability, because by then the line that divided the social classes
was vanishing; people were flocking into the country
from every corner of the globe, drawn by the miasma
of petroleum. Growth in the capital was uncontrolled,
fortunes were made and lost in the blink of an eye, and
it was no longer possible to ascertain the ancestry of
every individual. Even so, the old families kept their
distance from the Toros, despite the fact they themselves had descended from other immigrants whose
only merit was to have reached these shores a half-
century sooner. They attended Domingo and Abigail's
banquets and sometimes sailed around the Caribbean in
the yacht piloted by the firm hand of the Dutch captain,
but they did not return the invitations. Abigail might
have been forced to resign herself to second-class
status had an unforeseen event not changed their luck.

On a late August afternoon Abigail had awakened
unrefreshed from her siesta; it was unbearably hot and
the air was heavy with presages of a coming storm. She
had slipped a silk dress over her corset and ordered
her chauffeur to drive her to the beauty salon. They
drove through the heavy traffic with the windows
closed, to forestall any malcontent who might spit at
the *señora* through an open window—something that
happened more and more frequently. They stopped
before the salon at exactly five o'clock, which Abigail
entered after instructing the chauffeur to come for her
one hour later. When he returned to pick her up, Abigail
was not there. The hairdresser said that about five
minutes after she had arrived, the *señora* had said she
had a brief errand to run, and had not returned. Mean-

while, in his office Domingo Toro had received a call from the Red Pumas, an extremist group no one had heard of until then, announcing that they had kidnapped his wife.

That was the beginning of the scandal that was to assure the Toros' reputation. The police had taken the chauffeur and the hairdressers into custody, searched entire barrios, and cordoned off the Toros' mansion, to the subsequent annoyance of their neighbors. During the day a television van blocked the street, and a throng of newspaper reporters, detectives, and curiosity seekers trampled the lawns. Domingo Toro appeared on television, seated in a leather chair in his library between a globe of the world and a stuffed mare, imploring the kidnappers to release the mother of his children. The cheapgoods magnate, as the press had labeled him, was offering a million in local currency in exchange for his wife—an inflated amount considering that a different guerrilla group had obtained only half that much for a Middle East ambassador. The Red Pumas, however, had not considered the sum sufficient, and had doubled the ransom. After seeing Abigail's photograph in the newspaper, many believed that Domingo Toro's best move would be to pay the ransom—not for the return of his wife, but to reward the kidnappers for keeping her. Incredulity swept the nation when the husband, after consultations with bankers and lawyers, accepted the deal despite warnings by police. Hours before delivering the stipulated sum, he had received a lock of red hair through the mail, with a note indicating that the price had gone up another quarter of a million. By then, the Toro children had also appeared on television, sending desperate filial messages to their mother. The macabre auction was daily rising in pitch, and given full coverage by the media.

The suspense ended five days later, just as public curiosity was beginning to be diverted by other events. Abigail was found, bound and gagged, in a car parked in the city center, a little nervous and bedraggled but without visible signs of harm and, if anything, slightly more plump. The afternoon that she returned home, a small crowd gathered in the street to applaud the husband who had given such strong proof of his love. In the face of harassment from reporters and demands from the police, Domingo Toro had assumed an attitude of discreet gallantry, refusing to reveal how much he had paid, with the comment that his wife was beyond price. People wildly exaggerated the figure, crediting to him a payment much greater than any man would have given for a wife, least of all his. But all this speculation had established the Toros as the ultimate symbol of opulence; it was said they were as rich as the President, who for years had profited from the proceeds of the nation's oil and whose fortune was calculated to be one of the five largest in the world. Domingo and Abigail were raised to the peak of high society, the inner sanctum from which they had previously been excluded. Nothing clouded their triumph, not even public protests by students, who hung banners at the University accusing Abigail of arranging her own kidnapping, the magnate of withdrawing millions from one pocket and putting them into another without penalty of taxes, and the police of swallowing the story of the Red Pumas in order to frighten the populace and justify purges against opposition parties. But no evil tongue could destroy the glorious result of the kidnapping, and a decade later the Toro-McGoverns were known as one of the nation's most respectable families.

INTER-
MINABLE
LIFE

THERE are all kinds of stories. Some are born with the telling; their substance is language, and before someone puts them into words they are but a hint of an emotion, a caprice of mind, an image, or an intangible recollection. Others are manifest whole, like an apple, and can be repeated infinitely without risk of altering their meaning. Some are taken from reality and processed through inspiration, while others rise up from an instant of inspiration and become real after being told. And then there are secret stories that remain hidden in the shadows of the mind; they are like living organisms, they grow roots and tentacles, they become covered with excrescences and parasites, and with time are transformed into the matter of nightmares. To exorcise the demons of memory, it is sometimes necessary to tell them as a story.

Ana and Roberto Blaum had grown old together. They were so close that over the years they had come to look like brother and sister; they had the same expression of benevolent surprise, the same wrinkles, the same hand gestures, the same slope of the shoulders; they had been shaped by similar habits and desires. For the greater part of their lives they had shared each day, and from having walked so far hand in hand, and having slept so long in each other's arms, they could agree to rendezvous in the same dream. They had never been apart since their meeting a half-century before. At that time, Roberto had been studying medicine, and already exhibited the passion that ruled his life: to purify the world and serve his fellowman. Ana was one of those virginal young girls whose innocence makes everything about her more beautiful. They discovered each other through music. Ana was a violinist in a chamber orchestra and he—who came from a family of virtuosos and himself enjoyed playing the piano—never missed a concert. One night he had seen on the stage a girl dressed in black velvet with a white lace collar; she was playing with her eyes closed, and he had fallen in love at first sight. Months passed before he dared speak to her, but when he did, a few words were enough for them both to realize they were destined to form a perfect bond. The war interrupted their lives before they could marry and, like thousands of Jews suffering the specter of persecution, they had to flee Europe. They sailed from a Dutch port with no luggage but the clothing on their backs, a few of Roberto's books, and Ana's violin. The ship wandered the seas for two years, denied permission to dock in any port because none of the hemisphere's nations wanted to accept its cargo of refugees. After sailing in circles, the ship finally reached the coasts of the Caribbean. By then her hull was a cauliflower of shells and lichens; dampness oozed from her as from a great cheese; her engines had turned green, and all the crew and passengers—with the exception of Ana and Roberto, whose love had sheltered them from despair—had aged two hundred years. The captain, resigned to the idea of roaming aimlessly for all eternity, had anchored his transatlantic inner tube in the inlet of a bay facing a beach of phosphorescent sands and svelte, feather-crowned palm trees to allow some of the crew to go ashore by night and load on fresh water. That was as far as they got. At dawn the following day they were unable to start the engines, which were corroded from the wear and tear of running on a blend of salt water and gunpowder, for want of better fuels. About mid-morning, authorities from the nearest port motored up in their launch, a handful of cheerful mulatto men with unbuttoned uniform jackets and the best will in the world, who in accord with regulations ordered them to leave their territorial waters. When they learned the unhappy fate of the voyagers, however, and saw the deplorable state of the ship, they suggested to the captain that they ride at anchor for a few days enjoying the sun, and see whether by giving free rein to their difficulties things might right themselves, as they usually do. That night all the occupants of that ill-starred ship slipped ashore in lifeboats, stepped onto the warm sands of a country whose name they could scarcely pronounce, and headed inland through voluptuous vegetation, eager to shave off their beards, divest themselves of their moldy clothing, and leave behind them the oceanic winds that had tanned their souls to shoe leather.

That was how Ana and Roberto Blaum had begun their destinies as immigrants: first working as laborers in order to survive, and later, once they had learned the ways of that easygoing society, putting down roots, enabling Roberto to complete the medical studies interrupted by the war. They subsisted on bananas and coffee and lived in a small boardinghouse in a tiny room whose window framed a streetlamp. Roberto used that light to study at night; Ana, to sew. When their day's work was over, Roberto would sit and gaze at the stars above the neighboring rooftops while Ana played familiar melodies on her violin, a custom they retained as long as they lived. Years later, when the name of Blaum was famous, those days of severe poverty became the basis of romantic references in prologues to his books, or in newspaper interviews. Their luck changed, but they never lost their humility; they could not erase the memories of what they had suffered, or escape the feeling of insecurity so common among exiles. They were both the same height, with pale eyes and strong bones. Roberto looked like a scholar: an unruly mane formed a halo above his ears, he wore thick eyeglasses with round tortoise-shell frames, he always dressed in a gray suit that he replaced with an identical one when Ana refused to keep mending the cuffs, and he carried a bamboo cane a friend had brought him from India. He was a man of few words, as precise in speaking as in all his other habits, but with a delicate sense of humor that took the edge off the weight of his learning. His students would remember him as the most generous of their professors. Ana was merry and trusting; she was incapable of imagining evil of anyone, and thus was herself immune to it. Roberto recognized that his wife was endowed with an admirable practical sense and from the beginning delegated to her the major decisions and administration of their finances. Ana cared for her husband the way a mother babies her child: she cut his hair and fingernails, worried over his health, his food, and his sleep, and was always at his beck and call. Each found the other's company so indispensable that Ana gave up her musical career because it would have obliged her to travel, and played the violin only in the privacy of their home. She developed the habit of accompanying Roberto at night to the morgue or university library where his research kept him for hours. Both cherished the solitude and silence of deserted buildings. Later they would walk home through the empty streets to the poor barrio where they lived. With the uncontrolled growth of the city, that sector had become a nest of drug traffickers, prostitutes, and thieves, where not even police cars patrolled after sunset, but the Blaums walked there at all hours of the night with impunity. Everyone knew them. There was no illness or problem that had not been brought to Roberto, and no child who had grown up without tasting Ana's cookies. Someone always warned strangers in the barrio that for sentimental reasons the old couple was not to be touched. They would add that the Blaums were a source of national pride, that the President in person had decorated Roberto, and that they were so highly regarded that not even the *guardia* disturbed them when they roared into the sector with their military vehicles, searching houses one by one.

I met the Blaums in the late sixties, when in a mad fit my poor *madrina* had slit her own throat. We had taken her to the hospital with blood bubbling from her wound, with no real hope of saving her. By good fortune, Roberto Blaum was there and proceeded calmly to sew her head back in place. To the amazement of the other doctors, my *madrina* recovered. I spent many hours beside her bed during the weeks of her convalescence, and had many occasions to talk with Roberto. Gradually we developed a solid friendship. The Blaums had no children, and I think they must have longed for them, because with time they came to treat me as if I were their daughter. I often visited them— rarely at night, because I did not dare venture alone into that neighborhood—and they always surprised me with some special dish for lunch. I liked helping Roberto in the garden and Ana in the kitchen. Sometimes she took up her violin and played for me for an hour or two. They gave me the key to their house, and when they were away I looked after their dog and watered their plants.

Even though the war had delayed his studies, Roberto Blaum's successes had begun early in his career. When another physician might just have begun practicing, Roberto had published several respected articles. His true reputation, however, was the result of his book on the right to a peaceful death. He was not tempted by private practice, except in the case of some friend or neighbor, but preferred to pursue his profession in public hospitals where he could attend a greater number of sick and every day learn something new. Long hours in the wards of terminal patients had instilled in him a great compassion for those fragile bodies chained to life-support machines, with all the torture of their needles and tubes, patients whom science had denied their final dignity under the pretext that they must be kept breathing at any cost. It troubled him not to be able to help such people depart this world but to be forced, instead, to hold them against their will on their deathbeds. On occasion, the suffering imposed on his patients became so intolerable that he could think of nothing else. At night, when he slept, Ana would have to wake him when he cried out. In the refuge of their bed, he would embrace his wife, burying his face in her breasts, despairing.

"Why don't you disconnect the tubes and relieve that poor man's suffering? It is the most merciful thing you can do. He's going to die anyway, sooner or later . . ."

"I can't do it, Ana. The law is very clear; no one has the right to take another's life, although in my mind, this is a matter of conscience."

"We've been through this before, and every time you suffer the same remorse. No one will know; it will take only a minute or two."

Whether Roberto ever did, only Ana knew. In his view, death, with its ancestral weight of terrors, is merely the abandonment of an unserviceable shell at the time the spirit is reintegrated into the unified energy of the cosmos. The end of life, like birth, is a stage in a voyage, and deserves the compassion we accord to its beginnings. There is absolutely no virtue in prolonging the heartbeat and tremors of a body beyond its natural span, and the physician's labor should be to ease our passing, rather than contribute to the objectionable bureaucracy of death. These decisions, however, should not be left solely to the judgment of professionals or the compassion of family members; the law must establish a set of criteria.

Blaum's proposal evoked an uproar from priests, lawyers, and doctors. Soon the matter transcended scientific circles and spilled over to public debate, sharply dividing opinions. For the first time someone had spoken out on the subject; until then, death had been a taboo topic. One wagered on immortality, with the secret hope of living forever. As long as the discussion was maintained at a philosophical level, Roberto Blaum participated in public forums to argue his thesis, but once the subject became a diversion of the masses, he took refuge in his work, offended by the shamelessness with which his theory was being exploited for commercial purposes. Death took center stage; stripped of all reality, it became *fashionable*.

One element of the press accused Blaum of promoting euthanasia and compared his tenets to those of the Nazis, while another element acclaimed him as a saint. He ignored the tumult and continued his research and work at the hospital. His book was translated into several languages and published in other countries, where it provoked similarly impassioned reactions. His photograph appeared frequently in scientific journals. That year he was offered a Chair in the Medical School, and soon was the professor most sought after by students. There was not an ounce of arrogance in Roberto Blaum nor of the exultant fanaticism of mediums of divine revelation, only the scholar's placid conviction. The greater Roberto's fame, the more reclusive the Blaums' life became. The impact of that brief celebrity startled them, and they admitted fewer and fewer into their intimate circle.

Roberto's theory was forgotten by the public as quickly as it had become faddish. The law was not changed; the problem was not even debated in Congress, but in the academic and scientific worlds Blaum's prestige steadily grew. In the following thirty years, Blaum trained several generations of surgeons, developed new drugs and surgical techniques, and organized a system of mobile consultation facilities—vans, boats, and planes equipped for treating everything from childbirth to epidemics—that formed a network across the nation, bringing help to areas where previously only missionaries had chanced. He obtained numerous prizes, for a decade was Rector of the University, and for two weeks he was Minister of Health—the amount of time necessary to gather evidence of administrative corruption and misappropriation of funds and to present the facts to the President, who had no alternative but to destroy them: he could not shake the foundations of the government merely to please an idealist. Through all that time Blaum continued his research on the dying. He published various articles on the obligation to inform the terminal patient of his true condition, so he would have time to prepare his soul and not be stunned by the surprise of dying, and on respecting suicide and other forms of ending one's own life without undue pain and stridency.

Blaum's name again became a household word when

he published his last book, which not only rocked traditional science but evoked an avalanche of hope across the nation. In his long hospital practice Roberto had treated innumerable cancer patients and had observed that while some were defeated by death, others given the same treatment survived. In his book Roberto attempted to demonstrate the relationship between cancer and state of mind: he argued that sorrow and loneliness facilitate the reproduction of the deadly cells, because when a patient is depressed, the body's defense system is weakened; if, on the other hand, he has good reason to live, his organism battles tirelessly against the disease. He reasoned that a cure for cancer, therefore, should not be limited to surgery, chemistry, or medical resources, which address only physical manifestations, but that state of mind must be given prime consideration. In the last chapter he suggested that the best results are to be found among those blessed with a loving partner, or some other source of affection, since love has a beneficial effect unsurpassed by even the most powerful drugs.

The press immediately appreciated the limitless possibilities of this theory and placed words in Blaum's mouth that he had never spoken. If his book on death had caused an uproar, now a second, equally natural aspect of life was to be treated as an innovation. All the virtues of the philosophers' stone were attributed to love; it was claimed that it could cure all ills. Everyone talked about Blaum's book, but very few had read it. The simple proposition that affection can be good for the health was perverted according to what each individual wanted to add to or remove from the equation, until Blaum's original idea was lost in a tangle of absurdities that created a colossal confusion in the average mind. There was, naturally, no shortage of swindlers willing to take advantage of all this interest, appropriating love as if it were their personal invention. New esoteric sects proliferated, schools of psychology, courses for beginners, clubs for the lonelyheart, pills for fatal attraction, devastating perfumes, and a multitude of garden-variety diviners who used cards and crystal balls to sell cheap fortunes. As soon as it was discovered that Ana and Roberto Blaum were an amiable old couple who had been together for the best part of their lives and had preserved bodily and mental health *and* the strength of their love, they were lionized as living examples of Blaum's theory. With the exception of the scientists who analyzed the book to the point of exhaustion, the only people who read it for nonsensationalist purposes were people actually suffering from cancer. For them, however, the hope of a definitive cure became an atrocious joke; in fact, no one could tell them where to find love, how to attain it, even less, how to keep it. Although Blaum's idea was not without logic, in practice it was inapplicable.

Roberto was dismayed by the extent of the publicity, but Ana reminded him of what had happened with the first book and convinced him it was only a question of waiting awhile until the hubbub subsided. Which it did. The Blaums, however, were out of the city when the clamor finally died down. Roberto had already retired

THE STORIES OF EVA LUNA

from his work at the hospital and university, using the excuse that he was tired and at an age when he wanted to live a more tranquil life. He had not, however, been able to escape his own celebrity; his house was invaded at all hours by potential patients, newspaper reporters, students, professors, and curiosity seekers. Roberto told me he needed quiet to work on another book, and I said I would help him find a peaceful refuge. We found a small house in La Colonia, a strange village set into the side of a tropical mountain, a replica of a nineteenth-century Bavarian village, an architectural oddity of painted wood houses, cuckoo clocks, window boxes filled with geraniums, and Gothic-lettered signs; it was inhabited by a race of blonds with the same Tyrolean clothing and rosy cheeks their great-grandparents had brought with them from the Black Forest. Although La Colonia was already the tourist attraction we know today, Roberto was able to rent a cottage far from the weekend traffic. He and Ana asked me to look after things in the capital: I collected his retirement check, their bills, and the mail. At first I visited them fairly often, but soon I realized they were feigning a rather forced cordiality very different from the warmth of my usual welcome. I knew it was nothing personal; I had no doubts about the trust and affection they felt for me. I simply came to the conclusion they wanted to be alone, and found it easier to communicate with them by letter and telephone.

When Roberto Blaum last called me, I had not seen them for a year. Although I often had long conversations with Ana, I had spoken very little with him. I would tell Ana the latest news, and she would tell me stories from their past, which seemed increasingly vivid for her, as if all those distant memories had become part of the present in the silence that now surrounded her. From time to time she sent me the oatmeal cookies she had always baked for me, and sachets of lavender to perfume my closets. Recently she had sent me tender little gifts: a handkerchief her husband had given her years before, photographs of herself as a girl, an antique brooch. I suppose that the gifts, more than their strange remoteness and the fact that Roberto had avoided speaking of the progress of his book, should have been my clue, but in fact I never suspected what was happening in that little house in the mountains. Later, when I read Ana's diary, I learned that Roberto had not written a single line. All that time he had devoted himself solely to loving his wife, but his love had not been able to alter the course of events.

On weekends, the trip to La Colonia becomes a pilgrimage of overheated cars creeping along with wheels barely turning. On weekdays, however, especially during the rainy season, it is a solitary drive along a route of hairpin curves that knife through peaks between surprising ravines and forests of sugar cane and palm trees. That afternoon, clouds trapped among the hills cloaked the landscape in cotton. The weather had stilled the birds, and the only sound was the slap of the rain against the windshield. As I ascended, the air grew cool, and the storm suspended in the fog felt more like the climate of a different latitude. Suddenly, at a bend in the road, I saw that Germanic-looking village with roofs pitched to support a snow that would never fall. To reach the Blaums' house I had to drive through town, which was apparently deserted at that hour. Their cottage was similar to all the others: dark wood with carved eaves and lace-curtained windows. There was a well-tended flower garden in front of the house, and a small plot of strawberries in the rear. A cold wind was whistling through the trees, but I saw no smoke rising from the chimney. The Blaums' old dog did not move when I called; he raised his head and looked at me without wagging his tail, as if he did not recognize me, but followed when I opened the unlocked door and went inside. It was dark. I felt along the wall for the light switch and turned on the lights. Everything was in order. Fresh eucalyptus branches filled the vases, saturating the air with a sharp, clean scent. I walked through the living room of this rented house in which nothing betrayed the Blaums' presence except the stacks of books and Ana's violin, and I was puzzled that in a year and a half my friends had left no trace of their presence.

I climbed the stairs to the main bedroom, a large room with high ceilings and rustic beams, stained wallpaper, and inexpensive furniture in a vaguely provincial style. A lamp on the night table lighted the bed where Ana lay in a blue silk dress and the coral necklace I so often saw her wear. In death she had the same expression of innocence as in the wedding photograph taken long ago, the day the ship's captain had married them seventy miles off the coast, that splendid afternoon when flying fish announced to the refugees that the promised land was near. The dog, who had followed me, curled up in a corner, moaning softly.

On the night table, beside an unfinished embroidery

and the diary of Ana's life, I found a note to me from Roberto in which he asked me to look after the dog and to bury his wife and himself in one coffin in the cemetery of that fairy-tale village. They had decided to die together; Ana was terminally ill with cancer and they preferred to travel to the next stage of their lives hand in hand, as they had always done, so that at the fleeting instant in which the spirit disengages, they would not run the risk of losing each other in some warp in the vast universe.

I ran through the house, looking for Roberto. I found him behind the kitchen in the small room he used for a study, seated at a wooden desk, his head in his hands, sobbing. On the desk lay the syringe he had used to inject his wife, now filled with the dose intended for him. I rubbed the nape of his neck; he looked up and stared into my eyes for an endless moment. It seemed clear that he had wanted to prevent Ana's terminal suffering and had prepared their farewell so that nothing would alter the serenity of the moment; he had cleaned the house, cut fresh branches for the vases, dressed his wife and combed her hair, and when everything was ready he had given her the injection. Consoling her with the promise that a few minutes later he would be joining her, he had lain beside her and held her until he was certain she was no longer alive. He had refilled the syringe, pushed up his shirtsleeve, and located the vein, but then things had not gone as he planned. That was when he had called me.

"I can't do it, Eva. You're the only one I can ask. Please . . . Help me die."

A
DISCREET
MIRACLE

The Boulton family was descended from a Liverpool businessman who had emigrated in the mid-nineteenth century with enormous ambition as his only fortune but had amassed great wealth from a fleet of cargo ships in the most distant and southernmost country in the world. The Boultons were prominent members of the British colony and, like so many English away from their island, had preserved their traditions and language with absurd tenacity until a commingling with local blood had diluted their arrogance and substituted for Anglo-Saxon names others more typical of their adopted land.

Gilberto, Filomena, and Miguel had been born during the height of the Boulton family fortunes, but their lifetimes witnessed the decline of maritime traffic, along with a substantial part of their incomes. Although they were no longer truly wealthy, they were able to maintain their style of life. It would be difficult to find three persons of more widely divergent appearance and character than these three Boultons. In their old age the idiosyncrasies of each were exaggerated, but despite their obvious disparities their souls were basically in harmony.

Gilberto was over seventy, a poet with delicate features and the carriage of a dancer who had lived amid art books and antiques, indifferent to the necessities of life. He was the only one of the three who had been educated in England, an experience that had marked him deeply. He retained for a lifetime, for example, the vice of tea. He had never married, in part because he did not find soon enough the pale young girl who so often moved through his youthful verses, and by the time he had renounced that illusion it was already too late, his bachelor habits were too deeply rooted. He ridiculed his blue eyes, his blond hair, and his ancestry, saying that most of the Boultons had been common merchants who from having pretended so long to be aristocrats ended by believing they in fact were. Nevertheless, he always wore tweed jackets with leather elbow patches, he played bridge, read the *Times*—three weeks late—and cultivated the irony and phlegm attributed to British intellectuals.

Filomena was as plump and uncomplicated as a farm girl, a widow with a number of grandchildren. She was endowed with a great tolerance that allowed her to accept, on the one hand, Gilberto's Anglophile whims and, on the other, Miguel's having holes in his shoes and his shirt collars in shreds. She always found energy to minister to Gilberto's indispositions or to listen to him recite his strange verses, and to collaborate in

Miguel's innumerable projects. She tirelessly knit warm
sweaters for her younger brother, which he wore once
or twice and then gave to someone more needy. Her
knitting needles were an extension of her hands; they
moved with a sprightly rhythm, an uninterrupted *tick-
tack* that announced her presence and accompanied her
always, like the scent of her jasmine cologne.

Miguel Boulton was a priest. Unlike his brother and
sister, he was dark skinned, short, with hair so thick
over all his body that he would have seemed bearlike
had he not had such a gentle face. He had abandoned
the advantages of the family hearth at sixteen, and
returned only to eat Sunday dinners with his parents or
to be cared for by Filomena on the rare occasions he
was seriously ill. He was not at all nostalgic for the
comforts of his youth, and although he had fits of bad
humor, he considered himself a fortunate man and was
content with his life. He lived near the city dump, in a
miserable district on the outskirts of the capital where
the streets were unpaved and there were no sidewalks
or trees. His shack was constructed of boards and
sheets of zinc. Sometimes in summer the fetid gases
that filtered underground from the dump issued up
through the floor. His furniture consisted of a cot, a
table, two chairs, and planks for books, and the walls
displayed revolutionary posters, tin crucifixes crafted
by political prisoners, modest hangings embroidered by
the mothers of the *desaparecidos,* and pennants with
the name of his favorite soccer team. A red flag hung
beside the crucifix where every morning he took solitary communion and every night thanked God for the
good fortune of being alive. Padre Miguel was one of

those beings set apart by a terrible passion for justice. Throughout a long life he had accumulated so much vicarious suffering that he was incapable of thinking of his own, a quality which when added to the certainty he was acting in the name of God made him a man to be reckoned with. Every time the military searched his house and arrested him for subversive activities, they had to gag him, because not even beatings could muzzle the flow of insults interlarded with his quotations from the gospel. He had been arrested so often, had joined in so many hunger strikes in solidarity with the prisoners, had sheltered so many persecuted, that according to the law of probabilities he should have died many times over. His photograph, seated before a local police station and holding a placard announcing that people were tortured there, had been published around the world. There was no punishment capable of intimidating him, and the authorities did not dare "disappear" him as they had so many others, because he was too well known. At night, when he knelt before his small altar to converse with God, he agonized over whether he was motivated solely by love for his fellowman and thirst for justice, or whether there might not also be an element of satanic pride in his actions. This man who was capable of singing a baby to sleep with boleros, or of sitting up all night with the sick, had no faith in the gentleness of his own heart. All his life he had combated a rage that thickened his blood and erupted in ungovernable outbursts. Secretly, he wondered what would have become of him if circumstances had not offered him such ready pretexts for releasing his anger. Filomena hovered over him, but Gilberto was of the opinion that if nothing too serious had happened to Miguel in his almost seventy years of walking a tightrope, there was little reason to worry, since his brother's guardian angel had proved to be very efficient.

"Angels don't exist. They are an error of semantics," Miguel would argue.

"Don't be a heretic, Miguel."

"They were just ordinary messengers until Saint Thomas Aquinas came up with all that humbug."

"Do you mean to tell me that the feather of the Archangel Saint Gabriel they venerate in Rome was plucked from the tail of a buzzard?" laughed Gilberto.

"If you don't believe in angels you don't believe in anything. You should be in a different profession," Filomena chimed in.

"Several centuries have been lost in arguing how many of those creatures can dance on the head of a pin. Who cares? A man shouldn't waste his energy on angels, he should help people!"

Miguel had been gradually losing his vision and now was nearly blind. He saw nothing with his right eye and very little with his left; he could not read, and he had great difficulty outside his neighborhood, because he lost his way. He depended more and more on Filomena to get around. She either went with him or sent the car and chauffeur, Sebastián Canuto, alias El Cuchillo, an ex-convict for whom Miguel had obtained a parole, then rehabilitated, and who now had worked for the family twenty years. During the recent political turbulence El Cuchillo had become the priest's discreet bodyguard. Whenever she heard a rumor about an upcoming protest march, Filomena gave the chauffeur the day off and he went straight to Miguel's district, equipped with a bludgeon and a pair of brass knuckles hidden up his sleeves—having abandoned the knife that had earned him his nickname. He would post himself in the street to wait for the priest to leave and then follow at a distance, ready to rush to his defense or to drag him to safety if the situation demanded. It was just as well that the nebula in which Miguel lived prevented his being too aware of these lifesaving measures; they would have infuriated him. He would have thought it unjust that he received protection while his fellow protesters bore the brunt of the beatings and water cannon and tear gas.

As the date of his seventieth birthday approached, Miguel suffered a hemorrhage in his left eye and in a few seconds was in total darkness. He had gone to the church for a night meeting with the residents of the neighborhood, who were organizing to confront the City Sanitation Department with a petition saying they could not continue to live amid all the flies and stench of rotting garbage. Many of those who attended were in the opposite camp from the Catholic church; in truth, they had no evidence of the existence of God. To the contrary, the suffering in their lives was irrefutable proof that the universe was one long free-for-all, but at the same time they regarded the parish church as the natural neighborhood meeting place. The cross Miguel wore about his neck seemed only a minor aberration, a kind of extravagance on the old man's part. That night the priest was pacing back and forth, which was his custom when speaking, when he felt his blood pumping in his heart and at his temples and at the same time broke out in a clammy sweat. He attributed it to the heat of the discussion and wiped at his forehead with his sleeve and closed his eyes. When he opened them, he felt as if he were caught in a whirlpool at the bottom of the ocean: all he could see were undulating waves, spots, black upon black. He held out an arm, groping for support.

"The lights have gone out," he said, thinking of sabotage at the power plant.

His friends grouped around him, frightened. Padre Boulton was a formidable comrade who had lived among them as long as they could remember. They had come to believe he was invincible, a strong, robust, muscular man with a drill sergeant's booming voice and a bricklayer's hands that even joined in prayer seemed to have been made for a fight. Suddenly they realized how much he had aged; he was shrunken, small, a child with wrinkles. A choir of women administered first aid; they made him lie down, they placed wet cloths on his head, they gave him warm wine to drink, and massaged his feet. None of this had the desired effect; just the opposite: because of their overzealous attention he could scarcely get his breath. Finally, Miguel convinced everyone to stand back, and struggled to his feet, prepared to confront this new misfortune face to face.

"I've fucking well had it," he said, but without losing his calm. "Please call my sister and tell her I have a problem. But don't give her any details. I don't want her to worry."

An hour later Sebastián Canuto arrived, tight-lipped and reticent as always, bearing the message that *señora* Filomena had not wanted to miss the current episode of her soap opera and that she had sent money and a basket of provisions for his people.

"That's not it this time, Cuchillo. I think I've been struck blind."

The chauffeur helped him into the car and without a single question drove him back through the city to the Boulton mansion, which rose elegantly from the middle of a slightly overgrown but still majestic park. He honked to alert the household, then helped the sufferer from the car and almost carried him inside, touched to see the priest so frail and docile. Tears were running down his rough, debauched face as he told Gilberto and Filomena what had happened.

"I swear on my whoring mother's head, *don* Miguelito's gone blind. As if we needed that," wept the chauffeur, unable to contain himself.

"Don't curse in front of the Poet," chided the priest.

"Take him up to bed, Cuchillo," Filomena ordered. "I'm sure this is nothing serious. It's probably a cold. That's what you get for not wearing a sweater!"

"Time has ceased to flow / Night and day are eternal winter / There is naught but the pure silence / Of antennae in the blackness . . ."* Gilberto improvised.

"Go tell cook to prepare some chicken broth," his sister said, to silence him.

The family physician determined that it was not a cold and recommended that Miguel see an ophthalmologist.

*From the poem "Aunque es de noche," © by the Chilean poet Carlos Bolton.

The next morning, after an impassioned exposition on the subject of health—God's gift and the people's right—which the infamous regime in power had made into a privilege of caste, the stricken man agreed to see a specialist. Sebastián Canuto drove all three to the Southside Hospital, the only place Miguel approved of because there they treated the poorest of the poor. His sudden blindness had put the priest in an unusually bad humor; he could not understand the divine design that would make him an invalid just when his services were most needed. Christian resignation never entered his mind. From the beginning he had refused to allow anyone to lead him or support him; he preferred to stumble along, even at the risk of breaking his neck, more than for any reason of pride, to accustom himself as quickly as possible to this new limitation. Filomena had given the chauffeur secret instructions to take a different route and drive them to the German Clinic, but her brother, who knew all too well the smell of poverty, was suspicious the minute they stepped inside the building, and his suspicions were confirmed when he heard music in the elevator. His brother and sister had had to rush him out of the clinic before he threw the king of all fits. At Southside they waited four hours, time that Miguel used to inquire into the misfortunes of his fellow patients in the waiting room, Filomena to begin another sweater, and Gilberto to compose the poem about the antennae in the blackness that had welled up in his heart the night before.

"The right eye is hopeless, and to restore any vision to the left we will have to operate again," said the doctor who finally attended them. "He's already had three operations, and the tissue is greatly weakened; this will require special techniques and instruments. I believe the only place where it can be done is in the Military Hospi—"

"Never!" interrupted Miguel. "I will never set foot in that den of callous vipers!"

Startled, the doctor winked apologetically at the nurse, who smiled complicitously.

"Don't be difficult, Miguel," scolded Filomena. "It will only be for a day or two; I don't think that would betray your principles. No one goes to hell for a stay in the hospital!" But her brother replied that he would rather be blind for the rest of his days than give the military the pleasure of restoring his eyesight. At the door the doctor held his arm a moment.

"Look, Padre. Have you ever heard of the Opus Dei clinic? They have modern equipment there, too."

"Opus Dei?" the priest exclaimed. "Did you say Opus Dei?"

Filomena tried to lead him outside the consulting room, but he planted himself in the doorway to inform the doctor that there was another place he would never dream of asking a favor.

"But, why . . . ? Aren't they Catholics?"

"Reactionary Pharisees is what they are."

"S-s-sorry," stammered the doctor.

Back in the car Miguel lectured his brother and sister, and the chauffeur, on how the Opus Dei was a nefarious organization more concerned with soothing the conscience of the upper classes than with feeding the starving and on how it was easier for a camel to pass through the eye of a needle than for a rich man to enter the Kingdom of Heaven, or however that went. He added that their experience was further proof of how bad things were in a country where only the privileged could get well with dignity, and the rest had to be content with the herbs of poverty and poultices of humiliation. And to cap it off he asked them to take him straight home, because he had to water the geraniums and prepare his Sunday sermon.

"I agree," commented Gilberto, depressed by the hours of waiting and the vision of misfortune and ugliness he had witnessed in the hospital. He was not accustomed to activities of this sort.

"You agree with what?" asked Filomena.

"That we cannot go to the Military Hospital. That would not be wise. But we could offer the Opus Dei the opportunity, don't you think?"

"What are you saying!" his brother sputtered. "I told you what I think of them."

"People will say we can't afford to pay!" Filomena objected, close to losing her patience.

"There's nothing to lose by inquiring," suggested Gilberto, running a cologned handkerchief around his neck.

"Those people are so busy moving fortunes around in banks and embroidering priests' chasubles in gold thread that they don't have any energy left to devote to the needy. Heaven is not won with genuflections, but with—"

"But you're not poor, *don* Miguelito," interrupted Sebastián Canuto, not relaxing his grip on the wheel.

"Don't *you* insult me, Cuchillo. I'm as poor as you are. But turn around, then, and take us to the damned clinic, to prove to the Poet that as usual he's got his head in the clouds."

They were received by a pleasant woman who asked them to fill out some forms and offered them a cup of coffee. Fifteen minutes later they were in the consulting room.

"First of all, Doctor, I want to know whether you're a member of the Opus Dei, or whether you just work here," the priest asked.

"Yes, I do God's Work," the doctor smiled meekly.

"Then how much is the consultation?" The priest's tone did not mask his sarcasm.

"Do you have financial problems, Father?"

"Just tell me how much."

"Nothing, if you're not able to pay. Donations are voluntary."

For a brief instant Padre Boulton lost his aplomb, but his bafflement was short-lived.

"This doesn't have the look of a charity ward."

"No, it's a private clinic."

"Uh *hunh*! So only people able to make donations come here."

"Look, Father, if you don't like it here, I suggest you leave," the doctor replied. "But before you go, let me examine you. If you want, bring all your sheep to me and we'll deal with them to the best of our abilities; that's why those who are able to pay, pay. And now, sit very still and open your eyes wide."

After a painstaking examination the doctor confirmed the earlier diagnosis, and he was not optimistic.

"We have the very best equipment here, but this is a

very delicate operation. I won't deceive you, Father. Only a miracle can restore your eyesight."

Miguel was so crestfallen that he scarcely heard what the doctor was telling him; Filomena, however, seized on that one hope.

"A miracle, you say?"

"Well, that's a manner of speaking, *señora*. The truth is that no one can guarantee he will see again."

"If what you want is a miracle, I know where to get one," said Filomena, stuffing her knitting back in her bag. "Thank you very much, Doctor. Please proceed with preparations for the operation. We will not be gone long."

Once again in the car, with Miguel speechless for the first time in recent memory and Gilberto fatigued by the shocks of the day, Filomena ordered Sebastián Canuto to drive toward the mountains. He glanced at her from the corner of his eye and smiled enthusiastically. More than once he had driven the *señora* in that direction, never happily, because the road was a writhing serpent, but now he was animated by the thought that he was helping the person he valued most in the world.

"Where are we going now," murmured Gilberto, calling on all his British discipline to keep from swooning with exhaustion.

"Why don't you nap; it's a long trip. We're going to the grotto of Juana of the Lilies," his sister explained.

"You must be crazy!" the priest exclaimed.

"She's a saint."

"That's out-and-out nonsense. The Church still hasn't made up its mind about her."

"It takes the Vatican something like a hundred years to acknowledge sainthood. We can't wait that long," Filomena concluded.

"If Miguel does not believe in angels, he's even less likely to believe in some local saint, particularly since your Juana came from a family of wealthy landowners," Gilberto sighed.

"That is not relevant; she lived in poverty. Don't put ideas in Miguel's head," said Filomena.

"If it weren't for the fact that her family is prepared to spend a fortune to have its own saint, no one would've ever heard of her," the priest interjected.

"She's more miraculous than any of your foreign saints."

"Whatever the case, it would be arrogant of me to ask for special treatment. Sick as I am, I'm nobody, and I have no right to stir up heaven with personal demands," grumbled the priest.

Juana's fame had arisen after her premature death when the *campesinos* of the region, impressed by her piety and charitable works, had begun praying to her for favors. Soon the news spread that the dead girl could work miracles, and her notoriety grew until it culminated in the Miracle of the Explorer, as it was referred to. A man had been lost in the mountains for two weeks, and when the rescue teams had given up the search and were about to declare him dead, he appeared, hungry and nearly prostrate, but safe. In his statements to the press, he had declared that in a dream he had seen the vision of a girl wearing a long dress and carrying a bouquet of flowers in her arms. When he awakened he had smelled a strong aroma of lilies and had known beyond doubt that it was a message from heaven. Following the penetrating perfume of the flowers he had made his way out of the labyrinth of passes and ravines and finally come within sight of a road. When he was shown a photograph of Juana, he swore that she and the girl in his vision were one and the same. The girl's family had made it their business to disseminate the story, to construct a grotto on the site where the explorer had emerged, and to mobilize all resources at hand to present the case to the Vatican. To date, nevertheless, the Jury of Cardinals had not replied. The Holy See did not believe in hasty judgments; for many centuries it had exercised power cautiously and looked forward to doing so many more in the future; therefore, it never acted precipitously in any matter, especially beatifications. Rome had received numerous testimonies from South America, where every so often prophets, hermit saints, preachers, stylites, martyrs, virgins, anchorites, and other unique and locally revered figures appeared, but it would not do to be overenthusiastic about each case. Great caution was required in such matters because one misstep could lead to ridicule, especially in these pragmatic times when skepticism prevailed over faith. Juana's devoted, however, had not awaited a verdict from Rome before elevating her to the rank of saint. They sold pictures of her and medals with her portrait, and every day notices were published in the newspapers thanking her for some favor granted. So many lilies had been planted around the grotto that the odor went to the pilgrims' heads and caused sterility in domestic animals for miles around. Oil lamps and candles and torches filled the air with smoglike smoke, confounding condors in their flight. Within a brief time the site had been filled with memorial plaques, with orthopedic devices and miniature replicas of organs that believers had left as proof of a miraculous cure. Through public subscription, money had been raised to pave the route, and within a couple of years there was a road, sinuous but passable, linking the capital with the shrine.

The Boultons reached their destination at nightfall. Sebastián Canuto helped the three elderly people along the path that led to the grotto. Despite the late hour, worshipers were still present: some inching their way forward on their knees, aided by a solicitous relative; others praying aloud or lighting candles before the plaster statue of the revered girl. Filomena and El Cuchillo knelt to compose their pleas, Gilberto sat on a bench to cogitate upon the strange turns of life, and Miguel stood muttering that if they were going to ask for miracles, why not just pray for the fall of the tyrant and the return of democracy.

Several days later the physicians of the Opus Dei clinic operated on Miguel's left eye, without charge, after notifying the family that they must not be overly hopeful. The priest appealed to Filomena and Gilberto not to say a word about Juana of the Lilies; it was enough to bear the humiliation of accepting aid from his ideological rivals. As soon as he was discharged, Filomena took Miguel to the family home, ignoring his protests. Miguel was wearing an enormous patch that covered half his face and was weakened by the experience, but his humility was not diminished. He declared that he did not want to be attended by hands that accepted pay, so they had to dismiss the nurse they had engaged for his recovery. Filomena and the faithful Sebastián Canuto themselves assumed responsibility for Miguel's care—not an easy task, since he was in a foul humor: he could not tolerate staying in bed and had lost his appetite.

The priest's presence radically altered the household routine. Opposition radios and the shortwave Voice of Moscow blared constantly and an endless file of sympathetic neighbors came to visit their sick friend. Miguel's room soon filled with humble gifts: schoolchildren's drawings, cookies, herb teas, flowers grown in tin cans, a hen for chicken soup, even a two-month-old puppy that urinated on the Persian rugs and gnawed furniture legs, which someone had brought with the idea of training as a Seeing Eye dog. All in all, the convalescence progressed rapidly, and fifty hours after the operation, Filomena called the surgeon to tell him that her brother was seeing quite well.

"But I told him not to touch the patch," the doctor protested.

"Oh, he's still wearing the patch. He's seeing with the other eye," Filomena clarified.

"What other eye?"

"Well, the one that's not covered, Doctor; the one he was blind in."

"That can't be. I'll be right over. Don't move him for any reason!" ordered the surgeon.

In the Boulton mansion he found a very spirited patient eating fried potatoes and watching soap operas with the puppy in his lap. Incredulous, the doctor verified that the priest's vision was unimpaired in the eye that had been blind for eight years, and when he removed the patch it was evident Miguel could also see with the eye that had been operated on.

Padre Miguel celebrated his seventieth birthday in the parish church of his barrio. His sister, Filomena, and her friends formed a caravan of cars filled with cakes, pies, tasty morsels, baskets of fruit, and jugs of chocolate, led by El Cuchillo, who had brought liters of wine and liquor disguised in barley-water bottles. The priest had sketched the story of his eventful life on large posters and hung them inside the church. There, with a touch of irony, he had recounted the ups and downs of his vocation, beginning with the moment when at fifteen the call of God had fallen on his head with the force of a lead pipe, continuing with his struggles against the cardinal sins—first, greed and lust; later, anger—and ending with his recent adventures in police cells at an age when other old men were sitting in rocking chairs counting the stars. He had hung a portrait of Juana, crowned by a garland of flowers, beside his ubiquitous red flags. The festivities began with a mass—enlivened by four guitars—which all the neighborhood attended. Loudspeakers had been set up to allow the crowd that spilled out into the street to follow the ceremony. After the benediction, people began coming forward to testify to new cases of abuse of authority, until Filomena marched forward to announce that there had been enough lamentation, it was time to celebrate. Everyone went outside to the patio, someone put on a record, and immediately the dancing and feasting began. The ladies from exclusive neighborhoods served the food, while El Cuchillo set off fireworks, and Miguel, surrounded by well-wishers and friends, danced the Charleston to prove that not only were his eyes as sharp as a hawk's but, in addition, no one could best him when it came to a party.

"Plebian fiestas have no poetry about them," observed Gilberto after the third glass of fake barley water, but his English-lord affectations did not entirely disguise the fact he was having a good time.

"Here now, Padre Miguel, tell us the miracle!" someone shouted, and all the rest joined in.

Miguel asked for the music to be turned off, straightened his clothing, smoothed down the few hairs that still crowned his head, and in a voice quavering with gratitude told the story of Juana of the Lilies, without whose intervention all the craft of science and technology would have come to naught.

"If only she was a proletarian holy lady, we could trust her a lot easier," someone spoke up, and loud laughter seconded his quip.

"I don't want to hear any shit about my miracle," roared an indignant Padre Miguel. "You'll get my saint mad and I'll be blind as a bat again! And now, all of you line up, because you're going to sign this letter to the Pope for me!"

And so, amid guffaws and tipping of wineglasses, all the priest's neighbors signed the petition for the beatification of Juana of the Lilies.

REVENGE

O<small>N</small> the radiant day that
Dulce Rose Orellano was crowned with the jasmine of
the Queen of Carnival, the mothers of the other candi-
dates had grumbled that the competition was rigged,
that the title had been given to her only because she
was the daughter of Senator Anselmo Orellano, the
most powerful man in all the province. They admitted
that the girl had charm and that she could play the piano
and dance like no one else, but other girls who had
sought the same prize were much more beautiful. They
watched her standing there on the dais in her organza
dress and flower crown, waving to the crowd, and
cursed her under their breath. That was why some
were not at all unhappy when several months later
misfortune fell upon the house of the Orellanos, sowing
so much death and calamity that it took twenty-five
years to reap it.

On the night of the queen's election, there was a

dance at Santa Teresa's Mayoral Hall, and young men flocked from miles around to meet Dulce Rosa. She was so happy, and danced so gracefully, that many of them did not perceive that in truth she was not the most beautiful, and when they returned home they told everyone they had never seen a face like hers. And so she had won undeserved fame as a beauty, and no later assertion would ever disprove it. Exaggerated descriptions of her translucent skin and crystal-clear eyes circulated from mouth to mouth, and every teller added some bit from his own fancy. Poets in remote towns composed sonnets to a hypothetical maiden by the name of Dulce Rosa.

The rumor of the beauty flowering in the home of Senator Orellano eventually reached the ears of Tadeo Céspedes, who never dreamed he would meet her, because at no time in his life had he had time to learn verses or look at women. His sole preoccupation was the civil war. From the time he had first shaved his mustache, he had carried a weapon in his hand, and for years now he had lived amid the roar of gunpowder. He had forgotten his mother's kisses, even the music of the mass. He did not always have cause to fight, because during brief periods of truce there were no adversaries within reach of his troops; even in those times of forced peace, however, he lived the life of a corsair. He was a man habituated to violence. He crisscrossed the country fighting visible enemies, when there were such, and shadows, when he had to invent them, and he would have continued forever had his party not won the presidential election. Overnight he passed from hiding out to prominence, and lost all pretexts for shooting up the countryside.

Tadeo Céspedes's last mission was a punitive raid against Santa Teresa. With a hundred and twenty men he rode into town by night to make an example of the town and to wipe out the leaders of enemy factions. His troops shot out the windows of public buildings; they battered down the church door and rode right up to the high altar, in the process running down Padre Clemente, who stood in their way, then clattered on toward Senator Orellano's villa rising proudly on the crown of the hill.

After unleashing the dogs and locking his daughter in the farthest room of the farthest patio, the Senator, backed by a dozen loyal servants, prepared to make his stand against Tadeo Céspedes. In that moment, as at so many other times of his life, he lamented not having male descendants who could take up weapons with him and defend the honor of his house. He felt very old, but he had no time to dwell on such thoughts, because on the slopes of the hill he saw the awesome glimmer of a hundred and twenty torches spreading fear in the night. In silence he handed out the last store of ammunition. Everything had been said, and each man knew that before the dawn he must die like a man at his post.

"The last person will take the key to the room where my daughter is hidden and do what must be done," the Senator said at the sound of the first shots.

All those men had been with him when Dulce Rosa was born; they had held her on their knees when she could barely walk; they had told her ghost stories on winter afternoons, listened to her practice the piano, and wildly applauded on the day of her coronation as Queen of Carnival. Her father could die in peace, because the girl would never be taken alive by Tadeo Céspedes. The only possibility Senator Orellano had not considered was that despite his fierceness in the fighting he would be the last to die. He watched his friends fall one after another and recognized when it was futile to continue to resist. He had a bullet in his belly and his sight was clouding over; he could barely make out the shadows climbing the high walls of his property, but he was conscious enough to drag himself to the third patio. The dogs recognized his scent through layers of sweat, blood, and sorrow and opened a path to let him pass. He put the key in the lock, pushed open the heavy door, and through the mist blurring his eyes saw Dulce Rosa waiting for him. She was wearing the organza dress she had worn at Carnival, and the flowers of her crown adorned her hair.

"It's time, daughter," the Senator said, cocking his pistol as a pool of blood formed about his feet.

"Don't kill me, Father," Dulce Rosa replied in a firm voice. "Let me live to avenge you, and myself."

Senator Anselmo Orellano studied the face of his fifteen-year-old daughter and imagined what Tadeo Céspedes would do to her, but there was unflinching fortitude in Dulce Rosa's clear eyes, and he knew she would survive and punish his executioner. The girl sat back down on the bed, and he sat beside her, gun pointed toward the door.

With the last howls of the dying dogs, the wooden bar yielded, the bolt flew off the door, and the first men burst into the room. The Senator managed to fire off six shots before he lost consciousness. Tadeo Céspedes thought he must be dreaming when he saw the angel in a jasmine crown holding a dying old man in her arms while her white dress slowly turned red, but he could not summon enough pity for a second glance: he was drunk with violence and bone weary from hours of fighting. "The woman is mine," he said, before his men set hands on her.

Friday dawned to a leaden sky stained by the glare of fire. Silence lay heavy on the hilltop. The last moans had faded when Dulce Rosa struggled to her feet and walked to the garden fountain; the day before it had been surrounded by magnolia blossoms, but now it was a bubbling pool in the midst of rubble. Her dress hung in shreds; she removed it slowly and stood naked. She sank into the cold water. The sun appeared through the birch trees and Dulce Rosa watched the water turn pink as she washed away the blood from between her legs and that of her father, crusted in her long hair. Once she was clean and calm and had dried her tears, she returned to the ruined house, looked for something to cover her nakedness, pulled a linen sheet from the clothespress, and went outside to look for her father's remains. The marauders had tied him by the feet and then galloped up and down the hill, dragging his body until it was nothing but pitiable, battered flesh, but guided by love his daughter unerringly recognized him. She wrapped his remains in the sheet and sat beside him to watch the day brighten. That was how her neighbors from Santa Teresa had found her when they dared climb the hill to the Orellanos' villa. They helped Dulce Rosa bury the dead and extinguished the last coals of the fires; then they begged her to go live with her godmother in another town where no one would know her story. When she refused, the townspeople formed crews to rebuild the house and gave her six fierce dogs to defend herself.

From the instant they had borne away her still-living father and Tadeo Céspedes closed the door and unbuckled his leather belt, Dulce Rosa had lived for revenge. That memory caused her sleepless nights and consumed her days, but it never completely stilled her laughter or diminished her good nature. Her reputation as a beauty continued to grow; musicians wandered the byways giving her magnified charms, until they had made of her a living legend. She rose every morning at four to oversee the work in the fields and the household; to ride over her property; to buy and sell, haggling like a Syrian; to breed stock and cultivate magnolias and jasmine in her gardens. When dusk fell, she would remove her riding trousers, boots, and pistol, and dress in exquisite gowns shipped from the capital in trunks perfumed with aromatic herbs. As night fell, her visitors would arrive to find her playing the piano, while servants prepared trays of pastries and glasses of cool drinks. At first, people wondered why she was not in the sanatorium in a straitjacket, or a novice with the Carmelite nuns, but as there were frequent parties in the Orellano villa, with time people stopped talking about the tragedy and erased the murdered Senator from their memories. A few gentlemen of good name and sizeable fortune were able to overlook the stigma of rape and, drawn by Dulce Rosa's sensitivity and reputation as a beauty, propose marriage. She rejected them all, because her one mission in this world was revenge.

Neither could Tadeo Céspedes rid himself of the memory of that fatal night. The sweeping tide of the slaughter and the excitement of the rape evaporated as he was riding back to the capital to make his report of the havoc he had wrought on his foray. He thought of the girl in the ball gown and crown of sweet jasmine who had suffered him in silence in that dark room suffused with the smell of gunpowder. He saw her again, as he had left her, sprawled on the floor, half-naked in her bloodied rags, sunk in the compassionate sleep of unconsciousness; that was how he was to see her for the rest of his life at the moment of falling asleep. Peace, governing, and power turned Céspedes into a composed and hard-working man. With the passing of time, memories of the civil war faded, and people began to address him as *don* Tadeo. He bought a hacienda on the far side of the mountains, dedicated himself to administering justice, and was elected mayor. If it had not been for the tireless ghost of Dulce Rosa Orellano, he might have achieved a measure of happiness, but all the women he met along his path, all the women he took in his arms in search of consolation, all the loves he pursued through the years—all had the face of the Queen of Carnival. To add to his torment, from time to time he heard her name in the verses of wandering poets, making it impossible to eradicate her from his heart. The image of the young girl grew within him, filled him completely, until the day came when he could bear no more. He was sitting at the head of a long banquet table, celebrating his fifty-seventh birthday, surrounded by friends and colleagues, when he thought he saw a naked girl lying on the tablecloth among the jasmine blossoms, and he realized that this nightmare would not leave him in peace, not even after death. He pounded the table with a fist that made the china tremble, and asked for his hat and his cane.

"Where are you going, *don* Tadeo?" his Chief Administrator asked.

"To atone for an old injury," he replied, and left without bidding anyone goodbye.

He did not have to go in search of Dulce Rosa, because he had always known he would find her in the house of her misfortune, and it was there he drove. By then, good highways had been built across the country, and distances seemed much shorter. The landscape had changed in twenty-five years, but as he turned the last corner of the hill, the Orellano villa appeared, just as he remembered seeing it before his band stormed the hill. There stood the solid walls of river rock he had destroyed with charges of dynamite; there were the dark wood beams he had set fire to; there the trees from which he had strung the bodies of the Senator's men; there the patio where he had massacred the dogs. He stopped his car a hundred meters from the door; he could go no farther, he felt as if his heart was exploding in his chest. He was about to turn and drive back where

308

he had come from, when from among the rosebushes emerged a figure enveloped in a swirl of skirts. He shivered, hoping with all his might that she would not recognize him. In the soft light of evening he watched Dulce Rosa Orellano float toward him along the garden path. He saw her hair, her bright face, the harmony of her movements, the fluttering dress, and he felt as if he were suspended in a dream he had been dreaming for twenty-five years.

"You've come at last, Tadeo Céspedes," she said when she saw him. She was not deceived by the black mayor's suit or the gray hair of a gentleman; his corsair's hands were unchanged.

"You have pursued me relentlessly. I have never been able to love anyone but you," he whispered in a voice hoarse with shame.

Dulce Rosa Orellano breathed a sigh of satisfaction. She had called him in her mind night and day all those years, and finally he had come. It was her hour. But she looked into his eyes and could not find any trace of the executioner, only welling tears. She searched deep in her own heart for the hatred she had nurtured and could not find it. She evoked the moment when she had asked her father to sacrifice her and let her live to collect a debt; she relived the rough embrace of the man she had so often cursed and the early morning when she had wrapped her father's pitiful remains in a linen sheet. She reviewed the perfect plan of her revenge, but she did not find the expected happiness. To the contrary, she felt profoundly sad. Tadeo Céspedes took her hand and softly kissed her palm, wetting it with his tears. She realized then, to her horror, that from having thought of him so long, from having savored his punishment before the fact, her emotions had made a complete circle and she had come to love him.

In the days that followed, both lifted the floodgates on the love they had never released, and for the first time in their unhappy fates allowed another being close to them. They strolled through the gardens, talking about themselves, not avoiding the fatal night that had twisted the course of their lives. At dusk Dulce Rosa would play the piano as Tadeo Céspedes smoked, and as he listened he felt his bones grow weak and happiness enfold him like a blanket, erasing all his old nightmares. After dinner he would drive back to Santa Teresa, where no one remembered any longer the old horror story. He took rooms in the best hotel and there made plans for their wedding. He wanted a celebration with all possible fanfare, extravagance, and enthusiasm, a fiesta in which the whole town would participate. He had discovered love at an age when other men lose hope, and that discovery had restored the vigor of his youth. He wanted to surround Dulce Rosa with love and beauty, to lavish on her all the pleasures money could buy, to see whether in her later years he could compensate for the harm he had done her as a young girl. Occasionally he would be overcome by panic. He would search her face for signs of rancor, but found only the light of shared love and was reassured. A happy month went by in this way.

Two days before the wedding, when the tables for the wedding party were being set up in the garden, the fowls and hogs were being slaughtered for the feast, and the flowers being cut to decorate the house, Dulce

Rosa Orellano tried on her wedding dress. She gazed at herself in the mirror, so like the day of her coronation as Queen of Carnival that she could not go on deceiving her own heart. She knew she would never be able to carry out the revenge she had planned, because she was in love with the assassin, but neither could she silence the Senator's ghost. She dismissed the seamstress, picked up the scissors, and walked to the room in the third patio that had been empty so many years.

Tadeo Céspedes looked for her everywhere, calling her frantically. The barking of the dogs led him to the far end of the house. With the help of the gardeners he kicked down the bolted door and rushed into the room, where once he had seen an angel crowned with jasmine blossoms. He found Dulce Rosa just as she was in his dreams every night of his life, in the same bloody organza dress, and he knew he would live to be ninety and pay for his guilt with the memory of the only woman who had ever touched his heart.

LETTERS
OF
BETRAYED
LOVE

THE mother of Analía Torres had died of delirium following her delivery. Her father had not been able to endure the grief and two weeks later had shot himself in the chest. For several days he lay dying with his wife's name on his lips. His brother Eugenio was left in charge of the family estate and arranged the fate of the tiny orphan according to his own standards. Until she was six, Analía had clung to the skirts of an Indian nursemaid in the servants' quarters of the house of her guardian; later, as soon as she was old enough to go to school, she had been sent to the capital as a boarding student with the Sisters of the Sacred Heart, where she spent the next twelve years of her life. She was a good student and she loved the discipline, the austerity of the stone convent, the chapel with its court of saints and aroma of wax and lilies, the bare corridors, the shaded patios. What she liked least was the noisiness of the pupils and the acrid odor of the classrooms. Every time she was able to escape the nuns' vigilance, she hid in the attic among decapitated statues and broken-down furniture to tell herself stories. In those stolen moments she sank into silence with the sensation of indulging herself in a sin.

Every six months she received a brief note from her uncle Eugenio exhorting her to comport herself well and honor the memory of her parents, who had been good Christians in life and who would be proud that their only daughter was dedicating her life to the highest precepts of virtue, that is, preparing to enter the convent as a novice. At the first hint of this plan, however, Analía had informed her uncle that she was not inclined to follow it; out of pure contrariness, she adamantly maintained that position, because deep in her heart she enjoyed the religious life. Hidden behind the habit, in the ultimate solitude of total renunciation of pleasure, she might, she thought, find lasting peace; her instinct, nevertheless, warned her against her guardian's counsel. She suspected that his actions were motivated more by greed than by family loyalty. She mistrusted any idea that originated with him: there was bound to be a trap hidden somewhere.

When Analía was sixteen, her uncle came for the first time to visit her at school. When the Mother Superior called the girl to her office she found it necessary to introduce them; each had changed so much from the days of the Indian nursemaid in the back patios that they did not recognize one another.

"I see that the Little Sisters have looked after you well, Analía," her uncle commented, stirring his cup of chocolate. "You look healthy, you might even say pretty. In my last letter I notified you that beginning with this birthday, you will receive a monthly sum for your expenses, just as my brother, may he rest in peace, stipulated in his will."

"How much?"

"A hundred pesos."

"Is that all my parents left me?"

"No, of course not. You know that the hacienda belongs to you, but agriculture is no task for a woman, especially not in these times of strikes and revolutions. For the moment, I shall send you a monthly allowance that will increase every year until you reach your majority. Then we shall see."

"We shall see what, Uncle?"

"We shall see what is best for you."

"What choice do I have?"

"You will always need a man to oversee the hacienda, my girl. I have done that all these years; it has not been an easy task, but it was my duty. I promised my brother in his last hours, and I am prepared to continue doing it for you."

"You will not be forced to do it much longer, Uncle. When I marry I shall take charge of my estate."

"When she marries, the child says? Tell me, Sister, does she have a suitor, then?"

"What a thing to say, *señor* Torres! We look after our girls very closely. It's just a manner of speaking. How the girl goes on!"

Analía Torres rose, smoothed the pleats of her uniform, made a rather mocking curtsy, and left the room. The Mother Superior served her visitor another cup of chocolate, commenting that the only explanation for such discourteous behavior was that the girl had had so little contact with members of her family.

"She is the only student who never goes home for vacation, and the only one who has never received a Christmas present," the nun added curtly.

"I am not one for pampering a child, but I assure you I hold my niece in the highest esteem, and I have looked after her interests like a father. But you are right, my niece needs more affection; women are sentimental creatures."

A month later the uncle again presented himself at the school. On this occasion he did not ask to see his niece but merely notified the Mother Superior that his own son wished to enter into correspondence with Analía and asked her to see that the letters were delivered, with the hope that a friendship with her cousin would strengthen family ties.

The letters began to arrive with regularity: plain white paper and black ink, rounded characters, and a large, firm hand. Some letters spoke of life in the country, of seasons and animals; others of poets now dead, and of their ruminations. Sometimes the envelope included a book, or a sketch featuring the same firm hand as the calligraphy. Analía intended not to read them, faithful to the idea that some danger lurked behind anything connected with her uncle, but amid the boredom of school the letters represented her only opportunity for escape. She hid in the attic, not to invent improbable tales but to read and reread her cousin's notes until she knew by heart the slant of the letters and texture of the paper. At first she did not reply, but as time went by she could not help herself.

The contents of the correspondence grew more and more subtle in order to escape the censorship of the Mother Superior, who opened all mail. An intimacy developed between the correspondents, and soon they devised a secret code in which they began to speak of love.

Analía Torres did not remember ever having seen the cousin who signed himself Luis, because when she had lived in her uncle's house the youth had been in the capital attending school. She was sure he must be an ugly man, perhaps sickly or humpbacked, because it seemed impossible that so fine a sensibility and such a clear mind should be combined with a handsome appearance. She tried to sketch in her mind an image of her cousin: plump, like his father, his face scarred by smallpox, lame, and partly bald: the more defects she added the more she was inclined to love him. Radiance of spirit was all that really mattered; that was the only thing that survived the passage of time without deteriorating, the only thing that continued to grow with the years. The beauty of the dashing heroes of her stories was no virtue at all and might even become the source of frivolity, Analía concluded, although she could not help being slightly uneasy in regard to this reasoning. She wondered how much deformity she would be capable of accepting.

The correspondence between Analía and Luis Torres lasted two years, at the end of which the girl had a hatbox filled with letters and a heart lost beyond recall. If the idea had passed through her mind that the relationship might have been planned by her uncle to ensure that the estate she had inherited from her father would pass into the hands of Luis, she immediately rejected it, ashamed of such ignoble thoughts. On her eighteenth birthday, the Mother Superior called her to the refectory to tell her a visitor was waiting to see her. Analía Torres guessed who it was and for a moment had the impulse to run and hide in the garret of the forgotten saints, terrified by the eventuality of finally coming face to face with the man she had so long imagined. When she entered the drawing room and stood before him, it took her several minutes to overcome her disillusion.

Luis Torres was not the malformed dwarf she had constructed in her dreams and learned to love. He was a well-built man with a pleasant face: regular features, a still boyish mouth, a dark, well-trimmed beard, and light eyes fringed with long eyelashes but empty of expression. He looked a little like the saints in the chapel—rather too pretty and slightly foolish. Analía recovered from her shock and decided that if in her heart she had accepted a hunchback, she could love even more this elegant young man who kissed her on one cheek, leaving a lingering scent of lavender water.

From the day she was married, Analía detested Luis Torres. When he crushed her between the embroidered sheets of a too-soft bed, she knew that she had fallen in love with a ghost and that she could never transfer her imaginary passion to the reality of marriage. She fought these sentiments with determination, first putting them out of her mind as immoral and then, when it became impossible to ignore them any longer, trying to delve into the depths of her own soul and pull them out by the roots. Luis was an agreeable man, at times even entertaining. He did not harass her with outrageous demands nor try to modify her bent toward solitude and silence. She herself admitted that with a little good will on her part she could find a certain happiness in their relationship, at least as much as she would have known in a nun's habit. She had no precise reasons for the strange repulsion she felt toward the man she had loved for two years before meeting. Neither could she put her emotions into words, and even had she been able to do so she would have had no one to tell them to. She felt tricked by her inability to reconcile the image of the epistolary suitor with that of her flesh-and-blood husband. Luis never mentioned the letters, and if she raised the subject he would close her lips with a quick kiss and some flippant observation about romantic love's being unsuited to married life, in which trust, respect, shared interests, and the good of the family were much more important than adolescent love letters. There was no true intimacy between them. During the day each carried out his or her own duties, and at night they met among the feather pillows, where Analía—accustomed to her convent school cot—felt she was suffocating. Sometimes they hurriedly embraced: she motionless and tense, he with the attitude of one who is satisfying bodily demands in lieu of any other recourse. Luis would immediately fall asleep; she lay staring into the darkness, with an unvoiced protest in her throat. Analía tried various schemes to overcome the revulsion she felt for her husband, from the exercise of fixing in her memory every detail about her husband, with the aim of loving him out of sheer determination, to that of emptying her mind of all thoughts and transporting herself to a dimension where he could not reach her. She prayed this was merely a temporary repugnance, but the months went by and instead of the longed-for relief her animosity grew to loathing. One night she dreamed of being caressed by a repulsive man with black ink-stained fingers.

The Torreses lived on the property Analía's father had acquired when the region was still a half-savage territory belonging to soldiers and bandits. Now it was close to a main highway and a short distance from a prosperous town that was the seat of annual agricultural and cattle fairs. Legally, Luis was the administrator of the hacienda, but in reality it was Analía's uncle Eugenio who fulfilled that function, since Luis was bored by the details of country life. After the midday meal, when father and son installed themselves in the library to drink cognac and play dominoes, Analía would hear her uncle making decisions about investments, herds, crops, and harvests. On the rare occasions when she dared interrupt to offer an opinion, the two men listened with professed attention, assuring her they would keep her suggestions in mind, but then did as they pleased. At such times Analía would gallop through the pastures to the foot of the mountain, wishing she had been a man.

The birth of a son did not in any way improve Analía's feelings for her husband. During the months of her pregnancy, her withdrawn nature became more pronounced, but Luis was patient with her, attributing it to her condition, and anyway, he had other matters to occupy him. After the baby was born, she moved into a separate room furnished with nothing but a hard narrow cot. When their son was a year old, however, and Analía still locked the door of her room and avoided any occasion that meant being alone with him, Luis decided it was time to demand more considerate treatment; he warned his wife that she had better change her attitude before he shot the lock off her door. She had never seen him so outraged. She obeyed without comment. Through the next seven years the tension between them intensified to such a degree that they found they were secret enemies but, being well-mannered, in the presence of others they treated each other with exaggerated courtesy. Only the boy suspected the dimension of his parents' hostility, and at midnight would often wake up crying because he had wet the bed. Analía enclosed herself in a shell of silence and felt as if she was drying up inside. Luis, in contrast, became more expansive and irresponsible; he abandoned himself to his many appetites, he drank too much, and for days he disappeared on unmentionable escapades. When he no longer tried to disguise his dissipation, Analía found good reason for distancing herself even more from him. Luis lost all interest in running the hacienda, and his wife took his place, happy with this new arrangement. On Sundays her uncle Eugenio would sit after dinner discussing decisions with her, while Luis sank into a long siesta from which he revived at nightfall, bathed in sweat, his stomach churning, but ready for renewed revelry with his friends.

Analía taught her son the rudiments of writing and

arithmetic and tried to direct him toward a taste for books. When the boy was seven, Luis decided it was time for a more formal education, away from his mother's babying; he tried to send him to school in the capital, to see if he would grow up a little sooner, but Analía opposed him with such ferocity that he had to accept a less drastic solution. The boy was sent to school in the nearby town, where he stayed from Monday to Friday; on Saturday mornings a car was sent to bring him home for the weekend. After the first week Analía anxiously observed her son, searching for excuses to keep him with her, but she could find none. The child seemed happy; he talked about his teacher and his schoolmates with genuine enthusiasm, as if he had always known them. He stopped wetting his bed. Three months later he came home with his first report card and a brief letter from the teacher congratulating him on his good performance. As Analía read the note, she trembled, and smiled for the first time in many days. Elated, she hugged her son, asking a thousand questions about his school: what were the dormitories like, what did he have to eat, was it cold at night, how many friends did he have, what was his teacher like? She seemed much more relaxed and did not again raise the question of removing him from the school. As the months went by, the boy continued to bring home good marks, which Analía hoarded like treasures and repaid with jars of marmalade and fruit for the entire class. She tried not to think about the fact that this compromise would suffice only for his elementary education and that within a few years she could not avoid sending him to school in the city, where she could see him only during vacations.

One night in town Luis Torres, who had drunk too much, began pirouetting another man's mount to demonstrate his horsemanship to a group of his drinking companions. The horse threw him and with one kick crushed his testicles. Nine days later, Torres, screaming with pain, died in the city clinic where he had been taken with the hope of curing his infection. Beside him was his wife, guiltily weeping for the love she could never give him and for relief that now she would not have to keep praying for him to die. Before taking the coffin back to the country to bury her husband in his own soil, Analía bought a white dress and packed it in the bottom of her suitcase. She arrived home wearing mourning, her face covered by a widow's veil so that no one could see the expression in her eyes; she wore the same attire to the funeral, holding the hand of her son, who was also in black. After the service her uncle Eugenio, who was in very good health despite seventy well-lived years, proposed to his daughter-in-law that she relinquish her lands and go to live in the capital on her income; there the boy could complete his education and she could forget the sorrows of the past.

"Because it did not escape me, Analía, that my poor Luis and you were never happy together," he said.

"You're right, Uncle. Luis deceived me from the beginning."

"For God's sake, child, he was always very discreet and respectful with you. Luis was a good husband. All men have their little adventures, but they are meaningless."

"That's not what I mean. I'm referring to an unforgivable deception."

"I don't want to know anything about it. In any case, I think that you and the boy would be much better off in the capital. You will want for nothing. I will look after the hacienda. I'm an old man but I still have my strength: to this day I can throw a steer."

"I shall stay here. My son will stay with me, because I need his help around the place. Recently I've been doing more in the fields than in the house. The only difference will be that now I shall make my own decisions, without consulting anyone. At last the land is mine alone. So I will tell you goodbye, Uncle Eugenio."

Analía spent a few weeks organizing her new life. She began by burning the sheets she had shared with her husband and moving her narrow cot into the main bedroom. Then she examined the accounts of the hacienda in great detail, and as soon as she had an exact idea of her wealth she looked for an overseer who would carry out her orders without question. When she felt that everything was nicely under control, she removed the white dress from her suitcase, ironed it meticulously, put it on, and, thus attired, was driven to her son's school, carrying an old hatbox beneath her arm.

Analía Torres waited in the patio for the five o'clock bell to announce the end of the last class of the day; immediately a flood of boys rushed out to play. Among them was her son, who stopped short when he saw her, because this was the first time his mother had visited the school.

326

"Show me your classroom. I want to meet your teacher," she said.

At the door Analía motioned that the boy was to leave, that this was a private matter, and walked in alone. She found herself in a large, high-ceilinged room with maps and biology charts on the walls. There was the same close, sweaty odor she remembered from her own childhood, but now it did not bother her; to the contrary, she breathed it in with delight. Following the school day, the desks were untidy, there were papers scattered on the floor, and uncapped inkwells. Columns of numbers had not been erased from the blackboard. And at the front of the room, at a desk on a raised platform, sat the teacher. He looked up, surprised, but did not rise, because his crutches were too far away to be reached without scraping his chair across the floor. Analía walked down the aisle between two rows of desks and stopped before him.

"I am Torres's mother," she said, because she could think of nothing better.

"Good afternoon, *señora*. I must take this opportunity to thank you for all the preserves and fruit you have sent us."

"You can forget that. I did not come to exchange courtesies," said Analía, placing the hatbox on the desk. "I have come to settle accounts."

"What is this?"

She opened the box and turned out the love letters she had guarded for years. For a long moment he studied the pile of envelopes.

"You owe me eleven years of my life," Analía said.

"H-how did you know that I wrote them," he stammered, when he was again able to speak.

"On my wedding day I discovered that my husband could not have written them, and when my son brought home his first report card I recognized the handwriting. And now that I see you, I am absolutely sure, because it is you I have seen in my dreams since I was sixteen years old. Why did you do it?"

"Luis Torres was my friend, and when he asked me to write a letter to his cousin, I could see no harm in it. And it was no different with the second and third letters; afterward, when you replied, it was too late to turn back. Those were the best two years of my life, the only time I have ever looked forward to anything. I looked forward to the mail."

"Ahhh."

"Can you forgive me?"

"That depends on you," said Analía, handing him his crutches.

The schoolmaster put on his jacket and stood up. They walked out into the bustle of the patio, where a late sun was still shining.

PHANTOM
PALACE

WHEN five centuries earlier the bold renegades from Spain with their bone-weary horses and armor candescent beneath an American sun stepped upon the shores of Quinaroa, Indians had been living and dying in that same place for several thousand years. The conquistadors announced with heralds and banners the "discovery" of a new land, declared it a possession of a remote emperor, set in place the first cross, and named the place San Jerónimo, a name unpronounceable to the natives. The Indians observed these arrogant ceremonies with some amazement, but the news had already reached them of the bearded warriors who advanced across the world with their thunder of iron and powder; they had heard that wherever these men went they sowed sorrow and that no known people had been capable of opposing them: all armies had succumbed before that handful of centaurs. These Indians were an ancient tribe, so poor that not even the most befeathered chieftain had bothered to exact taxes from them, and so meek that they had never been recruited for war. They had lived in peace since the dawn of time and were not eager to change their habits because of some crude strangers. Soon, nevertheless, they comprehended the magnitude of the enemy and they understood the futility of attempting to ignore them; their presence was overpowering, like a heavy stone bound to every back. In the years that followed, the Indians who had not died in slavery or as a result of the different tortures improvised to entrench the new gods, or as victims of unknown illnesses, scattered deep into the jungle and gradually lost even the name of their people. Always in hiding, like shadows among the foliage, they survived for centuries, speaking in whispers and mobilizing by night. They came to be so skillful in the art of dissimulation that history did not record them, and today there is no evidence of their passage through time. Books do not mention them, but the *campesinos* who live in the region say they have heard them in the forest, and every time the belly of a young unmarried woman begins to grow round and they cannot point to the seducer, they attribute the baby to the spirit of a lustful Indian. People of that place are proud of carrying a few drops of the blood of those invisible beings mingled with the torrential flow from English pirates, Spanish soldiers, African slaves, adventurers in search of El Dorado, and, later, whatever immigrant stumbled onto these shores with his pack on his back and his head filled with dreams.

Europe consumed more coffee, cocoa, and bananas than we as a nation could produce, but all that demand was no bonanza for us; we continued to be as poor as ever. Events took a sudden turn when a black man digging a well along the coast drove his pick deep into the ground and a stream of petroleum spurted over his face. Toward the end of the Great War there was a widely held notion that ours was a prosperous country, when in truth most of the inhabitants still squished mud between their toes. The fact was that gold flowed only into the coffers of El Benefactor and his retinue, but there was hope that someday a little would spill over for the people. Two decades passed under this democratic totalitarianism, as the President for Life called his government, during which any hint of subversion would have been crushed in the name of his greater glory. In the capital there were signs of progress: motorcars, movie houses, ice cream parlors, a hippodrome, and a theater that presented spectaculars from New York and Paris. Every day dozens of ships moored in the port, some carrying away petroleum and others bringing in new products, but the rest of the country drowsed in a centuries-long stupor.

One day the people of San Jerónimo awakened from their siesta to the deafening pounding that presaged the arrival of the steam engine. The railroad tracks would unite the capital with this small settlement chosen by El Benefactor as the site for his Summer Palace, which was to be constructed in the style of European royalty—no matter that no one knew how to distinguish summer from winter, since both were lived under nature's hot, humid breath. The sole reason for erecting such a monumental work on this precise spot was that a certain Belgian naturalist had affirmed that if there was any truth to the myth of the Earthly Paradise, this landscape of incomparable beauty would have been the location. According to his observations the forest harbored more than a thousand varieties of brightly colored birds and numerous species of wild orchids, from the *Brassia,* which is as large as a hat, to the tiny *Pleurothallis,* visible only under a magnifying glass.

The idea of the Palace had originated with some Italian builders who had called on His Excellency bearing plans for a hodgepodge of a villa, a labyrinth of countless columns, wide colonnades, curving staircases, arches, domes and capitals, salons, kitchens, bedchambers, and more than thirty baths decorated with gold and silver faucets. The railroad was the first stage in the enterprise, indispensable for transporting tons of materials and hundreds of workmen to this remote corner of the world, in addition to the supervisors and craftsmen brought from Italy. The task of putting together that jigsaw puzzle lasted four years: flora and fauna were transmuted in the process, and the cost was equivalent to that of all the warships of the nation's fleet, but it was paid for punctually with the dark mineral that flowed from the earth, and on the anniversary of the Glorious Ascent to Power the ribbon was cut to inaugurate the Summer Palace. For the occasion the locomotive of the train was draped in the colors of the flag, and the freight cars were replaced by parlor cars upholstered in plush and English leather, the formally attired guests included members of the oldest aristocracy who, although they detested the cold-blooded Andean who had usurped the government, did not dare refuse his invitation.

El Benefactor was a crude man with the comportment of a peon; he bathed in cold water and slept on a mat on the floor with his boots on and his pistol within arm's reach; he lived on roast meat and maize, and drank nothing but water and coffee. His black cigars were his one luxury; he considered anything else a vice befitting degenerates or homosexuals—including alcohol, which he disapproved of and rarely offered at his table. With time, nevertheless, he was forced to accept a few refinements, because he understood the need to impress diplomats and other eminent visitors if they were not to carry the report abroad that he was a barbarian. He did not have a wife to mend his Spartan ways. He believed that love was a dangerous weakness. He was convinced that all women, except his own mother, were potentially perverse and that the most prudent way to treat them was to keep them at arm's length. He had always said that a man asleep in an amorous embrace was as vulnerable as a premature baby; he demanded, therefore, that his generals sleep in the barracks and limit their family life to sporadic visits. No woman had ever spent the night in his bed or could boast of anything more than a hasty encounter. No woman, in fact, had ever made a lasting impression until Marcia Lieberman entered his life.

The celebration for the inauguration of the Summer Palace was a stellar event in the annals of El Benefactor's government. For two days and two nights alternating orchestras played the most current dance tunes and an army of chefs prepared an unending banquet. The most beautiful mulatto women in the Caribbean, dressed in sumptuous gowns created for the occasion, whirled through salons with officers who had never fought in a battle but whose chests were covered with medals. There was every sort of diversion: singers imported from Havana and New Orleans, flamenco dancers, magicians, jugglers and trapeze artists, card games and dominoes, and even a rabbit hunt. Servants released the rabbits from their cages, and the guests pursued the scampering pack with finely bred greyhounds; the chase came to an end when one wit blasted all the black-necked swans gliding across the lake. Some guests passed out in their chairs, drunk with dancing and liquor, while others jumped fully clothed into the swimming pool or drifted off in pairs to the bedchambers. El Benefactor did not want to know the details. After greeting his guests with a brief speech, and beginning the dancing with the most aristocratic lady present, he had returned to the capital without a farewell. Parties put him in a bad humor. On the third day the train made the return journey, carrying home the enervated *bons vivants*. The Summer Palace was left in a calamitous state: the baths were dunghills, the curtains were dripping with urine, the furniture was gutted, and the plants drooped in their flowerpots. It took the servants a week to clean up the ravages of that hurricane.

The Palace was never again the scene of a bacchanal. Occasionally El Benefactor went there to get away from the pressures of his duties, but his repose lasted no more than three or four days, for fear that a conspiracy might be hatched in his absence. The government required eternal vigilance if power was not to slip through his fingers. The only people left in all that enormous edifice were the personnel entrusted with its maintenance. When the clatter of the construction equipment and the train had stilled, and the echoes of the inaugural festivities died down, the region was once again calm, and the orchids flowered and birds rebuilt their nests. The inhabitants of San Jerónimo returned to their habitual occupations and almost succeeded in forgetting the presence of the Summer Palace. That was when the invisible Indians slowly returned to occupy their territory.

The first signs were so subtle that no one paid attention to them; footsteps and whispers, fleeting silhouettes among the columns, the print of a hand on the clean surface of a table. Gradually food began to disappear from the kitchens, and bottles from the wine cellars; in the morning, some beds seemed to have been slept in. The servants blamed one another but never raised their voices because no one wanted the officer of the guard to take the matter into his hands. It was impossible to watch the entire expanse of that house, and while they were searching one room they would hear sighs in the adjoining one; but when they opened that door they would find only a curtain fluttering, as if someone had just stepped through it. The rumor spread that the Palace was under a spell, and soon the fear spread even to the soldiers, who stopped walking their night rounds and limited themselves to standing motionless at their post, eyes on the surrounding landscape, weapons at the ready. The frightened servants stopped going down to the cellars and, as a precaution, locked many of the rooms. They confined their activities to the kitchen and slept in one wing of the building. The remainder of the mansion was left unguarded, in the possession of the incorporeal Indians who had divided the rooms with invisible lines and taken up residence there like mischievous spirits. They had survived the passage of history, adapting to changes when they were inevitable, and when necessary taking refuge in a dimension of their own. In the rooms of the Palace they at last found refuge; there they noiselessly made love, gave birth without celebration, and died without tears. They learned so thoroughly all the twists and turns of that marble maze that they were able to exist comfortably in the same space with the guards and servants, never so much as brushing against them, as if they existed in a different time.

Ambassador Lieberman debarked in the port with his wife and a full cargo of personal belongings. He had traveled with his dogs, all his furniture, his library, his collection of opera recordings, and every imaginable variety of sports equipment, including a sailboat. From the moment his new destination had been announced, he had detested that country. He had left his post as Vice Consul in Vienna motivated by the ambition to obtain an ambassadorship, even if it meant South America, a bizarre continent for which he had not an ounce of sympathy. Marcia, his wife, took the appointment with better humor. She was prepared to follow her husband throughout his diplomatic pilgrimage—even though each day she felt more remote from him and had little interest in his mundane affairs—because she was allowed a great deal of freedom. She had only to fulfill certain minimal wifely requirements, and the remainder of her time was her own. In fact, her husband was so immersed in his work and his sports that he was scarcely aware of her existence; he noticed her only when she was not there. Lieberman's wife was an indispensable complement to his career; she lent brilliance to his social life and efficiently managed his complicated domestic staff. He thought of her as a loyal partner, but he had never been even slightly curious about her feelings. Marcia consulted maps and an encyclopedia to learn the particulars of that distant nation, and began studying Spanish. During the two weeks of the Atlantic crossing she read books by the famous Belgian naturalist and, even before arriving, was enamored of that heat-bathed geography. As she was a rather withdrawn woman, she was happier in her garden than in the salons where she had to accompany her husband, and she concluded that in the new post she would have fewer social demands and could devote herself to reading, painting, and exploring nature.

Lieberman's first act was to install fans in every room of his residence. Immediately thereafter he presented his credentials to the government authorities. When El Benefactor received him in his office, the couple had been in the city only a few days, but the gossip that the Ambassador's wife was a beautiful woman had already reached the caudillo's ears. For reasons of protocol he invited them to dinner, although he found the diplomat's arrogance and garrulity insufferable. On the appointed night Marcia Lieberman entered the Reception Hall on her husband's arm and, for the first time in a long lifetime, a woman caused El Benefactor to gasp for breath. He had seen more lithe figures, and faces more beautiful, but never such grace. She awakened memories of past conquests, fueling a heat in his blood that he had not felt in many years. He kept his distance that evening, observing the Ambassador's wife surreptitiously, seduced by the curve of her throat, the shadow in her eyes, the movement of her hands, the solemnity of her bearing. Perhaps it crossed his mind that he was more than forty years older than she and that any scandal would have repercussions far beyond the national boundaries, but that did not discourage him; on the contrary, it added an irresistible ingredient to his nascent passion.

Marcia Lieberman felt the man's eyes fastened on her like an indecent caress, and she was aware of the danger, but she did not have the strength to escape. At one moment she thought of telling her husband they should leave, but instead remained seated, hoping the old man would approach her and at the same time ready to flee if he did. She could not imagine why she was trembling. She had no illusions about her host; the signs of age were obvious from where she was sitting: the wrinkled and blemished skin, the dried-up body, the hesitant walk. She could imagine his stale odor and knew intuitively that his hands were claws beneath the white kid gloves. But the dictator's eyes, clouded by age and the exercise of so much cruelty, still held a gleam of power that held her frozen in her chair.

El Benefactor did not know how to pay court to a woman; until that moment he had never had need to do so. That fact acted in his favor, for had he harassed

Marcia with a Lothario's gallantries she would have found him repulsive and would have retreated with scorn. Instead she could not refuse him when a few days later he knocked at her door, dressed in civilian clothes and without his guards, looking like a dreary great-grandfather, to tell her that he had not touched a woman for ten years and that he was past temptations of that sort but, with all respect, he was asking her to accompany him that afternoon to a private place where he could rest his head in her queenly lap and tell her how the world had been when he was still a fine figure of a macho and she had not yet been born.

"And my husband?" Marcia managed to ask in a whisper-thin voice.

"Your husband does not exist, my child. Now only you and I exist," the President for Life replied as he led her to his black Packard.

Marcia did not return home, and before the month was out Ambassador Lieberman returned to his country. He had left no stone unturned in searching for his wife, refusing at first to accept what was no secret, but when the evidence of the abduction became impossible to ignore, Lieberman had asked for an audience with the Chief of State and demanded the return of his wife. The interpreter tried to soften his words in translation, but the President captured the tone and seized the excuse to rid himself once and for all of that imprudent husband. He declared that Lieberman had stained the honor of the nation with his absurd and unfounded accusations and gave him three days to leave the country. He offered him the option of withdrawing without a scandal, to protect the dignity of the country he represented, since it was to no one's interest to break diplomatic ties and obstruct the free movement of the oil tankers. At the end of the interview, with the expression of an injured father, he added that he could understand the Ambassador's dilemma and told him not to worry, because in his absence, he, El Benefactor, would continue the search for his wife. As proof of his good intents he called the Chief of Police and issued instructions in the Ambassador's presence. If at any moment Lieberman had thought of refusing to leave without Marcia, a second thought must have made clear to him that he was risking a bullet in the brain, so he packed his belongings and left the country before the three days were up.

Love had taken El Benefactor by surprise at an age when he no longer remembered the heart's impatience. This cataclysm rocked his senses and thrust him back into adolescence, but not sufficiently to dull his vulpine cunning. He realized that his was a passion of sensuality, and he could not imagine that Marcia returned his emotions. He did not know why she had followed him that afternoon, but his reason indicated that it was not for love, and, as he knew nothing about women, he supposed that she had allowed herself to be seduced out of a taste for adventure, or greed for power. In fact, she had fallen prey to compassion. When the old man embraced her, anxiously, his eyes watering with humiliation because his manhood did not respond as it once had, she undertook, patiently and with good will, to restore his pride. And thus after several attempts the poor man succeeded in passing through the gates and lingering a few brief instants in the proffered warm gardens, collapsing immediately thereafter with his heart filled with foam.

"Stay with me," El Benefactor begged, as soon as he had recovered from fear of succumbing upon her.

And Marcia had stayed, because she was moved by the aged caudillo's loneliness, and because the alternative of returning to her husband seemed less interesting than the challenge of slipping past the iron fence this man had lived behind for eighty years.

El Benefactor kept Marcia hidden on one of his estates, where he visited her daily. He never stayed the night with her. Their time together was spent in leisurely caresses and conversation. In her halting Spanish she told him about her travels and the books she had read; he listened, not understanding much, content simply with the cadence of her voice. In turn he told her stories of his childhood in the arid lands of the Andes, and of his life as a soldier; but if she formulated some question he immediately threw up his defenses, observing her from the corner of his eyes as if she were the enemy. Marcia could not fail to note this implacable stoniness and realized that his habit of distrust was much stronger than his need to yield to tenderness, and so, after a few weeks, she resigned herself to defeat. Once she had renounced any hope of winning him over with love, she lost interest in him and longed to escape the walls that sequestered her. But it was too late. El Benefactor needed her by his side because she was the closest thing to a companion he had known; her husband had returned to Europe and she had nowhere to turn in this land; and even her name was fading from memory. The dictator perceived the change in her and his mistrust intensified, but that did not cause him to stop loving her. To console her for the confinement to which she was now condemned—her appearance outside would have confirmed Lieberman's accusations and shot international relations to hell—he provided her with all the things she loved: music, books, animals. Marcia passed the hours in a world of her own, every day more detached from reality. When she stopped encouraging him, El Benefactor found it impossible to embrace her, and their meetings resolved into peaceful evenings of cookies and hot chocolate. In his desire to please her, El Benefactor invited her one day to go with him to the Summer Palace, so she could see the paradise of the Belgian naturalist she had read so much about.

The train had not been used since the inaugural celebration ten years before and was so rusted that they had to make the trip by automobile, escorted by a caravan of guards; a crew of servants had left a week before, taking everything needed to restore the Palace to its original luxury. The road was no more than a trail defended by chain gangs against encroaching vegetation. In some stretches they had to use machetes to clear the ferns, and oxen to haul the cars from the mud, but none of that diminished Marcia's enthusiasm. She was dazzled by the landscape. She endured the humid heat and the mosquitoes as if she did not feel them, absorbed by a nature that seemed to welcome her in its embrace. She had the impression that she had been there before, perhaps in dreams or in another life, that she belonged there, that until that moment she had been a stranger in the world, and that her instinct had dictated every step she had taken, including that of leaving her husband's house to follow a trembling old man, for the sole purpose of leading her here. Even before she saw the Summer Palace, she knew that it would be her last home. When the edifice finally rose out of the foliage, encircled by palm trees and shimmering in the sun, Marcia breathed a deep sigh of relief, like a shipwrecked sailor when he sees home port.

Despite the frantic preparations that had been made to receive them, the mansion still seemed to be under a spell. The Roman-style structure, conceived as the center of a geometric park and grand avenues, was sunk in the riot of a gluttonous jungle growth. The torrid climate had changed the color of the building materials, covering them with a premature patina; nothing was visible of the swimming pool and gardens. The greyhounds had long ago broken their leashes and were running loose, a ferocious, starving pack that greeted the newcomers with a chorus of barking. Birds had nested in the capitals of the columns and covered the reliefs with droppings. On every side were signs of disorder. The Summer Palace had been transformed into a living creature defenseless against the green invasion that had surrounded and overrun it. Marcia leapt from the automobile and ran to the enormous doors where the servants awaited, oppressed by the heat of the dog days. One by one she explored all the rooms, the great salons decorated with crystal chandeliers that hung from the ceilings like constellations and French furniture whose tapestry upholstery was now home to lizards, bedchambers where bed canopies were blanched by intense sunlight, baths where moss had grown in the seams of the marble. Marcia never stopped smiling; she had the face of a woman recovering what was rightfully hers.

When El Benefactor saw Marcia so happy, a touch of the old vigor returned to warm his creaking bones, and he could embrace her as he had in their first meetings. Distractedly, she acceded. The week they had planned to spend there lengthened into two, because El Benefactor had seldom enjoyed himself so much. The fatigue accumulated in his years as tyrant disappeared, and several of his old man's ailments abated. He strolled with Marcia around the grounds, pointing out the many species of orchids climbing the tree trunks or hanging like grapes from the highest branches, the clouds of white butterflies that covered the ground, and the birds with iridescent feathers that filled the air with their song. He frolicked with her like a young lover, he fed her bits of the delicious flesh of wild mangoes, with his own hands he bathed her in herbal infusions, and he made her laugh by serenading her beneath her window. It had been years since he had been away from the capital, except for brief flights to provinces where his presence was required to put down some insurrection and to renew the people's belief that his authority was not to be questioned. This unexpected vacation had put him in a fine frame of mind; life suddenly seemed more fun, and he had the fantasy that with this beautiful woman beside him he could govern forever. One night he unintentionally fell asleep in her arms. He awoke in the early morning, terrified, with the clear sensation of having betrayed himself. He sprang out of bed, sweating, his heart galloping, and observed Marcia lying there, a white odalisque in repose, her copper hair spilling across her face. He informed his guards that he was returning to the city. He was not surprised when Marcia gave no sign of going with him. Perhaps in his heart he preferred it that way, since he understood that she represented his most dangerous weakness, that she was the only person who could make him forget his power.

El Benefactor returned to the capital without Marcia. He left behind a half-dozen soldiers to guard the property and a few employees to serve her, and he promised he would maintain the road so that she could receive his gifts, provisions, mail, and newspapers and magazines. He assured her that he would visit her often, as often as his duties as Chief of State permitted, but when he said goodbye they both knew they would never meet again. El Benefactor's caravan disappeared into the ferns and for a moment silence fell over the Summer Palace. Marcia felt truly free for the first time in her life. She removed the hairpins holding her hair in a bun, and shook out her long hair. The guards unbuttoned their jackets and put aside their weapons, while the servants went off to hang their hammocks in the coolest corners they could find.

For two weeks the Indians had observed the visitors from the shadows. Undeceived by Marcia Lieberman's fair skin and marvelous curly hair, they recognized her as one of their own but they had not dared materialize in her presence because of the habit of centuries of clandestinity. After the departure of the old man and his retinue, they returned stealthily to occupy the space where they had lived for generations. Marcia knew intuitively that she was never alone, that wherever she went a thousand eyes followed her, that she moved in a ferment of constant murmuring, warm breathing, and rhythmic pulsing, but she was not afraid; just the opposite, she felt protected by friendly spirits. She became used to petty annoyances: one of her dresses disappeared for several days, then one morning was back in a basket at the foot of her bed; someone devoured her dinner before she entered the dining room; her watercolors and books were stolen, but also she found freshly cut orchids on her table, and some evenings her bath waited with mint leaves floating in the cool water; she heard ghostly notes from pianos in the empty salons, the panting of lovers in the armoires, the voices of children in the attics. The servants had no explanation for those disturbances and she stopped asking, because she imagined they themselves were part of the benevolent conspiracy. One night she crouched among the curtains with a flashlight, and when she felt the thudding of feet on the marble, switched on the beam. She thought she saw shadowy, naked forms that for an instant gazed at her mildly and then vanished. She called in Spanish, but no one answered. She realized she would need enormous patience to uncover those mysteries, but it did not matter because she had the rest of her life before her.

A few years later the nation was jolted by the news that the dictatorship had come to an end for a most surprising reason: El Benefactor had died. He was a man in his dotage, a sack of skin and bones that for months had been decaying in life, and yet very few people imagined that he was mortal. No one remembered a time before him; he had been in power so many decades that people had become accustomed to thinking of him as an inescapable evil, like the climate. The echoes of the funeral were slow to reach the Summer Palace. By then most of the guards and servants, bored with waiting for replacements that never came, had deserted their posts. Marcia listened to the news without emotion. In fact, she had to make an effort to remember her past, what had happened beyond the jungle, and the hawk-eyed old man who had changed the course of her destiny. She realized that with the death of the tyrant the reasons for her remaining hidden had evaporated; she could return to civilization, where now, surely, no one was concerned with the scandal of her kidnapping. She quickly discarded that idea, however, because there was nothing outside the snarl of the surrounding jungle that interested her. Her life passed peacefully among the Indians; she was absorbed in the greenness, clothed only in a tunic, her hair cut short, her body adorned with tattoos and feathers. She was utterly happy.

A generation later, when democracy had been established in the nation and nothing remained of the long history of dictators but a few pages in scholarly books, someone remembered the marble villa and proposed that they restore it and found an Academy of Art. The Congress of the Republic sent a commission to draft a report, but their automobiles were not up to the grueling trip, and when finally they reached San Jerónimo no one could tell them where the Summer Palace was. They tried to follow the railroad tracks, but the rails had been ripped from the ties and the jungle had erased all traces. Then the Congress sent a detachment of explorers and a pair of military engineers who flew over the area in a helicopter; the vegetation was so thick that not even they could find the site. Details about the Palace were misplaced in people's memories and the municipal archives; the notion of its existence became gossip for old women; reports were swallowed up in the bureaucracy and, since the nation had more urgent problems, the project of the Academy of Art was tabled.

Now a highway has been constructed that links San Jerónimo to the rest of the country. Travelers say that sometimes after a storm, when the air is damp and charged with electricity, a white marble palace suddenly rises up beside the road, hovers for a few brief moments in the air, like a mirage, and then noiselessly disappears.

AND OF
CLAY
ARE WE
CREATED

THEY discovered the girl's head protruding from the mudpit, eyes wide open, calling soundlessly. She had a First Communion name, Azucena. Lily. In that vast cemetery where the odor of death was already attracting vultures from far away, and where the weeping of orphans and wails of the injured filled the air, the little girl obstinately clinging to life became the symbol of the tragedy. The television cameras transmitted so often the unbearable image of the head budding like a black squash from the clay that there was no one who did not recognize her and know her name. And every time we saw her on the screen, right behind her was Rolf Carlé, who had gone there on assignment, never suspecting that he would find a fragment of his past, lost thirty years before.

First a subterranean sob rocked the cotton fields, curling them like waves of foam. Geologists had set up their seismographs weeks before and knew that the

353

mountain had awakened again. For some time they had predicted that the heat of the eruption could detach the eternal ice from the slopes of the volcano, but no one heeded their warnings; they sounded like the tales of frightened old women. The towns in the valley went about their daily life, deaf to the moaning of the earth, until that fateful Wednesday night in November when a prolonged roar announced the end of the world, and walls of snow broke loose, rolling in an avalanche of clay, stones, and water that descended on the villages and buried them beneath unfathomable meters of telluric vomit. As soon as the survivors emerged from the paralysis of that first awful terror, they could see that houses, plazas, churches, white cotton plantations, dark coffee forests, cattle pastures—all had disappeared. Much later, after soldiers and volunteers had arrived to rescue the living and try to assess the magnitude of the cataclysm, it was calculated that beneath the mud lay more than twenty thousand human beings and an indefinite number of animals putrefying in a viscous soup. Forests and rivers had also been swept away, and there was nothing to be seen but an immense desert of mire.

When the station called before dawn, Rolf Carlé and I were together. I crawled out of bed, dazed with sleep, and went to prepare coffee while he hurriedly dressed. He stuffed his gear in the green canvas backpack he always carried, and we said goodbye, as we had so many times before. I had no presentiments. I sat in the kitchen, sipping my coffee and planning the long hours without him, sure that he would be back the next day.

He was one of the first to reach the scene, because

while other reporters were fighting their way to the edges of that morass in jeeps, bicycles, or on foot, each getting there however he could, Rolf Carlé had the advantage of the television helicopter, which flew him over the avalanche. We watched on our screens the footage captured by his assistant's camera, in which he was up to his knees in muck, a microphone in his hand, in the midst of a bedlam of lost children, wounded survivors, corpses, and devastation. The story came to us in his calm voice. For years he had been a familiar figure in newscasts, reporting live at the scene of battles and catastrophes with awesome tenacity. Nothing could stop him, and I was always amazed at his equanimity in the face of danger and suffering; it seemed as if nothing could shake his fortitude or deter his curiosity. Fear seemed never to touch him, although he had confessed to me that he was not a courageous man, far from it. I believe that the lens of the camera had a strange effect on him; it was as if it transported him to a different time from which he could watch events without actually participating in them. When I knew him better, I came to realize that this fictive distance seemed to protect him from his own emotions.

Rolf Carlé was in on the story of Azucena from the beginning. He filmed the volunteers who discovered her, and the first persons who tried to reach her; his camera zoomed in on the girl, her dark face, her large desolate eyes, the plastered-down tangle of her hair. The mud was like quicksand around her, and anyone attempting to reach her was in danger of sinking. They threw a rope to her that she made no effort to grasp until they shouted to her to catch it; then she pulled a hand from the mire and tried to move, but immediately sank a little deeper. Rolf threw down his knapsack and the rest of his equipment and waded into the quagmire, commenting for his assistant's microphone that it was cold and that one could begin to smell the stench of corpses.

"What's your name?" he asked the girl, and she told him her flower name. "Don't move, Azucena," Rolf Carlé directed, and kept talking to her, without a thought for what he was saying, just to distract her, while slowly he worked his way forward in mud up to his waist. The air around him seemed as murky as the mud.

It was impossible to reach her from the approach he was attempting, so he retreated and circled around where there seemed to be firmer footing. When finally he was close enough, he took the rope and tied it beneath her arms, so they could pull her out. He smiled at her with that smile that crinkles his eyes and makes him look like a little boy; he told her that everything was fine, that he was here with her now, that soon they would have her out. He signaled the others to pull, but as soon as the cord tensed, the girl screamed. They tried again, and her shoulders and arms appeared, but they could move her no farther; she was trapped. Someone suggested that her legs might be caught in the collapsed walls of her house, but she said it was not just rubble, that she was also held by the bodies of her brothers and sisters clinging to her legs.

"Don't worry, we'll get you out of here," Rolf promised. Despite the quality of the transmission, I could hear his voice break, and I loved him more than ever. Azucena looked at him, but said nothing.

During those first hours Rolf Carlé exhausted all the resources of his ingenuity to rescue her. He struggled with poles and ropes, but every tug was an intolerable torture for the imprisoned girl. It occurred to him to use one of the poles as a lever but got no result and had to abandon the idea. He talked a couple of soldiers into working with him for a while, but they had to leave because so many other victims were calling for help. The girl could not move, she barely could breathe, but she did not seem desperate, as if an ancestral resignation allowed her to accept her fate. The reporter, on the other hand, was determined to snatch her from death. Someone brought him a tire, which he placed beneath her arms like a life buoy, and then laid a plank near the hole to hold his weight and allow him to stay closer to her. As it was impossible to remove the rubble blindly, he tried once or twice to dive toward her feet, but emerged frustrated, covered with mud, and spitting gravel. He concluded that he would have to have a pump to drain the water, and radioed a request for one, but received in return a message that there was no available transport and it could not be sent until the next morning.

"We can't wait that long!" Rolf Carlé shouted, but in the pandemonium no one stopped to commiserate. Many more hours would go by before he accepted that time had stagnated and reality had been irreparably distorted.

A military doctor came to examine the girl, and

observed that her heart was functioning well and that if she did not get too cold she could survive the night.

"Hang on, Azucena, we'll have the pump tomorrow," Rolf Carlé tried to console her.

"Don't leave me alone," she begged.

"No, of course I won't leave you."

Someone brought him coffee, and he helped the girl drink it, sip by sip. The warm liquid revived her and she began telling him about her small life, about her family and her school, about how things were in that little bit of world before the volcano had erupted. She was thirteen, and she had never been outside her village. Rolf Carlé, buoyed by a premature optimism, was convinced that everything would end well: the pump would arrive, they would drain the water, move the rubble, and Azucena would be transported by helicopter to a hospital where she would recover rapidly and where he could visit her and bring her gifts. He thought, She's already too old for dolls, and I don't know what would please her; maybe a dress. I don't know much about women, he concluded, amused, reflecting that although he had known many women in his lifetime, none had taught him these details. To pass the hours he began to tell Azucena about his travels and adventures as a newshound, and when he exhausted his memory, he called upon imagination, inventing things he thought might entertain her. From time to time she dozed, but he kept talking in the darkness, to assure her that he was still there and to overcome the menace of uncertainty.

That was a long night.

* * *

Many miles away, I watched Rolf Carlé and the girl on a television screen. I could not bear the wait at home, so I went to National Television, where I often spent entire nights with Rolf editing programs. There, I was near his world, and I could at least get a feeling of what he lived through during those three decisive days. I called all the important people in the city, senators, commanders of the armed forces, the North American ambassador, and the president of National Petroleum, begging them for a pump to remove the silt, but obtained only vague promises. I began to ask for urgent help on radio and television, to see if there wasn't *someone* who could help us. Between calls I would run to the newsroom to monitor the satellite transmissions that periodically brought new details of the catastrophe. While reporters selected scenes with most impact for the news report, I searched for footage that featured Azucena's mudpit. The screen reduced the disaster to a single plane and accentuated the tremendous distance that separated me from Rolf Carlé; nonetheless, I was there with him. The child's every suffering hurt me as it did him; I felt his frustration, his impotence. Faced with the impossibility of communicating with him, the fantastic idea came to me that if I tried, I could reach him by force of mind and in that way give him encouragement. I concentrated until I was dizzy—a frenzied and futile activity. At times I would be overcome with compassion and burst out crying; at other times, I was so drained I felt as if I were staring through a telescope at the light of a star dead for a million years.

I watched that hell on the first morning broadcast, cadavers of people and animals awash in the current of new rivers formed overnight from the melted snow. Above the mud rose the tops of trees and the bell towers of a church where several people had taken refuge and were patiently awaiting rescue teams. Hundreds of soldiers and volunteers from the Civil Defense were clawing through rubble searching for survivors, while long rows of ragged specters awaited their turn for a cup of hot broth. Radio networks announced that their phones were jammed with calls from families offering shelter to orphaned children. Drinking water was in scarce supply, along with gasoline and food. Doctors, resigned to amputating arms and legs without anesthesia, pled that at least they be sent serum and painkillers and antibiotics; most of the roads, however, were impassable, and worse were the bureaucratic obstacles that stood in the way. To top it all, the clay contaminated by decomposing bodies threatened the living with an outbreak of epidemics.

Azucena was shivering inside the tire that held her above the surface. Immobility and tension had greatly weakened her, but she was conscious and could still be heard when a microphone was held out to her. Her tone was humble, as if apologizing for all the fuss. Rolf Carlé had a growth of beard, and dark circles beneath his eyes; he looked near exhaustion. Even from that enormous distance I could sense the quality of his weariness, so different from the fatigue of other adventures. He had completely forgotten the camera; he could not look at the girl through a lens any longer. The pictures we were receiving were not his assistant's but those of other reporters who had appropriated Azucena, bestowing on her the pathetic responsibility of embodying the horror of what had happened in that place. With the first light Rolf tried again to dislodge the obstacles that held the girl in her tomb, but he had only his hands to work with; he did not dare use a tool for fear of injuring her. He fed Azucena a cup of the cornmeal mush and bananas the Army was distributing, but she immediately vomited it up. A doctor stated that she had a fever, but added that there was little he could do: antibiotics were being reserved for cases of gangrene. A priest also passed by and blessed her, hanging a medal of the Virgin around her neck. By evening a gentle, persistent drizzle began to fall.

"The sky is weeping," Azucena murmured, and she, too, began to cry.

"Don't be afraid," Rolf begged. "You have to keep your strength up and be calm. Everything will be fine. I'm with you, and I'll get you out somehow."

Reporters returned to photograph Azucena and ask her the same questions, which she no longer tried to answer. In the meanwhile, more television and movie teams arrived with spools of cable, tapes, film, videos, precision lenses, recorders, sound consoles, lights, reflecting screens, auxiliary motors, cartons of supplies, electricians, sound technicians, and cameramen: Azucena's face was beamed to millions of screens around the world. And all the while Rolf Carlé kept pleading for a pump. The improved technical facilities bore results, and National Television began receiving sharper pictures and clearer sound; the distance seemed suddenly compressed, and I had the horrible sensation that Azucena and Rolf were by my side, separated from me by impenetrable glass. I was able to follow events hour by hour; I knew everything my love did to wrest the girl from her prison and help her endure her suffering; I overheard fragments of what they said to one another and could guess the rest; I was present when she taught Rolf to pray, and when he distracted her with the stories I had told him in a thousand and one nights beneath the white mosquito netting of our bed.

When darkness came on the second day, Rolf tried to sing Azucena to sleep with old Austrian folk songs he had learned from his mother, but she was far beyond sleep. They spent most of the night talking, each in a stupor of exhaustion and hunger, and shaking with cold. That night, imperceptibly, the unyielding floodgates that had contained Rolf Carlé's past for so many years began to open, and the torrent of all that had lain hidden in the deepest and most secret layers of memory poured out, leveling before it the obstacles that had blocked his consciousness for so long. He could not tell it all to Azucena; she perhaps did not know there was a world beyond the sea or time previous to her own; she was not capable of imagining Europe in the years of the war. So he could not tell her of defeat, nor of the afternoon the Russians had led them to the concentration camp to bury prisoners dead from starvation. Why should he describe to her how the naked bodies piled like a mountain of firewood resembled fragile china? How could he tell this dying child about ovens and gallows? Nor did he mention the night that he had seen his mother naked, shod in stiletto-heeled red boots, sobbing with humiliation. There was much he did not tell, but in those hours he relived for the first time all the things his mind had tried to erase. Azucena had surrendered her fear to him and so, without wishing it, had obliged Rolf to confront his own. There, beside that hellhole of mud, it was impossible for Rolf to flee from himself any longer, and the visceral terror he had lived as a boy suddenly invaded him. He reverted to the years when he was the age of Azucena, and younger, and, like her, found himself trapped in a pit without escape, buried in life, his head barely above ground; he saw before his eyes the boots and legs of his father, who had removed his belt and was whipping it in the air with the never-forgotten hiss of a viper coiled to strike. Sorrow flooded through him, intact and precise, as if it had lain always in his mind, waiting. He was once again in the armoire where his father locked him to punish him for imagined misbehavior, there where for eternal hours he had crouched with his eyes closed, not to see the darkness, with his hands over his ears, to shut out the beating of his heart, trembling, huddled like a cornered animal. Wandering in the mist of his memories he found his sister Katharina, a sweet, retarded child who spent her life hiding, with the hope that her father would forget the disgrace of her having been born. With Katharina, Rolf crawled beneath the dining room table, and with her hid there under the long white tablecloth, two children forever embraced, alert to footsteps and voices. Katharina's scent melded with his own sweat, with aromas of cooking, garlic, soup, freshly baked bread, and the unexpected odor of putrescent clay. His sister's hand in his, her frightened breathing, her silk hair against his cheek, the candid gaze of her eyes. Katharina . . . Katharina materialized before him, floating on the air like a flag, clothed in the white tablecloth, now a winding sheet, and at last he could weep for her death and for the guilt of having abandoned her. He understood then that all his exploits as a reporter, the feats that had won him such recognition and fame, were merely an attempt to keep his most ancient fears at bay, a stratagem for taking refuge behind a lens to test whether reality was more tolerable from that perspective. He took excessive risks as an exercise of courage, training by day to conquer the monsters that tormented him by night. But he had come face to face with the moment of truth; he could not continue to escape his past. He *was* Azucena; he was buried in the clayey mud; his terror was not the distant emotion of an almost forgotten childhood, it was a claw sunk in his throat. In the flush of his tears he saw his mother, dressed in black and clutching her imitation-crocodile pocketbook to her bosom, just as he had last seen her on the dock when she had come to put him on the boat to South America. She had not come to dry his tears, but to tell him to pick up a shovel: the war was over and now they must bury the dead.

"Don't cry. I don't hurt anymore. I'm fine," Azucena said when dawn came.

"I'm not crying for you," Rolf Carlé smiled. "I'm crying for myself. I hurt all over."

*   *   *

The third day in the valley of the cataclysm began with a pale light filtering through storm clouds. The President of the Republic visited the area in his tailored safari jacket to confirm that this was the worst catastrophe of the century; the country was in mourning; sister nations had offered aid; he had ordered a state of siege; the Armed Forces would be merciless, anyone caught stealing or committing other offenses would be shot on sight. He added that it was impossible to remove all the corpses or count the thousands who had disappeared; the entire valley would be declared holy ground, and bishops would come to celebrate a solemn mass for the souls of the victims. He went to the Army field tents to offer relief in the form of vague promises to crowds of the rescued, then to the improvised hospital to offer a word of encouragement to doctors and nurses worn down from so many hours of tribulations. Then he asked to be taken to see Azucena, the little girl the whole world had seen. He waved to her with a limp statesman's hand, and microphones recorded his emotional voice and paternal tone as he told her that her courage had served as an example to the nation. Rolf Carlé interrupted to ask for a pump, and the President assured him that he personally would attend to the matter. I caught a glimpse of Rolf for a few seconds kneeling beside the mudpit. On the evening news broadcast, he was still in the same position; and I, glued to the screen like a fortune-teller to her crystal ball, could tell that something fundamental had changed in him. I knew somehow that during the night his defenses had crumbled and he had given in to grief; finally he was vulnerable. The girl had touched a part of him that he himself had no access to, a part he had never shared with me. Rolf had wanted to console her, but it was Azucena who had given him consolation.

I recognized the precise moment at which Rolf gave up the fight and surrendered to the torture of watching the girl die. I was with them, three days and two nights, spying on them from the other side of life. I was there when she told him that in all her thirteen years no boy had ever loved her and that it was a pity to leave this world without knowing love. Rolf assured her that he loved her more than he could ever love anyone, more than he loved his mother, more than his sister, more than all the women who had slept in his arms, more than he loved me, his life companion, who would have given anything to be trapped in that well in her place, who would have exchanged her life for Azucena's, and I watched as he leaned down to kiss her poor forehead, consumed by a sweet, sad emotion he could not name. I felt how in that instant both were saved from despair, how they were freed from the clay, how they rose above the vultures and helicopters, how together they flew above the vast swamp of corruption and laments. How, finally, they were able to accept death. Rolf Carlé prayed in silence that she would die quickly, because such pain cannot be borne.

By then I had obtained a pump and was in touch with a general who had agreed to ship it the next morning on a military cargo plane. But on the night of that third day, beneath the unblinking focus of quartz lamps and the lens of a hundred cameras, Azucena gave up, her eyes locked with those of the friend who had sustained her to the end. Rolf Carlé removed the life buoy, closed her eyelids, held her to his chest for a few moments, and then let her go. She sank slowly, a flower in the mud.

You are back with me, but you are not the same man. I often accompany you to the station and we watch the videos of Azucena again; you study them intently, looking for something you could have done to save her, something you did not think of in time. Or maybe you study them to see yourself as if in a mirror, naked. Your cameras lie forgotten in a closet; you do not write or sing; you sit long hours before the window, staring at the mountains. Beside you, I wait for you to complete the voyage into yourself, for the old wounds to heal. I know that when you return from your nightmares, we shall again walk hand in hand, as before.

And at this moment in her story, Scheherazade
saw the first light of dawn, and discreetly
fell silent.

Born in Peru, Isabel Allende is Chilean. She worked as a journalist for many years and only began to write fiction in 1981. The result was the widely acclaimed international bestseller *The House of the Spirits,* which was soon followed by the novels *Of Love and Shadows* and *Eva Luna.* She left her homeland after the coup of 1973 and lived for many years in Caracas. She now lives near San Francisco, where she is completing her fourth novel.